FORTY WEEKS

LORI BEASLEY BRADLEY

PROLOGUE

Twelve-year-old Charlotte McCleod, Charlie to those who knew her well, stood shivering with fear and rage on the back of a buckboard, held in place by the firm hand of black-clad Reverend Talley.

Standing on a wooden crate beneath a colossal oak was Rebecca McCleod. The Reverend and his men had beaten her, stripped her naked, and shaved the golden curls from her head. Charlie had been shocked to see they'd shaved the golden triangle between her thighs as well.

Talley was the stern minister of the Church in the Hollow, who held sway over the small settlement of Fern Hollow, Tennessee. Everyone feared him. Charlie hated him.

Rebecca's eyes only met those of her daughter once, but they conveyed a sense of defiance and pride Charlie knew well. Her mother had fought these men and wanted her to fight as well.

The Reverend stepped forward to address the gathered crowd of dirt-farmers from the Hallow. He pointed at Rebecca. "All of you know this cursed woman to be a witch," he yelled in his deep, commanding voice and raised his hand that held his Bible above his head, "and God's Holy Word commands us not to suffer a witch to live amongst us."

Charlie stared at her mother, who stood with her shoulders squared and her bald head high. What was this man going to do to her?

"On Monday last," the Reverend continued, "my young wife, Amelia informed me, to my great joy, that she finally carried my child."

Charlie heard the murmuring of the crowd. She knew Amelia. The girl and her family had been neighbors. The Reverend had decided he wanted the pretty young girl and paid her father a handsome price to give his daughter over to him to be his new wife.

Amelia hadn't wanted to be the tyrannical man's wife, but her father couldn't pass up the money the Reverend offered. It had broken Charlie's heart to see her friend's tears on her wedding day and the bruises she wore on her face and body in the weeks after.

The Reverend dug his fingers into Charlie's shoulder as he went on. "The witch there, somehow enchanted my wife and lured her into her Godless home where she tore my child from her womb, causing my poor Amelia to perish in turn."

Charlie wanted to scream. Amelia had come to them, begging for her mother to help rid her of the unwanted child in her belly. She refused to bear the child of that beast of a man. People in the Hollow knew Rebecca as a wise woman who could give a woman herbs to rid her of an unwanted child in her womb. Rebecca had warned Amelia the process would be painful and could even make her barren. Amelia had begged even harder. She didn't want the Reverend's child in her belly, and she never wanted another.

Rebecca had given Amelia the pennyroyal oil and sat with her through the excruciating hours while expelling the child from her womb.

"This witch stole my child, and in her hate of me and the

God I revere, killed my poor wife." His voice grew even louder. "For this, she must die."

The Reverend nodded, and a man on horseback rode up to her mother and slipped a knotted rope around Rebecca's neck. As he rode away, the rope tightened.

Reverend Talley bent to whisper in Charlie's ear. "Watch close, child, or this will be your fate as well."

Charlie's eyes grew wide as she watched her struggling mother lifted off the box, gagging, twitching, and gasping for air. Her naked body rose above the cheering crowd and thrashed for minutes until it finally stopped with an expulsion of urine and feces that dripped onto the crate below.

Charlie wept and struggled in the Reverend's strong hand. "In the name of our Lord," he told the gawking crowd, "I claim this girl as my new wife. She is the witch's get, but her father was a good, God-fearing soul. I know he would want his child taken into my care and taught to be a proper Christian woman.

"No, he wouldn't," Charlie gasped through her tears. "He'd kill you for what you did to my mama."

William McCleod, a trapper, had taken his son Thomas and traveled to the Oregon Territory five years earlier with the promise to return for his wife and daughter when he'd established himself there. He hadn't returned, and Rebecca and Charlie held little hope after so long that he ever would.

"Let me go," Charlie screamed and struggled to get away from the man. "Amelia hated you and didn't want your foul get in her belly." She heard gasps from the people standing around the wagon. "She begged Mama to take it out of her womb and make her so that she couldn't conceive again."

Charlie saw looks of understanding on the faces of women. "She told me you beat her and forced yourself on her in the most unnatural ways when she didn't want you to."

The man shook Charlie and slapped her. "I intend to take you in every way also, little witch," he mumbled into her ear, "and you'll take it just like that little bitch, Amelia, and your witch mother did."

The Reverend shoved Charlie aside into the arms of another man. "Lower the witch," he yelled, and the man backed his horse until Rebecca's body touched the soiled crate once more. The Reverend jumped from the wagon with a jug of kerosene in his hands and proceeded to pour it over Rebecca's slumped body.

"The witch hunters in Europe knew how to destroy the festered soul of a witch," he yelled as he took a torch from one of the men. "She cannot rise from Hell if her body is sent there in flames." He touched the torch to Rebecca, and fire consumed her body.

Charlie screamed at the sight and slumped unconscious in the arms of the man holding her.

Charlie was startled awake with a bucket of cold water. The rope holding her mother in the air had burned through, and Rebecca now sprawled on the leaf-strewn ground, charred black and smoldering. More tears washed down Charlie's face as the Reverend yanked her to her feet.

"I now take this poor Godless girl, Charlotte McCleod, as my wife," he yelled. "My announcement makes it so and by consummating our union this night upon returning to my home." He grinned at Charlie, and she wanted to vomit. "From this day forth, she shall be addressed as Charlotte Talley, my consummated wife."

From out of the darkness, a man on horseback rode through the crowd and stopped at the wagon. "You can't take her for your wife, Talley. She's already mine."

Charlotte heard gasps from those assembled on the ground below as she stared at the handsome Davis Byrde.

"What do you mean by she's already *yours*?" Talley demanded. "The witch didn't say anything about her belonging to another already."

Davis glanced at the smoldering heap of flesh and bones

on the ground. "Why should she? Charlotte and I consummated our betrothal weeks ago."

Talley glared down at Charlie. "You've already allowed yourself to be sullied by this filthy half-breed bastard?"

Charlie glanced from the grinning young man on the horseback to the scowling Reverend and smiled. "Several times, actually."

Charlie remembered Amelia telling her how Talley had ranted about prizing virginity in a girl and how he'd enjoyed taking hers.

The Reverend shoved Charlie away from him. "I denounce this trollop as a witch and a whore," he screamed as Davis Byrde put his arms around Charlie's waist and helped her onto his horse. "I command you all to shun her and this half-breed as fornicating sinners."

Being shunned by the people who watched her mother hanged and then burned was fine with Charlie. She knew they wouldn't shun Davis Byrde, though. His grandmother owned the largest farm in the county and employed a good many of them. Wayne and Sandra Byrde didn't own slaves. They preferred to have paid hands on their farm, and Charlie had respected that.

Davis was the son of the couple's daughter Melinda who'd been attacked by rogue Cherokees while she'd been out alone picking berries one day. She'd died in childbirth, but Sandra and Wayne had raised Davis, given him the Byrde name and everything that entailed. He would own the farm someday as their heir.

From that day forward, Davis Byrde had been Charlie's hero—her knight in shining armor. She'd moved into a room in the Byrde house, and she and Davis had married four years later in a private ceremony in the parlor by a priest brought from Nashville.

Davis had joined the Confederacy at the beginning of the War and died in a battle near the end. Wayne had passed away not long after Davis had enlisted, leaving Sandra and Charlie to manage the farm.

Sandra died of grief after they received the letter that Davis had been lost at Vicksburg. That left Charlotte Byrde, a twenty-four-year-old widow, the sole owner of the Byrde property.

Some days, it was all she could do to go on alone.

❧ I ❧

Charlie was just sitting down to Sunday Supper when someone pounded on the front door. Who would be knocking on her door this late on a Sunday?

She opened it to find three shabbily dressed men. "May I help you?"

"Is this the home of Mrs. Sandra Davis Byrde?" the older of the three asked.

"It is," she said, "but Grandmother Byrde passed away three years ago."

The man licked his dry, chapped lips as he stared Charlie up and down, making her feel very uncomfortable. "And just who might you be? I never knew Aunt Byrdie had a grand-daughter." He stuck out his hand. "I'm Clive Davis, Sandra's nephew, and these fine young men are my sons, Vernon and Floyd Davis." The two younger men nodded. Charlotte thought they might have been handsome had they bathed, shaved, and combed their hair.

"I'm Charlotte Byrde," Charlie said, introducing herself formally to these strangers, and took the man's hand. "I was married to Davis, Mrs. Byrde's grandson."

The man glanced over Charlie's shoulder into the parlor. "Oh, yeah, and where is he?"

"Davis died in the war," she replied.

"Is that so?" Clive said with an arched brow. "Well, then I reckon that makes us kin by marriage, Miss Charlotte."

"And kin usually invites other kin inside," Vernon spoke up from behind his father.

"Is that fried chicken I smell?" Floyd added. "It ain't right to leave kin out on the porch and deny 'em a meal if ya have one made. 'T ain't Christian, and you look to be a fine Christian woman."

Charlie certainly wouldn't claim that title, but she supposed she should invite these men inside if they were family of Grandmother Byrde's. They made her uneasy, but they were Grandmother Byrde's family. It wouldn't be right to leave them out on the porch. Against her better judgment, Charlie opened the door and allowed the men inside.

"I was just getting ready to sit down to supper," she said and motioned to follow her. "I hope there will be enough. I wasn't expecting company."

Clive stopped in front of the fireplace to stare up at the portrait of Sandra and William. "That's my Aunt Byrdie, all right," he said with a grin. "She was a right fine-lookin' woman in her day. It's no wonder she caught the eye of ol' William."

Young, dark-haired Davis sat smiling on his grandfather's knee, but the man made no mention of him. Floyd and Vernon glanced at the portrait but spent most of their time fondling the silver candlesticks on the mantle and the alabaster figurines.

"I'll set more places at the table," Charlie said to coax the men into the kitchen.

She took three more plates and cups from the china hutch and silver flatware from the velvet-lined box. She set everything out on the table, and the men dropped into seats.

Charlie filled bowls with mashed potatoes, cream gravy, and sweet green peas. She'd made a large batch of biscuits, so she'd have plenty for the next day or two. She put them all on a platter and took them and the plate of chicken she'd fried to the table.

The three men didn't wait for Charlie to sit before filling their plates and greedily shoving the food into their mouths. Charlie brought a pot of coffee to the table and filled their cups.

Charlie sat and began filling her plate. She did her best to ignore the slurping and smacking sounds of the men eating around her. She just wanted this meal over and these men out of her home.

"This is a right fine meal, Miss Charlotte," Clive said with a leering grin as he slurped coffee from the delicate china cup that looked out of place in his rough hand. "Your mama did a right fine job with your education in the womanly arts." He reached over with a greasy hand to finger the lace on her sleeve. "Did you make that dress, too, or do you have a servant woman here in the house to do that for you?"

Charlie pulled her arm away from the man. "I make my own clothes, sir," she said. "I don't have any house servants here on the farm. I'm perfectly capable of doing for myself."

Clive grinned and turned to his sons. "The yard out front looks neat and trimmed. Is that your doin' as well?"

Charlie sipped her coffee, wondering where the man was going with his questions. "I tend to the flowers and the kitchen garden," she said, "but one of the farmhands take care of the yard for me."

"You got niggers here, then?" Floyd asked, wiping grease from his mouth with the sleeve of his worn shirt.

"Lots of 'em stayed on at their master's expense after the emancipation," Vernon said as he glanced around the tidy kitchen.

"William and Sandra never kept slaves here on their

farm," Charlie said as she forked up some potatoes covered with cream gravy. "All my hands here are paid. I have a few Negroes who work in the fields," she said, "but they're all paid and live in their own homes."

Clive snorted. "Ol' man Byrde always was a strange sort." He shook his head. "I never understood his reckonin' that niggers was humans like us white men when everyone knows they ain't nothin' but a sort of ape from them wilds in Africa, meant to slave on the land for us humans like mules and horses slave for us."

Charlie refused to answer such a ridiculous statement. She didn't know many Negroes, but the ones she did know had much better table manners than these three supposed men.

"It also confounded me some that he let Aunt Byrdie have the runnin' of this place when women are inferior to men in the runnin' of a business like this fine farm, and don't have the head for figures and takin' care of money."

Charlie grinned to herself. "Grandmother Byrde did a fine job managing this farm after Grandfather Byrde died," she protested. "She and I kept it turning a profit during the war when others, run by men, floundered and folded."

"This used to be the Davis homestead," Clive said in a cold tone. "Did you know that, Miss Charlotte?"

"Grandmother Byrde mentioned it once," Charlie admitted. "She said her father willed it to her and William when he died and that they made many improvements over the years and expanded it."

"You and Aunt Byrdie got the money for the crops sold?" Clive asked with a raised brow.

This man was making Charlie very uneasy now that the subject of money had come up.

"Why ain't you got youngins?" Floyd asked. "You're young and look to be healthy."

Charlie's eyes widened at the too-familiar question from

the stranger. What gave him the right to ask such a question at her table?

"Davis and I were never blessed with children." She refused to admit she had been pregnant three times but lost the children in the first three months after conception. It was something that shamed Charlie terribly, though Davis had never held it against her in any fashion. They'd planned on trying again after he returned from the War, but that would never happen now, and Charlie batted back the tears stinging her eyes.

"Our Davis kin is buried here on this land, and a Davis man should be livin' here now."

"Grandmother Byrde left the farm to Davis and me," she said with an uneasy sigh. "But Davis died in the war, so it's just me now."

Clive snorted. "It's a sin the old bat gave that half-breed little bastard our good family name. They shoulda strangled him and buried him with his little whore mother who spread her legs for red heathens like she done."

Charlie's mouth fell open, and she dropped her fork into her plate. "I don't think it was like that at all, sir. Those Indians attacked her and left Davis in her belly."

"Is that a pie I see over there on the counter?" Vernon asked. "I'd sure like me a piece of pie with a little more coffee, girl."

Charlie had enough of this. She stood. "I'm not your girl, sir, and I'm withdrawing my invitation." She pointed toward the door. "I'd like you all to leave my house now."

Clive burst to his feet and grabbed Charlie's arm. "The way I see it, this house and farm are rightfully ours now as the Davis heirs to my Aunt Byrdie. Get my son his pie like he told ya to, woman." He shoved Charlie toward the counter.

Charlie's blood began to boil. This man had no right coming into her home and treating her this way after she'd shared her meal with him and his two sons. She picked up the blackberry pie, brought it back to the table, and dropped it in front of the smirking Vernon.

She returned to her seat and turned to Clive Davis. "This farm belonged to Sandra and William Byrde, sir. They willed it to their grandson Davis and me as his wife. If you'd like to contest that legal document in court," Charlie grinned, looking at their shabby clothes, "You can hire a lawyer and do just that." She stood again. "Now, I'd like you to please leave my home and take your sons with you."

Neither Clive nor his sons stood. He sat in deep thought, staring up at Charlie while chewing the meat from a chicken leg. He grabbed Charlie's wrist and yanked her back down into the chair. "I have me another thought on that matter. Me and my two fine sons here are all without wives at the moment."

Charlie's eyes darted to the two young men when they began to snicker. What was he going on about now?

"As I recall," he continued, "in the eyes of the law in the fine state of Tennessee, a woman can't rightfully hold property in her name."

"I don't believe that is true, sir, or Grandmother Byrde's attorney wouldn't have allowed her to put it in her will."

Charlie felt her stomach beginning to turn. Grandmother Byrde's attorney had warned her that if male Byrde relatives came forward, there could be trouble with the will. She'd assured him there were none, but she hadn't given thought to Grandmother Byrde's male relatives.

"Now, if you was to marry one of us fine Davis men and give us a male child to carry on the Davis name, then you could stay on here as the lady of the house."

Vernon chuckled as he shoveled pie from the pan into his mouth. "If she can fuck as good as she can cook, I'll marry up with her, Pa."

Charlie's eyes went wide, and her cheeks flamed at the young man's vulgarity. Did this man actually think she would marry one of them and allow him to rut atop her every night until she conceived a child? It was ridiculous.

Charlie stood again to glare down at Clive Davis. "I suggest you hire an attorney, sir. I'd never countenance having any of you filth as a husband. Now, please leave my home. I fear my hospitality has run its course, and I'd like you all to go."

Clive grinned up at her. "That's just it, Miss Byrde," he said in a calm and controlled voice, "this is *our* home, not yours, and we have no plans to leave it any time soon."

Charlotte stepped back with rage boiling inside her, knocking over her chair. She wanted to hit this man with something. "Get out of my house," she screamed.

As Charlie was about to reach for a butcher knife from the block on the counter, something hit the back of her head, and she fell into peaceful darkness.

❧ 2 ❧

C harlie woke to male voices she didn't recognize.
Her eyes fluttered open. She was in her room and on her bed, but something was strange. Where were her clothes? She never slept naked, not even in the hottest weather. The window was wide open with the breeze blowing the sheers into the room. She never slept with the window open without cheesecloth over it. The mosquitoes would eat her alive.

Charlie turned her head on the pillow, and pain blasted until she moaned and squeezed her eyes tight against it. What had happened? She heard the male voices again, and it began to come back to her—Clive and his sons. Charlie groaned again as she sat up.

"Wanna have another go at her, Vern?" Charlie heard one of the men say. It must have been Floyd.

Charlie pictured greasy blond hair, an unshaven face, and blue eyes. What did he mean by having a go at her? She touched her hand between her thighs and felt slimy deposits on her fingers. Charlie didn't need to put it to her nose to know what it was, and she shivered with rage.

"I'd like to have another go at that tight little asshole, but

Pa wants a baby in her, so I'd best settle for her cunny again."
She heard Vern say before both men laughed.

"Yeah," Floyd added. "I pumped her mouth a few times,
but it ain't the same when they're sleepin'."

"Which of us you think she'll pick to take to husband?"
Vern asked. "I think Pa wants her. Did ya see how fast he blew
his stuff both times?"

"Well, she's gonna know we've been at her when she
wakes," Floyd said, "and we Davis men tend to sprout our
seeds after the first plantin', so she's bound to be with child
after all the plantin' we done tonight."

Charlie's stomach turned as she heard the men laugh, and
she thought she would vomit. All three of them had taken
turns with her, and Clive had gone to find a minister to marry
her to one of them so that they could have the farm. She
refused to allow that to happen. This was her farm, and it
would never belong to them if she had anything to say
about it.

Charlie slid off the bed as quietly as possible and went to
the wardrobe. She knelt and pulled open the drawer where
she kept Davis's things. The room was dark, except for the
thin light of dawn coming through the open window. It didn't
matter. This had been her room for twelve years, and she
knew it like the back of her hand.

In the drawer, Charlie found what she was looking for and
eased Davis's two Colt revolvers out. She'd practiced with
them over the years and kept them loaded.

The men still talked out in the hall, and Charlie hurried
into a pair of bloomers, a camisole, and a dress. She buckled
Davis's holster around her waist and returned the Colts. As
she tied her boots onto her feet, the men returned to her
room.

"What the hell ya doin' outta bed with clothes on?" Vern
demanded. "My cock is hard again."

Charlie moved to put the bed between her and the two

naked brothers. "Get dressed and get out of my house," Charlie ordered as she eased the Colts from the holster, cocked them while the brothers laughed, and put her fingers over the triggers.

She'd only used her left hand to fire the gun a few times but was confident at this close range she could hit her target with ease. Perhaps it wouldn't be a kill shot, but it would certainly slow him down.

Vern noticed the guns in her hands and grinned. "What you think you're gonna do with them?

"Shoot your worthless balls off if you don't get out of my house," Charlie sneered as she pointed the revolvers at both men's crotches.

"Why would you wanna do that, sweetheart, when you was enjoyin' them balls so much earlier tonight?"

Both men laughed, and Charlie fired. She adjusted her aim, though, and the bullets took both men in the head. Blood and brains splattered the wall behind where they stood. They crumpled to the floor with wide-eyed looks of astonishment on what remained of their faces.

Charlie vomited in the porcelain chamber pot, then poured water into the basin and washed her face to calm her nerves. What was she going to do now?

She trudged down the stairs to find the kitchen a mess. The remnants of last night's supper remained on the table, the pie she'd taken so much time to bake half-eaten in the pan. How could she leave this fine house to men like this, who were little better than the pigs in the barn?

With a plan in her head, Charlie went to the barn and hitched the two gray mules to the wagon and took it back to the house. The sun was just above the horizon. She didn't have much time, but she knew Clive would have difficulty finding a minister today to come all the way out to the farm.

She hurried inside and began packing up the kitchen. In barrels of flour and oats, she buried the good china and silver.

She packed cook pots and skillets into wooden crates and used washcloths and linen kitchen towels to line mixing bowls and other crockery against breaking. Charlie carried it all and stacked it in the wagon.

In the parlor, Charlie wrapped the silver candlesticks and Sandra's favorite figurines in cloth and placed them in another crate. She carried them along with the portrait from above the fireplace to store in the wagon.

As quick as she could, Charlie ran things through her head she would need for a house in Oregon. She'd decided it was time to go in search of her father and brother. They'd been gone from Tennessee for nearly fifteen years without so much as a word, and Charlie suspected they were dead. At this point, she thought Oregon was the right choice. It was a long way from Tennessee and Clive Davis, and that suited Charlie now more than anything.

When the mantle clock Charlie had stacked on top of a crate struck nine, she had the wagon loaded with every useful thing she could think of. She had crates of canned vegetables and potatoes from the cellar, smoked pork, chickens, and sausages from the smokehouse. Her clothes and Davis's things she stored in trunks and packed near the rear of the wagon for easy access.

Most of the furniture was too heavy and awkward for Charlie to load. Still, she'd managed the smaller kitchen table and four chairs, a nice wingback chair and ottoman from the parlor, a vanity from one of the bedrooms with its pretty porcelain bowl and pitcher carefully wrapped with soft blankets from the bed.

For bedding, Charlie rolled a straw mattress and two feather beds together and tied them. Those would do her until she could find a real bed in Oregon. At the rear of the fully packed wagon, Charlie added a chamber pot, a crate with a skillet, coffee pot, coffee, eggs, potatoes, and a butcher knife. She also added a box with kindling and the makings for a fire.

Satisfied she had everything in the wagon she possibly could pack into it, Charlie went back to the barn and released all the animals into the pasture. She found a large canvas tarp in an old trunk, some rope, and a tin of kerosene.

Charlie threw the tarp over the wagon and secured it with the rope. The kerosene she took into the big farmhouse. She began by pouring the liquid over the bodies in her room, then splashed some around the other bedrooms and down the stairs. The last of it went into the kitchen and parlor.

With a straw, she lit in the cookstove, then ignited the kerosene pooled at the bottom of the stairs.

"I'm so sorry, Grandmother Byrde. I know you loved this house dearly," Charlie said with tears running down her face as she watched the blue flames whoosh up the stairwell and spread into the kitchen and parlor.

She hurried outside, climbed up into the wagon, and urged the mules toward the barn where she lit the straw piled in the loft. If Clive Davis wanted the farm, he could have it, but he would have to rebuild first.

Satisfied with her accomplishments, Charlie flicked the leather reins to set the mules toward the road. She turned them in the opposite direction she expected Clive to come and took the back way around to the main road north, away from Fern Hollow. When she got to Nashville, she'd find a mapmaker and buy a map to Independence, Missouri, where she could join up with a wagon train headed to Oregon.

❧ 3 ❧

*Z*achary Drake was hot and tired when he saw the glow of a campfire ahead.

The sun still glowed orange on the western horizon, but it was still too dark for him to make out much more than the shape of a wagon ahead. He'd crossed the Wabash into Illinois yesterday and had traveled all day. He hoped this fella didn't mind sharing his fire with another traveler.

"Ho, the wagon," he called when he came near, hoping for an affirmative greeting in return.

The person at the fire stood, and Zach saw it was a woman in skirts. She held a gun in her hand. "Stop right there," she called back in reply. "Who are you, and what do you want?"

"To share your fire," Zach called back, "and maybe a cup of that coffee I smell. I've been traveling since dawn, and Tess and me both could use a rest."

The woman studied him for a few minutes and then lowered her gun. "Come on over," she said. "You can stake your horse to rest down by the river with my mules."

Zack dismounted and walked Tess toward the fire. The

woman had gone to her wagon and returned with a cup she filled with coffee and handed it to him when he got to the fire.

"Much obliged, ma'am," he said when he took the cup. "I'm Zack Drake," he said as he offered his gloved hand, and she took it.

"Charlotte Byrde," she told him.

She was tall for a woman and slender. In the firelight, Zach thought her hair might be red, but upon closer inspection, it was blonde with a reddish turn to it. Maybe it was the fire. He'd have to see it in the sunlight to be sure. She was pretty too, with freckles splashed across her cheeks and eyes he couldn't be sure of either. At first glance, he thought they were blue, but then they appeared green. Zack thought of her as a mystery and smiled. He liked mysteries. She was younger than he'd first thought, as well.

Zack scanned the darkness for signs of another person. "You out here all alone, ma'am?"

She grinned and lifted two revolvers from their holsters at her hips. "I'm not quite alone."

"You know how to use those, I hope," he said uneasily. Zack watched her face fall a little as she stared at the two big guns in her hands.

"My husband taught me, and yes, I can use them just fine." She stood and returned to the wagon.

When she returned to the fire, she carried a skillet loaded with a slab of smoky bacon, some potatoes, and a big butcher knife.

"I tried to catch a fish," she said, nodding toward the river, "but they weren't biting. I hope you don't mind bacon and fried potatoes."

Zach smiled as his stomach made a loud, growling noise. "No, ma'am, bacon and fried potatoes sounds wondrous after a day of beef jerky that was like chewing on shoe leather, and water from my canteen."

"Please call me Charlie," the young woman said. "Ma'am

makes me feel like an old woman." She grinned up at him. "Why don't you unburden your poor horse and take her down by the river with my mules."

"You don't mind if I bed down by your fire then?"

She smiled across the fire. "Not at all. I have my bedding rolled out beneath the wagon."

Zach emptied his cup of coffee, stood, and unsaddled Tess. He dropped the saddle and bedroll by the fire and then walked the horse to the river, where he watched her drink her fill before he staked her out beside the woman's two gray mules in a grassy area near the water's edge. He left her enough lead to wander around a bit to enjoy the green grass and still get to the water.

The flat, low-lying area felt firm beneath Zach's boots, and he suspected it hadn't rained much lately. The river would rise quickly and spread across this area when it did.

The aroma of bacon frying made Zach's mouth water, and he headed back to the fire where Charlie was slicing potatoes into the hot bacon fat in the steaming skillet.

"Your wagon looks like it's loaded with all your worldly goods," he said when he dropped down by his saddle. "Where are you from, and where are you headed?" She nodded to the pot she'd set aside on a rock, and Zack refilled his cup. "If you don't mind my asking."

She took a deep breath before answering as she used a fork to turn the potatoes. "I grew up in Tennessee," she finally said. "My husband died in the war, and after his grandmother passed, I decided it was time to leave." She scooped some potatoes onto a plate already heaped with strips of crisp bacon and handed it to Zack. "My father and brother went to Oregon some years ago," she explained as she forked up a potato slices from the skillet and put it into her mouth, "and I plan to join a wagon train in Independence headed to Oregon to find them."

Zack picked up the fork he found on the plate and shoveled some of the potatoes into his mouth. They were salty from the bacon fat and hot—the first hot meal he'd had in weeks. He closed his eyes and enjoyed the feeling as he chewed.

"I hope they're all right," Charlie said as she bit off the end of a strip of bacon.

"You have no idea how good this is, ma'am," he said with a contented sigh. "It reminds me of my mama's cookin'."

Charlie smiled. "Now tell me where you're from and where you're headed. Turn about is only fair."

The woman's smile warmed his heart. She was genuine, and he liked that. Her smile wasn't something put on to entice a man the way Penny's had been. Zack filled his mouth again. He didn't want to think about Penny Sims. He'd loved the pretty brunette, and she'd broken his heart.

"I'm headed to Independence as well," he finally said. "A friend of mine works for a trail company there and got me on as an outrider for one of the wagon trains." He filled his mouth with coffee and swallowed. "I'm supposed to be there in three weeks to make one of the last trains out for the season."

"Perhaps we should travel together," Charlie said. "I'd like to join one of those trains."

Zack took off his hat and scratched his head. "I'm going to be traveling straight through without making any stops," he told her. "I don't know as your wagon, loaded down as it is, would be able to keep up and get there in three weeks."

"Tiny and Tot are good, strong mules," she said, "and I'll feed you every day for your time. I have plenty of foodstuff with me in the wagon."

Zack finished his meal and studied the plate and cup in the firelight. They were nice and probably cost her family a lot of money. He glanced up at the young woman again. Her clothes were nice too. This was no simple country girl. Could she handle the rigors of a long cross-country trip, driving those big old mules?

"Let me think on it overnight," Zack finally said. "Those mules don't give you any trouble hitchin' and unhitchin'?"

Charlie snorted in a very un-ladylike fashion. "Tot and Tiny are old sweethearts and I've been hitching and unhitching wagons for as long as I can remember."

She spoke with an accent, but it was a refined accent. Zach concluded this young woman had been educated. Nothing about her seemed to fit. She was pretty, wore nice clothes, had nice things, and spoke with a sophisticated accent, but she drove a wagon and handled a team of mules like an experienced farmhand. She'd managed to get from Tennessee to Illinois on her own.

Zack watched her carry the dishes to the river, squat at the water's edge, and wash them. She didn't look to be afraid of work either. She returned with the coffee pot filled with water for the morning and set it and the skillet beside the fire ring.

"All ready for breakfast in the morning," she said with a smile.

"I expect to be headin' out at the crack of dawn," Zach said as he rolled out his bedding beside the fire, Charlie had added some pieces of wood to it.

She walked to the wagon and crawled beneath it. "I'll be ready," she called back to Zack.

Yeah, we'll see about that. With his belly full and warmed by the safety of the fire, Zack fell asleep without much more thought of the pretty girl who slept only a few feet away.

Zack woke to the smell of coffee and the sound of bacon frying. He opened his eyes to see Charlie squatting by the fire where the coffee pot, a skillet, and a cast-iron Dutch oven set nestled in the coals.

He got up and rested the weight of his body on his elbow. "You're up already?"

She turned to him with a grimace on her pretty face. "You said you wanted to leave at daybreak. Didn't you?"

"What time is it? It ain't even daylight yet."

"My clock woke me at four," she said as she opened the Dutch oven and used a fork to test something. Satisfied with what she saw, she smiled and lifted the pot out of the coals.

Zach sat up and rubbed the sleep from his eyes. *She has a clock? Of course, she does. Doesn't every well-bred southern lady have a clock on her mantle? Charlotte Byrde certainly sounds like a well-bred southern name.*

She handed him a cup of coffee and a plate. "I didn't have any eggs, so I made biscuits." She offered him a ceramic crock. "There's no butter, but here's some peach jam."

She made biscuits? Zach smeared the sweet jam between the halves of the hot biscuits he gingerly pulled apart. If those old mules of hers could keep up with him and Tess, Zach thought this might not be such a bad bargain after all. He bit into the hot biscuit and sighed as he chewed. Not bad at all.

"I'll hitch up the mules as soon as we've eaten, and I've cleaned up."

"Take your time," Zach told her. "It won't be daylight for a good half hour yet."

"I just wanted you to have a good breakfast before we started out today."

Zach swallowed some coffee to wash down the biscuit and sweet jam. "I appreciate that, ma'am. This is really good."

"I made enough biscuits and bacon for a few lunches. I'll wrap them up in napkins, and you can put some in your saddlebag to eat along the way."

Zach smiled. She seemed to have a good head on her shoulders and thought things ahead.

"I'm going to have to stop in the next town," he advised, "to get the best directions to the Mississippi and where there's a crossing into Missouri."

Charlie grinned. "I have a map. I bought one in Nashville that shows the route all the way to Oregon."

"I'm gonna want to take a close look at that," he said with a smile. "But it will have to wait for daylight."

Charlie smiled at him across the fire. "I can come along with you, then?"

Zach lifted a strip of bacon from his plate. "How could I say no to cookin' like this?"

"Thank you, Mr. Drake," she said in reply. "I like to cook, and I hate to eat alone."

"Where's your husband, Charlie?" he finally asked.

Her pretty face fell and grew dark. "Killed in the war. I hated leaving him buried back there in an unmarked grave near Vicksburg, but I couldn't stay there any longer."

"A lot of good men died in that meaningless war," he said with a sigh.

"You fought?"

Zack nodded. "For the Confederacy."

Her face screwed up in confusion. "But I thought you said you were from Indiana. Indiana fought for the Union."

"Many men from southern Indiana," Zack said, "and southern Illinois sympathized and fought with the South."

"You believed in the slavery of your fellow human beings?" she asked, her eyes going cold and her smile becoming a firm line.

"No," he said, shaking his head, "but I believed a state had the right to make its own laws if it was what the majority of the people in that state wanted, and the government in Washington had no right to overstep the rights of the people in those states."

"I see," she said, but Zack was of the opinion she really didn't.

"Your husband fought for the South. Was he a slave owner?"

"No," she said, shaking her head. "The Byrdes kept no

slaves." She began to collect the dirty dishes. "My Davis was of much the same opinion as you, Mr. Drake, and that's why he fought … and died for the Confederacy."

"I'm so sorry, ma'am."

"And what of your family? Did they share your feelings about the War?"

Zach took a deep breath. "Sadly, no," he said. "My brother joined the Union Army and was killed at Shiloh." He was silent for a moment. "I was at Shiloh too, and when my parents found that out, my father threw me out of the house and told me never to come back." He poured more coffee into his empty cup, filled his mouth with the rich hot brew, and swallowed it, using the pain of it like a thrashing from his father. "It's why I took the job with the wagon train. I needed to get as far away from Indiana as I could."

Charlie gave him a sympathetic smile and patted his shoulder. "We have that in common. I need to get as far away from Tennessee as I can possibly get."

Without explaining, Charlie took the dishes over to the narrow, muddy river to wash. He wondered why she needed to leave her home, but it was none of his business, and decided to leave it alone. If the woman wanted to tell him, she would. Zack watched her squatting by the water and smiled, appreciating her form. He doubted she was a criminal, and even if she was, she was a good cook and damned nice to look at.

He wanted to take the measure of her and saddled Tess while Charlie harnessed the mules to the wagon. It surprised him how easily she accomplished the job. She tugged her bedding from beneath the wagon, rolled and secured it with a leather thong, and then stored it and her cooking supplies beneath the oiled tarp on the wagon.

She'd given him her map, and Zack studied it as the sun rose in the east. He plotted a course toward St. Louis, where there was a ferry, and showed it to Charlie.

"I'm gonna lead," he told her, "and if you fall behind too much, you're on your own."

She nodded her strawberry-blonde head as she returned the folded map to its place beside her on the seat. "I understand, Mr. Drake. I'll do my best to keep up."

Zack studied the woman for a minute and addressed something that came to him in the night. "You're a very pretty woman, Mrs. Byrde."

He watched her cheeks turn pink. "Thank you, Mr. Drake."

"I'm sayin' that because it could end up causin' us a lot of trouble."

"Trouble?" she said with her brow furrowed in confusion.

He took off his hat and ran his hand through his thick, brown hair. "That hair of yours is gonna attract a good bit of attention," he told her, "and probably from the wrong sorta fellas, if you catch my meanin'."

Charlie put a hand to her head. "My hair?"

"And those clothes aren't much better. Don't you have anything less provocative?"

Charlie's eyes narrowed as she stared down at her simple plaid day dress. "What's so provocative about this old thing?" she gasped. "It doesn't even have any lace on it, and I have it buttoned up to my chin."

Zack didn't know how to say what he wanted to say in a manner that wasn't offensive, so he just said it. "The whole get-up makes you look like a girl," he blurted, "and the open road is no place for a pretty girl alone."

Charlie sat on the wagon, staring at him with her pretty mouth agape. "What do you want me to do about it?" she demanded. "I am a girl. There's nothing I can do to change that."

Zack rode closer to the wagon. "You could cut that damned hair off, wear a man's hat, and some men's clothes. Do you have any of those by chance?"

Charlie stared at him for a few minutes. Zack saw her fists tighten on the reins. If she were strong enough to handle a team of mules, Zack wagered she could probably knock him off Tess with one good swing and backed the horse away from the wagon some. There was no good sense in taking chances with an angered woman.

Without saying a word, Charlie got down from the wagon, went to the back, and loosened the tarp. After rummaging beneath it for a while, she jumped down and stormed into the bushes with some things clutched in her arms.

Zach waited atop Tess as the sun rose in the clear blue morning sky. The wind was still as he listened to the river flow by and the chittering of birds in the bushes. He could smell the rich loamy soil beneath the nearby oaks and hickories.

The damned woman was throwing him off his schedule, but he dared not call to her and tell her to hurry it up—whatever it was she was doing.

❧ 4 ❧

Charlie could see his point, but it still troubled her to cut off her hair.

The sight of her mother, standing naked with her head shaved bald, kept returning to Charlie's mind as she used her sewing scissors to cut off her hair. Her hair wasn't as curly as her mother's had been, but Charlie had always been proud of her wavy locks, and Davis had loved running his hands through them as they made love.

The memory of it brought tears to her eyes that fell harder as the ground around her feet became covered with golden hair. Charlie dashed away the senseless tears. This Zack Drake was right. She'd be safer traveling as a young man than as a woman in the wilds of the west.

She stripped out of her dress and petticoat, folded them, and put on the things she'd taken from the trunk of Davis' things. They were clothes he'd worn as a younger man and fit Charlie's slender frame well enough. She attached suspenders to the old brown trousers and pulled them over the shoulders of an equally worn plaid cotton shirt. Over her newly shorn hair, she pulled an old wide-brimmed felt hat she'd found rolled in the trunk. She'd have to wear her feminine boots but suspected few people would be looking at her feet. Davis's feet had been much larger than hers, and there had been none of his boots in the trunk anyhow. She smelled of the camphor balls the clothes had been stored in but knew the air would weaken the odor as she traveled.

Charlie rolled cuffs in the trousers. Davis had been six inches taller than her. She returned the gun belt to her waist and cinched it tight before gathering her discarded female clothes to return to the wagon.

Zack sat atop his horse, and when she walked out from the bushes, his eyes went wide, and his mouth fell open.

"I hope this is more to your liking, Mr. Drake," Charlie said as she returned her dress to the wagon and retightened the canvas tarp. She turned toward the man. "Does my appearance meet with your satisfaction, and are we ready to travel now?"

Zack jumped from his horse, went to the firepit, and dabbed his hands into the ash. Then he walked up to Charlie and patted them on her cheeks, chin, and the area beneath her nose.

"May as well look like neither of us has had a shave in a day or two," he said with a grin. "That face was still too pretty, and there are men out there with a hankerin' for pretty boys too."

Charlie curled her lip. "Are you joshing me? Boys?"

Zack gave her an incredulous stare. "Have you never heard of catamites?"

"Oh," she said with a frown. "I have, but it's still disturbing."

Zack chuckled. "Just think how disturbed you'd be to find yourself bent over a barrel in some alley with your trousers pulled down and some big brute with his—"

Charlie raised a hand as her cheeks blazed red with embarrassment. "No need to elaborate, Mr. Drake. I get your meaning."

"Let's get goin' then, Charlie."

She noticed he put an emphasis on the mannish name and chuckled.

"We're burnin' daylight."

Zack rode ahead, and Charlie loosened the brake and flicked the reins to get the idle mules moving. She chided herself for not thinking of this disguise herself. Clive Davis would be chasing after a woman with long blonde hair—not a boy.

Charlie suspected the man would be one of those Southerners stuck in his Scottish or Irish past, who believed in blood feuds and would expect an eye for an eye when it came to the killing of any kin and especially his sons. A chill ran down her spine when she thought of the man. She found it hard to believe the three had been Grandmother Byrde's close kin. That genteel lady had always been so loving and kind to her.

Those men had come into her home, sat at her table, and eaten her food. Then they'd demanded she turn it over to them, and when she'd refused, they'd done the unthinkable. Charlie squeezed her eyes shut against the tears. They'd assaulted her in the bed she'd shared with Davis as his wife, they'd used her body in ways that sweet man would never have, and then they'd expected her to choose one of them to marry.

Charlie didn't know what she'd expected of them when she'd allowed them into her home, but as Grandmother Byrde's kin, she'd certainly expected something much more gentlemanly.

The bruises they'd left on her body had finally faded, but Charlie suspected the ones they'd left on her soul would last a lifetime. She still had nightmares, and the only relief she found was remembering their blood and brains splattering the wall when she'd shot them. It also gave her heart some ease to think of them burning along with the house.

After what the Preacher Talley had done to her mother,

Charlie knew it took a large flame to destroy a body. Would the inferno of the burning house have been enough? The burning of the Davis' bodies had brought Talley back to her mind, and after years without the nightmares of that night, they'd returned to plague Charlie's sleep. She had dreams of Talley pulling one arm and Clive Davis pulling the other, both screaming she owed them a child from her body.

Charlie swiped sweat from her brow when Zack fell back and told her to stop the wagon. In the wet road ahead, a wagon was mired in the mud up to the axle.

"You wait here while I go and see if I can be of help. I'll wave you forward if I need you."

"All right," Charlie said as she heard the clock chime twelve.

She watched Zack approach the men with the wagon, get off his horse, and stoop to inspect the mired wheel. Charlie drank some water from her canteen and took out the biscuit with jam and bacon she'd made from their breakfast. Zack had his on his horse, and she didn't know if he'd eaten already or not, but she was hungry and was going to eat hers.

As she chewed her final bite, Zack motioned her forward. She brushed the crumbs from her hands and retook the reins. When she neared the other wagon, Zack stopped her.

"They're stuck badly here, and they've only got the one old horse, which ain't much to speak of," he said with a shake of the head, "but I think we can pull them out if we hook 'em to our wagon and let the mules give 'em a good tug."

Charlie studied the sloppily loaded wagon, the panting, sway-backed old horse that had been pulling it, and the two shabbily dressed but clean men. "Doesn't look like they've done much to get themselves out, save stress the poor old beast," she said.

Zack rolled his brown eyes and smiled. "My thinking exactly, but helping that poor old beast, if not the men, is the Christian thing to do."

Charlie stared at the foamy sweat on the flanks of the old horse and frowned. Shooting the poor old thing in the head would probably be the more apt thing to do, but who was she to say.

One of the men, a skinny thing in ill-fitting clothes, greasy blond hair that fell to his collar, and a missing tooth from his top gum, ambled over to stare first at Charlie and then at her loaded wagon.

"Well, who we got here now?" he asked as he walked around the wagon, trying to lift and peek beneath the tarp.

"This is my cousin, Charlie," Zack said. "And Charlie, this here is Bob. Over yonder is his brother Tom. They're on their way to Independence."

He gave her a slight shake of the head, and she didn't say anything to the man. "I'm gonna let you tend to this wagon thing," she said in a soft voice. "I need to go find a bush. It's been a while since my coffee this morning."

Zack grinned. "I understand. Go on ahead but watch for snakes. Areas like this around the rivers are full of cotton-mouths and copperheads."

Charlie nodded as she wet a cloth with water from her canteen and wiped at her neck. "I need to cool down some too." When she moved to wipe her face, Zack grabbed her wrist and shook his head. She understood and returned the cool cloth to her neck.

She hopped down from the wagon and headed toward some honeysuckle-covered bushes near the muddy trail. Zack took the mules by their harnesses and began leading them toward the other wagon. Charlie needed to relieve herself so severely she only gave the ground a quick glance before unbuckling the gun belt, unbuttoning the trousers, unhooking the suspenders, and squatting.

She released a stream of fluid with a long sigh of delight. After putting herself back together, Charlie unbuttoned the shirt and then her camisole to wipe the sweat from her chest and beneath her bosoms.

"Damn, you're a gal," a male voice said, causing Charlie's heart to flutter in surprise.

Charlie yanked at the camisole and shirt to cover herself. She saw Bob staring at her with a gap-toothed smile on his greasy face. He took a step toward her. "I can do that for ya," he said, reaching for a bosom. "Them's real nice. Why don't ya let a fella have a little taste."

Charlie rolled her eyes in disgust. Honestly, was this all men thought about? Before Bob could come closer, Charlie pulled one of the pistols from the holster and pointed it at the slobbering man. Had he not seen her wearing them?

"Why don't you go back and help my cousin and your lazy brother get your wagon out of the mud?"

"Hey," he hissed, "who you callin' lazy? Why ain't you over there puttin' your back into it?"

"If you or your brother had put your backs into it," Charlie retorted, "you'd have mud all over your clothes." Charlie motioned toward the wagons with the pistol. "Now, get outta here and let me dress."

"You his whore?" Bob sneered. "If that's what ya are, me and my brother got money. We can pay for a poke."

"I think you really want another hole in your head," Charlie said and cocked the pistol with her thumb.

Bob raised his hands and turned away. "All right, all right, I'm goin'."

Charlie waited to hear his footsteps leave before she returned the pistol to its holster and began buttoning her camisole and shirt.

As she finished, a hand grabbed her shoulder. "Now, you put that gun away," Bob said with a rumbling chuckle, "Let's me an' you have some real—"

Charlie's elbow caught him beneath the chin with all the force she could muster, and he crumpled to the ground. She turned to stare down at the man and grinned. "Yes, let's have some real fun." She kicked the man in the mouth as hard as she could and then kicked him again and again for good measure.

"What the hell are you doing?" Zack said before she could kick the man's bloody face a fourth time.

"He followed me to the bushes and watched me take down my trousers and open my camisole to cool off," she said as her anger began to fade. "He tried to take liberties with me."

Zack glanced down at the man's bloody face and the tooth hanging by a fine piece of bloody tissue on his chin and chuckled. "I'll wager he won't try that again."

"Let's get back on the road," Charlie said as she pushed past the two men. "We're burnin' daylight."

❧

Zack mounted his horse with a broad grin on his face. The gal was feisty, that was for certain. He'd found her pretty in the firelight the night before, but in the light of day, he recognized true beauty. He'd hated to make her cut that golden hair, but she'd be safer dressed as a boy.

He thought back to Bob's bloody face and hoped the girl had learned her lesson. Men alone could be dangerous to a woman they thought vulnerable. He smiled again. Zack didn't think Bob would think of Charlie as vulnerable again any time soon.

He wanted to put as many miles as he could between them and the two brothers who were also on their way to Independence. He didn't want any trouble from them between here and there, and now that Bob knew Charlie was female and had a bone to pick with her, Zack realized there could be trouble. He'd also seen the envious looks the men had given Charlie's well-provisioned wagon and team.

Men like Bob and Tom, homeless after the War and

without a family's anchor, were dangerous. Zack had seen good men go wrong and had the distinct feeling these two were just that—bad.

He slowed his horse and let Charlie in the wagon catch up. "You all right?" he asked the sullen-faced young woman.

"I'm fine," she said. "What was your assessment of those two?"

"Bad news if we don't put plenty of miles between our two wagons."

Charlie nodded. "I was thinking much the same thing." She grinned up at him. "Ol' Bob might need a day or two to recover the use of his jaw, though."

Zack chuckled. "Let's hope so. They said they were up from Tennessee, and those ol' boys tend to hold grudges and are always keen to fight. We should make an effort to steer clear of 'em as best we can. I'd hate to think what they might have in mind to get even with you."

Charlie took the hat from her head and ran a hand through her cropped blonde curls. "Did they say they were headed for Independence too?"

"Yep," Zack said with a nod, "so we'd best make our way toward the river, so we can get a ferry across before they get there."

"My mules can out-pace their old nag, I'm sure."

"They should have had two beasts harnessed to that slip-shod load of theirs." Zack shook his head. "Treatin' a poor beast like that should be considered criminal."

5

They stopped for the evening in a clearing beside a slow-moving creek.

It had been a long day, and Charlie was exhausted, but she threw together a supper of sliced ham and fried yams from her stores. She found a thicket of dewberries growing along the creek and picked enough of the fat, sweet berries to make a couple of skillet pies to have with their coffee before retiring.

"Why do you want to go to Oregon?" Zack asked her as they sat by the fire. "Surely finding a new husband would have been easier back home than in the wilds of Oregon?"

"Who said I was looking for a new husband?" Charlie snapped. "From my experiences with men of late, a woman is better off on her own than saddled with one of them."

Zack grinned at her across the fire. "I hope I haven't done anything to foster that opinion."

"Not at all," she said as she scooped one of the little folded pies from the skillet and slid it onto his plate. "You've been a perfect gentleman, Mr. Drake, and I appreciate that more than you can know."

"What's this?" he asked, staring at the fat piece of fruit-filled dough.

"My mama called them fried skillet pies," she said with a smile. "I found some dewberries growing by the creek and thought pies would be nice with our coffee."

Zack used his fork to cut into the fried pie and smiled when the aroma of berries hit his nose. "Damn," he said with a smile, "it's nice having a cook along for the ride."

"You haven't even tasted it yet," Charlie said, rolling her eyes as she forked up a bite of her own and slid it into her mouth. "I'd be picking and putting up berries now if I was still back home."

"Again," he said between bites, "why Oregon?"

"My daddy and brother are up there somewhere," she finally replied. "I intend to find them and reunite my family if I can."

"Oregon's a big territory," he said with a whistle. "Do you have any idea where they are?"

"No," she admitted, "but Daddy and Tommy are trappers, so I'll start asking after them at the trading posts and fur markets we pass through."

"This is really good," he said, scraping his plate. "Your mama taught you well. Where is she?"

"Dead," Charlie said and hastily swallowed some coffee.

"I'm sorry to hear that."

"It was a long time ago," she said with a deep sigh as she began collecting the dirty dishes.

Charlie flinched and almost dropped the plate when a large cat screamed in the distance. "Was that a bobcat or a panther?"

Zack got to his feet. "I don't know," he said in a low voice, "but it was too damned close for my likin'." He got to his feet. "I'm gonna bring the animals in closer, and you should sleep beside the fire tonight too, instead of under the wagon."

"Do you think it smells the meat I have in the wagon?" Charlie asked, glancing at the wagon.

Zack shrugged. "It probably smells the warm blood in Tess and the mules."

"And in us," Charlie said with a shiver in her voice.

"Thus, my suggestion you sleep closer to the fire." Zack left her and went to collect the animals.

Charlie filled a pan with water to heat for dishes and collected her bedding from the back of the wagon while she waited for it to warm. She rolled out her mattress pad and shook out her blanket. The breeze brought the scent of honeysuckles along with it, and Charlie inhaled deeply. She hoped the cat kept its distance during the night.

When Zack returned with his horse and the two mules, he staked them nearby and squatted by the fire for one last cup of coffee.

He glanced at her bedding and grinned. "It must be nice to travel with such comfort."

"It's not nearly as nice as my four-poster bed in the house on the farm," she said, "but it does me fine. It was on Davis' bed from his childhood."

"It was a big farm?"

Charlie smiled sadly. "Over five hundred acres of prime farm and grazing land with a big house, barns, and sheds. We were lucky not to have lost any of it to the War, other than stock and stores taken by the armies when they came through."

Zach nodded. "My parents lost almost everything. If it weren't for my sister and her husband, they'd be on their own now that my brother is dead and I'm—"

"Your parting wasn't acrimonious?"

"More like the first shots at Fort Sumter in '61," he said with a soft chuckle that held no mirth.

"That damned war ruined too many families," Charlie hissed.

"I followed my convictions, as did my brother," Zack said

with a yawn. "I just wonder if my parents would have been as bitter with him if it had been me killed during that battle."

"And now they've lost both their sons instead of just one," Charlie said as she dropped to sit upon her mattress pad by the fire. "Did you have a good childhood?"

Zack stared at her with a raised brow. "As good as you can have with a strict father who expects you up before dawn, workin' until you drop into your bed at dusk." He smiled. "And you? How was your childhood on the big farm in Tennessee?"

"It didn't start out on the big farm," she said with a sigh. "It started in a one-room cabin in the Hollow, shared with my parents and my brother."

"And then your father and brother went off to Oregon and left you and your mother to fend for yourselves?"

"He was supposed to send for us when they were settled but never did."

"And then your mother died?"

"Was murdered," Charlie hissed and looked away.

"Good Lord," Zack gasped. "I'm so sorry. What happened, and how old were you?"

Charlie took a deep breath. "I was twelve," she said, "but woman enough for this child-loving minister to want to take me to wife."

When Zack's eyes went wide, Charlie went on to explain the circumstances of her mother's death and her rescue by Davis, the half-breed grandson of the Byrdes and owners of the farm.

"Davis Byrde was the best man I've ever known," Charlotte said, "but we were never blessed with children during our short marriage, and I don't know as I'd want to bring a child into this world as it is."

"Why?"

"Too damned much meanness and hatred," she said. "Those people watched Talley, a supposed man of God, burn my mama as a witch because she was pretty and made cures. They cheered him on for no good reason and laughed when my mama screamed in pain. They treated Davis like filth because of his mixed blood when he was better than all of them put together." Charlie pulled off her boots and set them up on the mattress before lying down and pulling the blanket up over her shoulders.

"I've had the one good man in my life I think I was allowed, and I'm content with that." She took a deep breath. "And children will be better off born to other women than me." She snuggled into her pillow and closed her eyes.

"How about you, Mr. Drake?" she asked with a coy smile on her lips. "Is there no young lady in Indiana pining after you?"

"She pined until my best friend made her a better offer," he said in a bitter tone, turned, and stalked to his bedroll on the other side of the fire.

৩৵৯

Zach crawled into his bedroll and rested his head upon his saddle, studying the pretty face of the woman across the fire from him. It had filled him with horror to hear her recite the events about what had happened to her poor mother. How could a child of twelve endure such a thing? Was it any wonder she'd given herself to the half-breed boy who'd saved her?

Zack had never known any Indians, but he had no cause to feel any ill-will toward them either. There hadn't been any Indian troubles in Indiana for almost a century, and he was reasonably certain his mother's family had some Indian blood in it. However, the woman would never have admitted it outside the walls of their fine home. She'd probably have been demoted in the ladies' sewing circle at Church if she had.

Indiana was known to be a very white-oriented state with

deep German and French roots. While the French were known to be racially tolerant, the Germans were not. Drake, he knew, was of English descent—Sir Francis Drake, the famous naval captain and paramour of Queen Elizabeth, being a touted family ancestor.

Zack wasn't certain how he felt about the girl having shared her body and her bed with an Indian man—even a half Indian. She could undoubtedly cook, though, and didn't fear a little hard work. That said more for her, in his way of thinking than who she'd been married to in the past.

She moaned and thrashed in her sleep, and Zack wondered if he should go to her. Bringing up the awful memories of her mother's death must be giving her nightmares. She was even pretty in the throes of a nightmare.

Penny's face came back to Zack as he lay, staring at Charlie, and he felt the stabbing pain of her abandonment again. He'd only been away for a month when he received his sister's letter telling him that Penny had married Doug Peters and moved into his parents' house. Penny had promised him she'd understood his position about going south to enlist with the Confederacy and that she'd wait for him to return. Zack knew her parents were staunch Unionists and had probably been the ones to push their daughter into the arms of Zack's best friend, but it had still hurt.

It had hurt even more when Zack had seen the two of them together with their young child and Penny's belly full with another after he'd returned home. She hadn't even had the decency to write and tell him or return the ring of engagement he'd given her.

"That ring," Penny had said when Zack had confronted her outside the mercantile, "was mine to do with as I saw fit, and I sold it so Doug and me could put a down payment on that little piece of land out by Miller Creek to start our farm."

"The piece of land you and I always talked about buyin'?" he'd gasped in surprise.

Penny had grinned, then sneered. "I always get what I want, Zackary. I wanted you, but your best friend Doug would do in a pinch, and my parents liked his politics better anyhow. I wanted that piece of land, and your ring bought it for us." She put a hand on her swollen belly. "I wanted Drake children, but Peters children will suffice."

Zack had shaken his head in disgust. "You and Doug deserve one another, Penny. I wish you all the best in your endeavors."

Before leaving for Independence, Zack had ridden by Doug and Penny's place on Miller Creek. The spring rains had flooded the creek, and because they'd built too close to the bank, their cabin, barn, and garden were flooded as well. Zack smiled at the memory of Penny wading through the mud with two infants on her hips to find dry ground.

Zack smiled to himself. He couldn't see his current traveling companion ever getting herself in that predicament. Charlie seemed too smart to build that close to a damned creek or marry a nit-wit like Doug.

❧ 6 ❧

They got to the ferry crossing and made it across the Mississippi, north of St. Louis without incident, much to Charlie's relief.

"How long will it take us to get from here to Independence?" she asked Zack as she fried bacon for their breakfast.

"I checked the map, and by my reckoning, we should get there in about nine days if our luck holds," he replied with a smile on his handsome face. "That bein' said, I'm goin' into town to pick up an extra wheel for the wagon here and some hardware for the hitch. I noticed some loose fittings need to be replaced. We can't afford to lose any time with broken equipment while we're goin' through the hills up ahead."

"Do you have a clean shirt?" she asked.

"What's wrong with this one?" he asked, brushing at a dirty spot on the front. "I'm just goin' to the blacksmith's."

Charlie grinned. "Aside from the fact it smells like unwashed man and horse? I'm gonna wash up some of my things in that creek over there and thought I'd do your shirt as well if you had a clean one to change into."

"Oh," he said and opened his saddlebag. He pulled out three shirts in much the same condition as the one he wore. "I can't say as any of these are in much better shape," he grinned.

Charlie rolled her eyes, took the bacon off the fire, and reached out. "Just give 'em all to me," she said as she stood to go to the wagon. "The smelly one on your body too."

When she returned, she tossed Zack a clean shirt that had belonged to Davis. "I think that should fit you," she said. "It was always a little big on Davis."

She saw him wrinkle his nose. "It smells like my grandma's storage closet."

"Camphor balls to keep out the bugs," she giggled. "It's bound to smell better than three days of sweat, horse, and road dust in cramped quarters, though."

"I reckon you have a point there," he said and stripped off his old shirt.

Charlie, who'd changed out of her male garb so that she could wash it, wore a skirt and blouse again. She fried some eggs and sliced some bread, which she toasted and smeared with jam.

They ate, and then Zack saddled his horse. "I'll be back in a few hours," he said. "Do we need anything else from town?"

"We could use some eggs." She handed him two silver coins. "There are only a few left in the box of straw in the wagon. Do you need more money for the new wheel?"

He tipped his hat. "I'll see what I can find," he said with a grin, "but this should more than cover it."

Charlie watched the man ride away. Before carrying her washing to the creek, she mixed up a bowl of bread dough and added some wood to the fire so that it would make a good bed of coals for the Dutch oven she would bake in when the dough had risen. She was glad for the break in travel to catch up on chores, but she couldn't honestly say she'd be getting any rest.

As she went through her trunk of clothes, Charlie came

across her bag of clouts and sat down hard. When had she had her last monthly? She struggled to remember. It had been three or four weeks since Clive and his bastard sons had shown up at her door. How long before that had it been?

Charlie rubbed at her temples deep in thought. She'd been traveling hard with little rest. Her body was probably stressed. She'd missed two monthlies after getting word of Davis's death and missed them regularly when busy with hard work on the farm. Missing a monthly because of stress and overexertion was nothing unusual. She was sure her body would right itself once they reached Independence, were teamed up with the wagon train and got on their way to Oregon.

Charlie put the clouts back into the trunk, scooped up her laundry, and headed to the creek. If a good man like Davis had never gotten her with a child that lived more than a few months in her belly, Charlie was confident three bad men like Clive and his sons hadn't either.

She spent the next two hours in the cold creek water washing Zack's shirts, the clothes of Davis's she'd been wearing, and her underthings. She soaped everything well and rinsed them, twisted the excess water from them, and then draped the wet clothes over the bushes along the creek to dry in the bright sunlight and gentle breeze.

Charlie returned to the wagon and put her bread into the Dutch oven. She placed it into the bed of hot coals and used a stick to rake up more to cover the cast-iron pot that would bake her bread.

As she attended to the bread, Charlie heard the sound of a wagon. She turned to see an old wagon with two men in the seat being pulled up the hill toward her by a sway-backed old horse.

Could it really be those two asinine brothers from back in Illinois? How could they possibly be on the same trail as she and Zack? It wasn't as though they were following a well-defined road or even trail. The map had shown Independence to be on a slightly northwest route from St. Louis, and that was the way they'd traveled, using Zack's compass. Charlie doubted these half-wits could read a map, much less a compass.

Charlie cleaned up her dishes and stored everything in the wagon. She slid a crocheted snood over her head in case these were not the odious brothers. She didn't want to look odd in a dress with her hair cut short like a boy. She made sure her gun belt was tight on her waist, however. She didn't intend to be unarmed with strangers in the area.

"Ho, there, wagon," one of them called as they slowed their wagon.

Taking a deep breath, Charlie stepped around the wagon for them to see. To her regret, she recognized the two brothers and smiled when she saw the heavy bruising that remained on Bob's face. Tom pulled on the reins, and the old horse stopped in its tracks. "We seen the smoke from your fire," he said. "Would you happen to have a bite to eat for a couple of hungry travelers?"

"I have some bread and coffee," she said, "but that's about all I can spare at the moment."

"That'd be much appreciated, ma'am," Tom said with a tip of his dusty, ragged hat.

"Hey," Bob shouted and jumped to his feet when he recognized either Charlie or the guns at her waist, "that's the bitch that kicked my face."

He jumped from the wagon and charged at her. "You owe me, whore," he snarled and grinned to show more than just one missing tooth now. "I aim to take my pleasure, and I ain't gonna pay for it neither like I offered before."

"Get back up here on this wagon, little brother," Tom yelled. "That gal bested ya once, and I don't aim to lose no more time nursin' ya after she does it again."

Bob frowned up at his brother. "Aw, come on, Tom, her man, ain't around. We can both get us a taste of her cunny, and I owe her a punch or two in the face for what she done to me back there."

"The lady said she had coffee and bread to share with us," Tom snapped at his brother, "now watch your mouth before she changes her mind. I ain't had a good cup of coffee since leavin' Memphis."

"I peeked in that there wagon before," Bob said, "and the bitch has a sight more than bread in it. I seen hams and bacon. She's got more than enough in there for two."

"Is that true?" Tom asked as he eyed the tarped wagon. "You got ham and bacon too?"

"None I can spare," Charlie said honestly. "It's our provisions to see us to Oregon."

"You see, Tom," Bob said with a toothless grin, "we can take her cunny and what's on her damned wagon too for our trip to Oregon. I bet the bitch has money hidden in that damned wagon too." He laughed maniacally. "The tramp can pay us for a poke instead of the other ways about."

Charlie lowered her hands to rest on the pistols. Tom saw it and smiled. "Get our damned cups, Bob, and let's get that cup of coffee before you piss the lady off, and she blows your damned fool head off."

"Damnit, Tom, she's—"

"She's offerin' us her coffee and bread, Bob," Tom yelled, "now get the damned cups."

Bob went to the rear of their wagon with a pout on his bruised face and returned with two enameled tin cups. Charlie stepped aside for the two men to pass and watched them pour themselves coffee when they got to the fire. She used the stick she had beside the pit to brush the cooled embers off the top of the Dutch oven and opened the pot to check her bread. It needed more time, and she returned the lid and added some more coals to the top to ensure it browned on the top.

"She ain't even gonna offer us none of the fresh bread, brother," Bob groaned as he glared at Charlie.

"It's still baking," she said and got to her feet. "Would you like jam on your bread? I have another loaf in the back." She smiled sweetly at Tom.

Bob offered a snort, reminding Charlie of an old boar they once had on the farm. She smiled to herself as she glanced at the sulking Bob. Hadn't the bacon and ham they'd been enjoying come from that old boar?

"Never mind him, ma'am," Tom said. "Mama said Daddy dropped him on his head when he was borned and yes, ma'am, the jam would be much appreciated as is this fine coffee."

Charlie went to the back of her wagon, sliced some bread, and smeared it with raspberry jam. She turned to find Bob standing behind her with a grin on his dirty, stubbled face as he craned his head to see what she had in the wagon beneath the tarp.

"You got lots more in there than hams and bacon, don't ya?" he asked brusquely.

"Take that to your brother," Charlie said, shoving the bread into his hands.

She followed him back to the fire where Tom waited. Bob handed his brother one of the thick slices of bread before licking off the jam and then stuffing the bread into his mouth.

Charlie refilled Tom's cup.

"Where's your man?" he asked her when she sat back down. "He your husband or your cousin, the way he said back in Illinois?"

"She's his damned whore," Bob said with his mouth full. "She's spreadin' her legs to pay her way to Oregon."

"Zack and I are traveling together until we get to Independence," she said. "He has a job lined up there as an outrider for one of the wagon trains."

"If the two of you aren't married up," Tom said with a nervous grin and a glance at the loaded wagon. "Maybe you'd consider marryin' up with me to make the trip. It's a long trip for a woman to make alone."

Bob snorted and wiped his nose with his grimy sleeve. "Women like her ain't never alone for long, Tom. She'll have some fool between her legs soon enough and leave you stranded high and dry somewhere along that damned trail." Bob grinned at Charlie. "Now, if she was to marry up with me, I'd keep her in line right." He suggestively squeezed his crotch. "And she wouldn't be wantin' to wander off with no strangers."

Charlie rolled her eyes. "Thank you for the offers," she said in her sweetest voice as her right hand slipped to the pistol at her waist, "but I'm not interested in marriage at this point."

"Not interested in marriage?" Tom said with his eyes wide. "What sorta gal ain't interested in marriage?"

Bob snorted again. "The kind with a wagon loaded with valuables already." He glanced at Charlie's wagon again with narrowed eyes. "I'm tellin' ya, Tom. We oughta just take her and this damned wagon. We'd be ridin' high on the hog all the way up ta ol' Oregon if we did." He gave Charlie another gap-toothed grin. "She could warm our beds at night and warm our coffee in the mornin'. She cooks and fucks too, I'd wager. She's prime and just sittin' out here for the takin'."

Charlie slipped one of the pistols from the holster. "I think it's time for you fellas to be on your way now," she said coolly as she raised and cocked it.

Tom slapped his brother on the back of the head. "Now see what ya went and done, you nitwit. You got her all riled up with your rude talk." He turned to Charlie as he stood and dragged his brother up with him. "I'm right sorry, ma'am. We'll be on our way all right, but first, we'd be obliged if you'd have a look at this here." He reached into his trouser pocket, pulled out a folded piece of paper, and handed it to Charlie.

"She's a fugitive from Tennessee wanted for murderin' some of our kin."

Charlie unfolded the paper and saw the face of a woman staring back at her. The poster read: *Wanted Dead or Alive for the crime of Murder Charlotte Bird 100.00 Reward.*

Charlie smiled to herself. The picture showed a woman with a full head of curly blonde hair, large shaded lips with a painted woman's sultry smile, and dark, round eyes with thick lashes. Was this how Clive Davis had seen her?

She handed the poster back to Tom. "I haven't seen her."

"Just keep an eye out. She's dangerous, and there is a passel of us out searchin' for her to collect that there reward and watch her strung up."

They heard a horse approach and looked up to see Zack. He gave Charlie a questioning glance, and she shrugged as she bent to brush coals from the Dutch over and lift it from the fire pit. "Look who happened by, Zack," she said in a cheery tone. "Our two friends from back in Illinois."

"I can see that," he said and slid off his horse. "How you boys doin'?"

"You havin' wagon troubles?" Tom asked when he saw the wheel tied across the back of one of the mules he'd taken with him.

"Just bein' prepared," he answered. "It's a long trip over rough terrain, and this old wagon didn't have a good spare."

"Always good to be prepared," Bob said as he stared at the tarped wagon again.

Tom handed Zack the folded poster. "Speakin' on bein' prepared," he said, "keep an eye out for that murderin' bitch, and if ya should come across her, we'd be right grateful to ya if you'd hang on to her for us. We'd even split that there reward with ya for your trouble."

Zack glanced at Charlie. "We'll keep that in mind," he said, "if we should run across her. Who'd she kill?"

"Close kin of ours," Bob said angrily, shaking his head.

"The whore cut their damned throats whilst they slept and then burnt their house down around 'em."

Zack bit his lip as he watched Charlie taking the loaf of bread from the oven to cool. "Is that so? We'll be sure to keep an eye open for her. What makes you think she'd be on the trail up here and not still in Tennessee?"

"She's supposed to have kin up in the northwest some-where, so we figure she's headed up there to join up with 'em."

"Her and thousands of others," Zack said with a deep sigh.

"My uncle said she'd stand out," Bob said. "She has a head of gold curls and is likely to flaunt 'em like any whore."

Zack returned the poster to Tom. "We'll be certain to keep our eyes open for her."

"Thank you for the coffee and bread, ma'am," Tom said, doffing his hat. "Me and my nitwit brother appreciate your kindness."

Tom and Bob got on the wagon and urged the old horse into movement as Zack turned to Charlie. "What the hell was that all about?"

❧ 7 ❧

Charlie dropped down beside Zack at the fire after he'd unloaded the mule, unsaddled his horse, and staked them out by the creek. "Those two are gonna be trouble if we can't shake them," she said and handed Zack a slice of the fresh bread she'd slathered with butter and jam. "Tom wants to marry me, and Bob just wants to—"

"Yeah, I know what Bob wants to do." Zack stared at Charlie. "Do you think they recognized you as the woman they're looking for?"

Charlie laughed. "From that ridiculous picture? I highly doubt it, and you've always called me Charlie, not Charlotte." She chuckled. "Clive couldn't even get the spelling of my name right—not that those two imbeciles could have read it."

"Why the hell would you invite them into the camp?" Zack demanded as he tore off a big bite of bread.

Charlie's eyes went wide. "They rode up, and what was I supposed to do? Shoot them?"

Zack raised a brow. "You should have told them to be on their way."

"That's easy for you to say," she snapped. "Maybe if you'd been here, there wouldn't have been a problem."

She got to her feet and strode in anger to the creek to collect her laundry. She checked each piece, and most of them were dry. She hated to get the damp trousers smoky at the fire but didn't want to leave them on the bushes overnight either, so she pulled them down and took them back to the wagon.

Zack came to her side as she stood, folding his freshly laundered shirts. "I'm sorry, Charlie. I know those two showing up wasn't your fault, and I shouldn't have snapped at you like that."

She handed him the folded shirts. "No, you shouldn't have."

"We're gonna need to give you another name besides Byrde," he said. "Charlie Byrde might not be good enough, even with your disguise." He reached up and pulled the snood from her head. "And more of that hair is gonna have to go. It gets curly when you sweat, and we can't take any chances of you being recognized if they're passing that poster around."

Zack went to his saddlebag and returned with a pair of scissors. "I use these to trim Tess's mane," he said with a chuckle. "I suppose they'll work for you as well." He roughed up her hair with his hand and then began clipping.

"McCleod," Charlie said as bits of golden hair fell to the ground around her. "My name before I married Davis was Charlotte McCleod."

Zack nodded and shoved her shoulder playfully. "McCleod is a good strong name for a good, strong boy."

Charlie felt the scissors' cold steel against the back of her neck and then up around her ears. Zack was being thorough with this haircut.

"I suppose that'll have to do," he said as he brushed the hair from her shoulders. "What's for supper, camp boy?" he asked with a soft chuckle.

"I guess I'd best get back into the shirt and trousers," she said with a deep sigh, "now that they're clean again. I want to let them dry a little more by the fire, though."

Zack grabbed her wrist. "I don't mind ya wearin' a dress when we're out in a camp like this." He motioned the vast empty landscape around them. "But when we're gonna be around other folks, you should go back to wearin' the britches." He smiled, and it traveled to include his warm brown eyes. "You look really nice in a dress, Miss Charlotte McCleod."

Charlie's breath caught in her throat, and she felt a tingling in her nether regions she hadn't felt in a good long while. "I'll try to find something for your supper," she said and hurried to the back of the wagon.

From the wood crate where she'd stored the meat that she'd taken from the smokehouse, Charlie grabbed a string of smoked beef sausages. A couple of those with slices of the fresh bread she'd baked would suffice.

She put a hand to the back of her head to feel her bare neck, and tears burned her eyes. Davis had loved her hair, and now it was all gone. Charlie swiped the tears away. Davis was gone now too, so what did it matter what he'd loved?

Charlie squatted and sliced the sausages in half lengthwise by the fire and arranged them in the skillet to warm. Soon, the aroma of smoky beef sausages filled the camp, and Charlie's mind moved from her empty heart to her empty stomach. She filled the coffee pot with water to warm, but she wanted tea rather than coffee.

"What's this?" Zack asked with his lip curled when she handed him the china cup with a silver tea ball floating in it.

"I had a hankering for tea rather than coffee with my supper tonight," she replied. "It's sweetened with a little honey."

"I know what tea is," he snapped and lifted the dainty cup. "I just never expected it on the trail, is all."

"I had a taste for it," she said with a sad smile. "Grandmother Byrde always loved her afternoon tea and cookies."

Zack wrapped sausage in the soft, fresh bread Charlie had

spread with some apple butter and took a bite before taking a sip of the tea. "These aren't cookies," he said with a grin, "but I like it."

"I'll bake up some biscuits and cornbread tomorrow to have while we're traveling," Charlie said, "and maybe another loaf of bread."

Zack nodded. "I saw several deer on my way back from town today, so I think I'll hunt tomorrow. Some fresh meat would be good, and I can set up a small smoke tent to cure some during our overnights." He took another bite. "You have salt in that wagon?"

"A keg or two, I think, ground fine." She smiled as she bit into the warm, savory sausage. The rest of Grandmother Byrde's fancy china tea service was hidden away in the kegs of flour and meal. The barrels of salt held her future. "I have a grinder and some skins. I could make up some deer sausage, too, if you get one."

Zack stared at her wide-eyed as he chewed his sausage and bread. "You know how to make deer sausage too?"

"My daddy was a trapper." She giggled. "We made sausage out of everything. Smoke and a few spices can do wonders to the meat of any critter."

He raised his brow and studied the sausage in his hand. "I'll keep that in mind."

Bob scowled as he stared into their meager campfire. They kept it small, so the girl and her man wouldn't notice it and know they'd only traveled over the next hill before stopping.

"What you think that is she's got cooked up over there?" Tom asked as he took another deep breath. "Sure smells good. We need us a woman who can cook."

Bob squeezed his cock. "I bet she's got somethin' that smells even better. We just need us a woman."

"You really think we oughta take her?" Tom took a sip from his canteen. "I doubt that man of hers is gonna leave her alone again after comin' upon us with her today."

"She's got that hair of hers cut short, but it's blonde. I'd wager we could pass her off as Uncle Clive's gal in that poster and collect the reward," Bob said with enthusiasm, "and while we had her in tow to the authorities in Memphis," he grinned and stroked his crotch, "we could use her as we saw fit."

Tom chuckled. "You'd have to get them guns off her waist first."

"Don't give that no, never mind, brother," Bob said with a broad grin. "She's gotta take her drawers down to piss sometime."

Tom inhaled the aroma of sausage in the air again. "Maybe you're right, Bob. Why don't we creep on over the hill early in the mornin' and wait to see if her man leaves again." He pulled a tattered blanket up over his shoulders and settled in for the night beside the low fire.

"I think that there is a damned good plan," Bob said as he stroked his hard cock beneath his blanket. "I know the first thing I'm gonna do with her when I get my hands on her. That little bitch owes me a debt, and I aim to collect on it."

Charlie made Zack a hardy breakfast of bacon, eggs, and biscuits.

"You're not happy I'm leaving you alone again, are you?" Zack asked as he secured the two warm biscuits with bacon and jam Charlie had wrapped for him in a linen napkin. He tucked them into his saddlebag along with his clean shirts.

She'd changed back into her trousers and shirt and wore her freshly cropped hair beneath the old felt hat. "I'll be fine," she said, sliding her hand down to touch the handle of the pistol on her hip.

"I won't be going too far," Zack said as he saddled his horse. "I saw those deer only about a mile or two away from here, though I might have to hunt for them in the woods."

"I'll be fine," she said with a sigh. "I'm gonna keep busy with some baking and rearrange the wagon some while we're just sitting here."

"A pot of stew would be nice for supper tonight. Do you have the fixins in there for stew in that stash of yours back there?" He nodded toward the bed of the wagon with a grin on his handsome boyish face.

Charlie smiled. "You know, I do. Some fresh venison would make a good stew, though." She giggled playfully.

"I'm taking one of the mules in anticipation of a good hunt," he said as he tied the mule's lead to the back of his saddle. He surprised her with a peck on the cheek. "I'll be back well before sunset," he advised. "Stay close to camp, and don't be inviting in any more vagrants."

"I invited you in once," she said with a grin.

He rolled his eyes and chuckled. "I bet you've been regretting that one." He got into his saddle and urged the horse with his booted feet to trot away, leading the mule.

Charlie touched a hand to her cheek. Why had he kissed her like that? She shook her head in wonder as she watched him ride away. Maybe because she was cooking for him and doing his laundry, he'd gotten it into his head they were something more than simple traveling companions. Would he be expecting something more from her next? The thought of rolling with Zack on her bed the way she'd rolled with Davis brought that tingling in her nether regions back again. She'd never thought about being with another man after Davis. Why this one now?

Clive and his boys were another story. If she'd been with them the way they said they'd been with her, she didn't remember it, so it didn't count. Those horrid men didn't count in any way that mattered.

Charlie stood, brushed off her behind, and went to the back of the wagon to mix up another batch of biscuit dough. They would be back on the trail tomorrow, and she wanted to have biscuits, cornbread, and loaf bread made up so she didn't have to worry about baking at night after they stopped. Maybe she'd go back down to the creek and look for more of those dewberries for skillet pies. Zack had liked them. She frowned to herself. Why was what he liked and didn't like becoming so important to her?

Charlie fit the biscuit pan into the Dutch oven and carried

it to the fire to set in the coals to bake. Once that was settled, she went back to the wagon and began a batch of bread dough. It would take an hour to rise in the warm sun, and that would give the biscuits time to bake.

She climbed into the wagon and found the box with the root vegetables she'd taken from the cellar. She filled a bowl with potatoes, carrots, and an onion. From the wooden crate she'd packed in the smokehouse, she pulled two more of the beef sausages and cut off a large chunk of smoked pork butt. That would make plenty of stew for the two of them.

Charlie carried the bowl of vegetables and the meat along with her sharpest butcher knife back to the fire, where she planned to get everything ready for her pot of stew. She settled herself beside the fire and began peeling potatoes.

Charlie loved to cook. Her mama had begun teaching her at an early age, and Grandmother Byrde had continued her culinary education after Charlie had moved into the big farmhouse.

Her mama's cooking had been simple fare, but Grandmother Byrde had cookbooks from France and taught Charlie how to make some very sophisticated and elegant meals. Meals with sauces rather than gravy over the meat. Charlie had always thought that funny, but Grandmother Byrde had loved her fine meals eaten on her fine china in her fine dining room.

Charlie checked her biscuits, took them off the fire, and replaced the biscuit pan with the bread pan. While her bread baked, Charlie peeled potatoes and carrots, chunked them, and dropped them in another pot.

As she reached for one of the sausages to slice, a shadow fell over her from behind, and a hand reached over her shoulder to snatch the link from her hand.

"What ya got there?" a male voice said.

Charlie jerked her head around to see the grinning faces of Tom and gap-toothed Bob. Tom was biting off the end of the sausage while Bob studied the other items in her bowl.

"I told ya the bitch had more in that damned wagon than bread and coffee."

"Her coffee is good," Tom said as he chewed, "Pour me a cup."

Bob shoved Charlie's shoulder. "You heard him, bitch," he said with a loud chuckle, "pour the man a cup of coffee."

With her heart pounding, Charlie reached for the coffee pot. Rather than pouring the coffee into a cup, Charlie slung the pot around and sent hot coffee into Bob's grinning face. He screamed and fell back with his hands on his scalded cheeks.

"Now, why'd ya have to go and do that?" Tom asked, staring at his brother writhing in the dirt. "We just wanted a little breakfast and," he grinned, "maybe a little cunny."

Tom reached for her, and Charlie grabbed the handle of the iron skillet she'd fried bacon and eggs in for Zack. Without thinking, she swung the skillet with all her might and struck the man in the temple. She heard the cracking sound like an egg breaking, and Tom fell. Charlie saw the deep dent in the man's head and the blood leaking from his ears and nose. She knew he was dead and no longer a threat.

Bob crawled to his knees and went to his brother. "You kilt him," he gasped as he glared up at Charlie. "You kilt Tom for no good reason." He pointed a trembling finger. "You are the murderin' bitch Uncle Clive is lookin' for." He pushed himself to his feet. "But Clive ain't gonna get to hang ya, cause I'm gonna do it first."

Charlie knelt and grabbed up the butcher knife she'd dropped.

"Your man's gonna come back and find your naked body hangin' in one of them trees down there by the crick," he sneered.

His words brought back the memory of her mother's

naked body being hauled up by the neck while she kicked and struggled. Charlie tightened her grip on the handle of the knife.

"I'm gonna strip ya naked and poke ya good before I string ya up, though. I've been thinkin' on givin' you a poke since Illinois," he said as he lunged.

Charlie heard a shot in the distance. Zack must have found the deer. The two pistols hung heavy at her waist, but she had the knife clutched in her hand. Why hadn't she used the pistols?

As Bob fell on her, Charlie pushed the knife into his soft abdomen. He grunted and stopped, exhaling his foul breath into her face. Charlie shoved deeper and twisted the blade. "There's a poke for ya, Bob," Charlie said as the man's body slid down beside his brother.

Her clothes and arm covered in blood, Charlie slid to the ground as well. Her heart pounded in her chest, and she felt light-headed. She glanced at the two men, and tears burned her eyes. She'd killed again. What did that make her? Was she going to burn in hell as a murderer? Was it murder if you were defending yourself?

She'd been defending her body against the unwanted advances and forced marriage to one of Clive's sons. She glanced at Bob. He'd wanted to use her body too. Tom wanted to steal her food from the wagon, but she had no doubt he would have joined in with his brother to ravage her had it come to that. They'd both gotten what they deserved.

The tears slipped down her cheeks. She couldn't feel sorry for these two any more than she could feel sorry for Clive's sons. She'd done what she had to do to save herself. Her stomach lurched, and Charlie threw up over Bob's lifeless body. She saw the blood on her hand and saw more saturating her shirt. She threw up again and then took off the bloody shirt to add to the fire.

She went to the creek and washed her hands, arms, and

face. Some blood had seeped through the shirt onto her camisole. Charlie took it off and washed it in the creek's cold water, getting most of the red stain out. Would she ever get the stain from her soul, though? She tossed the garment over a bush to dry in the sun and returned to the camp to find a fresh shirt in the wagon.

As she checked her bread, Zack rode up with a small buck draped over the mule. "I was successful," he said with a broad smile on his handsome face. He lost his smile when he saw the bodies by the fire pit.

"What the hell happened?" he demanded and slid off the horse.

"They snuck up on me and—" Charlie broke down in tears and fell into Zack's arms. "They were gonna rob us and—"

"Shhh," he said in a soothing tone as he patted her back. "I know what the bastards were gonna do."

"I didn't invite them," she sobbed. "I was cutting up vegetables and meat for the stew, and they were just *there*."

"Just finish what you were doing, and I'll take care of these two assholes," Zack whispered into her sweaty curls.

"Their wagon and horse must be close." Charlie wiped her nose on her sleeve. "They must have come up from behind me across the creek."

Zack nodded. "I'll go have a look."

They spent the remainder of the day working in silence. Zack buried the brothers, found their camp, and released their old horse to graze in the meadow and drink from the creek. He dressed his deer, cutting the meat into thin strips, and built a small smoke tent from an oiled tarp he found in the brother's wagon.

Charlie took some of the fresh deer meat to add to her stew and put the pot of meat and vegetables seasoned with fine salt and wild herbs over the fire to cook. She baked a pan of cornbread and another of biscuits.

They ate warm cornbread along with their stew that night.

"This is really good, Charlie," Zack said as he took his second slice from the pan. "You're a damned fine cook."

"Thank you," she said. "How long will you smoke the deer?"

"Overnight, and then again tomorrow night, but we need to get moving away from this place in the morning." He glanced at the two fresh graves. "There's not too many by this way so late in the season, but I don't think we want to take any chances." He stared at the poster he'd taken from Tom's body, tore it into pieces, and threw it in the fire.

"What did you do, Charlie?" he asked as he forked up some stew. "Did you really cut two fellas' throats and burn their house down around 'em?"

Charlie set her plate aside and took a deep breath, collecting her thoughts. "Well, first of all, it was my damned house, and I didn't cut their throats." Rage filled her as she thought back to that horrible morning. "I shot the bastards, and I'd do it again if given the chance."

"Oh," he said and took a long swallow of his coffee, "well, that makes all the difference."

Frustrated, Charlie launched into the whole story about Clive and his sons. She told him Clive wanted the farm and wanted to force her to marry one of them to take it legally. She left out the part about waking up brutalized in her bed and jumped to the part about the boys coming into her room for a little pre-wedding fun, so she could have an easier time deciding between the two.

"And those two assholes were related to them?" he asked and nodded toward the graves.

"Cousins from what I could figure," Charlie said.

Zack shook his head. "And I thought my family was messed up."

"I find it hard to believe Grandmother Byrde came from that line of scum," Charlie said. "She was such a sweet lady and loved Davis with all her heart though he was the half-breed son of men who'd beaten and abused her daughter."

"You certainly don't need to fret over ridding the world of that garbage." He nodded toward the fresh graves in the meadow.

Charlie wrung her trembling hands over the fire. "I've killed four men," she muttered. "I can certainly understand if you don't want to travel with me anymore, Zack."

Zack took her hand. "Don't be ridiculous. You were defending yourself. That's no more murder than the killing I did during the war."

"Yankees would call what you did murder," Charlie said with a sigh as she ran a hand through her short, sweaty curls.

He smiled at her across the fire. "That's why I'm so glad you're not a Yankee."

"I think it's time we called it a day," Charlie said as she got to her feet to collect her bedding. "We need to get an early start in the morning."

Zack glanced at the wagon and grinned. "I didn't realize you were in a hurry to get back into that wagon seat."

"I'm not, but this spot has lost its appeal." Her eyes drifted to the graves as she rolled out her mattress.

"Don't fret over it none, Charlotte," Zack whispered into her ear with his strong arms around her waist. "Those boys deserved what they got."

Charlie let the blanket slip from her fingers and drop onto the waiting mattress. She wanted to turn in his arms and gaze up into his warm, brown eyes. She wanted to taste his lips, but she knew she wouldn't. Charlie wasn't ready to let Davis go just yet.

A whippoorwill called from the brush along the creek, where a soft breeze rustled the leaves as it moved through the branches. Stars flashed in the sky above, and Charlie took a deep breath in an attempt to ignore the tingling between her thighs as Zack's warm arms held her close to his body.

She broke free from his grasp and bent to retrieve the blanket. "Good night, Zack." Charlie snatched up her blanket and spread it over the mattress, fluffed her pillow, and kicked off her boots.

Zack threw his blankets out beside the fire, settled onto them, and rested his head upon his saddle. "Good night, Charlie," he said softly as he pulled the blanket up over his shoulders and rolled his body to face the fire.

❧ 9 ❧

*Z*ack rode ahead of the wagon as they made their way into bustling Independence.

It had been a hard week of traveling, but they'd finally made it to what city folks were calling the Gateway to the West. He'd always thought that city to be St. Louis, but he supposed Independence made more sense as all the wagon trains departed from here.

The smells of the river filled his nose as he slowed his horse to wait for Charlie and the wagon to draw alongside.

"So, we made it," she said with a broad smile on her dusty face. Zack had made sure to powder her cheeks and chin with wood ash that morning to give her the appearance of a boy in need of a shave.

"I'm gonna go search out the train," he said. "I'd suggest you go find the livery and have ribs mounted to stretch over that old canvas of yours." He nodded to the bed of the wagon. "You'll need to start sleepin' inside from here on out."

Charlie glanced over her shoulder and groaned. It would take a lot of work to rearrange the wagon but sleeping beneath a canvas cover would be more appealing than outside on the ground, being eaten alive by mosquitoes the way they had been. She watched Zack ride away and urged the mules down the muddy street toward the building marked "Livery."

"What can I do for ya, young fella?" a middle-aged black man in a shirt with cut-off sleeves asked when Charlie walked in.

She smiled, happy Zack's disguise seemed to be working. "My cousin and I are joining the next train leaving west, and we need hoops installed for our canvas."

The man took in Charlie's dusty clothes and ran a gnarled hand over the gray stubble on his chin. "Them bows ain't cheap, boy," he said as he stepped closer to crane his head to get a look at her wagon. "Damned old rig too. Not sure I got the outfit for somethin' that old."

The old man brushed past Charlie to study the wagon. "Where the hell you come up with an old schooner like her?"

"In the family since they migrated west from Carolina," she replied.

He raised a gray brow and frowned. "You and your cousin are Southerners, then?"

"If you count southern Indiana and Illinois as Southern." She grinned uneasily.

The old man shrugged as he continued to study the wagon. "Your money all spends the same, if you got any. Might I know your name, boy?"

"Charles," she said uneasily. "Charlie McCleod. How much do you need?" Charlie asked as she fished into her pocket for the leather pouch she kept gold and silver coins in.

"These bolt holes are old and worn, but I think I might have an old set of bows to fit this rig out back in my scrap heap." He fingered the canvas covering her supplies. "This the original canvas?"

Charlie nodded. "My grandmother kept it stored in a trunk in the barn with camphor balls."

"Smart woman, your grandmother, Charlie McCleod," he

said with a grin. "Kept out the mice and the silverfish. It looks damn near new."

Charlie sighed with relief. She remembered Grandmother Byrde telling her the old wagon and canvas had brought the family from Carolina to Tennessee after the rebels defeated the British. They'd lived in it for almost a year while clearing the land and building the original homestead. That would have been close to ninety years ago. She wondered for the first time if it had been the Byrde or Davis family that had made that trip in the wagon all those years ago. Hadn't Clive said the farm had been the Davis family's original homestead?

The old man took one of the mules by the halter and began to lead the wagon behind the building.

"You're gonna need to add four more mules to your team," the man said. "This old rig was meant to be hauled by a team of six oxen, not two old mules." He patted Tiny's sweaty flank. "I'm surprised you didn't kill these two trying to get them over the hills here in Missouri. They'll never make it over the mountains in Wyoming."

Charlie furrowed her brow in thought. The old man was a good salesman.

He went to a pile of rusted iron and began to root through it, pulling out several narrow, arched pieces.

"Looks as I've got what ya need here." he said with a raised brow. "If you and your cousin got the coin to pay for it."

"How much?" she asked, expecting it to be too much.

"Twenty dollars," he replied without looking her in the eye.

"Twenty dollars for that pile of rusted scrap?" Charlie gasped, her eyes wide.

"Rusted scrap you'll only find here on this side of the Missouri, boy. That old rig of yourn has been out of service for nigh on my lifetime, and if you had to have new iron fitted to it, you'd pay double that or better."

Charlie walked over to study the ends of the rusted ribs. "Are these going to hold bolts?"

"They will," the old man said with a sly grin, "but the bolts are gonna cost ya extra."

"I'll give you ten dollars gold, but that has to include the bolts and you fitting them to the wagon."

The old man studied her face closer. "Fifteen gold, and I'll bolt 'em up and stretch the canvas for ya."

Charlie extended her hand. "Done," she said.

"Let me see your money before I do any shakin', boy."

Charlie shook fifteen dollars in gold coin into her palm, and the old man reached for it. "I'll pay when the work is completed," she said, closing her hand around the coins. "Now, let's talk on the prices of four more mules and harnesses."

⚜

Zack found the bustling encampment of wagons near the river. He spotted his friend Morgan seated at a table in the shade of the lead wagon.

"Hey, Morgan." Zack extended his hand as he approached. "We finally made it."

Morgan stood. "Well, it's about damned time," he said in a mock grumble as he grasped Zack's outstretched hand. "I was about to think I'd have to leave without you." The burly man with much gray in his hair and whiskers glanced past Zack's shoulder. "What do you mean by 'we'? Did you and that gal of yours get hitched before you left home?"

The thought of his lost fiancé burned Zack's gut. "No, she married someone else while I was away. Didn't Ellie tell you that?"

Morgan's face lost its smile. "Yeah, I was sorry to hear that, buddy, but it's happened to plenty of fellas while they were gone to fight for whichever cause they happened to choose."

"Yeah," Zack sighed, glad Morgan had never reprimanded him for choosing the Confederacy and not the Union. "I reckon so."

Someone climbed from the back of Morgan's wagon, and Zack held his breath. "Hello, Zackary," his sister Ellen said with a frown on her face that resembled their mother's.

"Hello, Sis," he said softly. "How are you?"

"Busy," she answered as a boy of ten followed her from the wagon and ran to join Morgan at the table. "We were expecting you sooner," she said in her critical tone as she stood with her hands on her hips, glaring at him.

"I was surprised when Mama said you were taking Henry and joining Morgan on this trip to Oregon." Zack smiled down at the boy's table.

"It was time for us to move on," Ellen said with a shrug. "Morgan will lead wagon trains up during the season, and I'll tend the business from that end."

"I just never thought you'd go off and leave Mama and Daddy there on the farm," he said.

Ellen snorted. "Did you happen to see Penny and Doug before you left?"

Zack grinned, remembering the sight of Penny slogging through the flooded yard with her two children on her hips. "Yeah, I saw them, but we didn't speak much."

"They're moving in with Mama and Daddy," Ellen said with a loud sniff. "Penny is taking my place, and Doug is taking yours. I imagine Daddy will probably write my children and me out of his will and replace them with their brats." She turned on her heel to storm back to her wagon but stopped, took a breath, and returned to her seat beside Morgan. "I'm sorry, Zackary," she said ruefully, "I'm just a little miffed about the whole situation with Penny and Doug, I suppose."

Zack took his sister's hand. "You're not the only one, Sis.

Did you know she sold the ring I gave her to buy that piece of creek land for Doug?"

Ellen grinned. "Didn't the stupid bitch know it flooded every spring?"

Zack shrugged. "I have no idea, but Doug should have."

"Did you bring me another outrider then?" Morgan asked with a hopeful grin on his suntanned face when he returned to the table with his son, who'd needed to go and relieve himself.

Zack took a seat in the chair across from his friend. "Not exactly," he answered with a sigh as he went on to explain Charlotte's situation.

Ellen shook her brunette head, and her frown deepened. "I can't believe you brought an unmarried woman to join Morgan's train, Zackary. Don't you see how unseemly that is and how it will reflect badly on him if she causes trouble with loose ways?"

Morgan scratched his chin. "I don't usually take on single women," he said with a glance at his wife. "They cause too much upset on a long trip. Men try to crawl into their wagons at night, and the other women complain to no end." He shook his head with a glance at his stern-faced wife. "I don't know as I can do it, Zack."

"And you shouldn't have to, Morgan," Ellen hissed, "Zackary should have known better than to have brought her and put you into this position."

"It's why we had her hair cut and dressed her as a boy," Zack explained. "Charlie won't be any trouble with the men or the other women." He grinned at his frowning sister and shrugged. "He's my younger cousin, and we're traveling north together."

Ellen shook her head. "That sounds about like one of your outlandish schemes, Zackary," she scolded as Charlie pulled up in the wagon.

"Damn, if that ain't an old rig," Morgan said with a

whistle and a grin on his face. "I'm surprised the old heap made it this far."

Zack turned his head at his friend's chuckle to see a canvas-covered wagon arriving. Its ribs were broader and squatter than the more streamlined newer ones. He recognized two of the old mules pulling the wagon but noted with surprise that Charlie had added four more of the large animals. He recognized the driver as well and smiled. "That wagon has been better maintained than you'd ever imagine, Morgan."

He watched Charlie set the brake and jump to the ground. "I'd like you to meet Charlie McCleod," he said when Charlie arrived at the table. "Charlie, this is my friend Morgan. He's the wagon master of this organization, and this is his wife and my older sister, Ellen."

Charlie extended her hand. "It's a pleasure to meet you, sir, ma'am."

Morgan stood and studied her before taking her hand. "Zack's explained your situation, Mrs. Byrde," he said with a furrowed brow, "but I'm still not certain I can allow a single woman on my train."

"It's unseemly and will rile the married women in the group," Ellen snapped. "Zackary should have known better than to have brought you here and put my husband and me in the situation of turning you away."

Charlie fished the leather bag from her pocket and dropped it with a heavy clink onto the table in front of the wagon master. "I have the money if that's what you're worried about. How much does it cost to join a train, sir?"

"Thirty-five dollars," Morgan replied in a firm voice as he ignored the protesting sighs of his wife and stared at the pouch on the table, "and you're responsible for the care and feeding of your animals along the way." He glanced up at the old wagon and smiled. "As well as the upkeep of your wagon. We can't slow the group, trying to keep your old rig in repair."

"My wagon is as sound as any new rig out there," Charlie snapped, "and I have a new replacement wheel on board as well as an old one, should I require it." She picked up the pouch and shook out some coins. "I understand my situation is unusual, sir, and I'm willing to pay you for any inconvenience." She slapped two gold eagles and another half eagle onto the table. "Will fifty dollars cover any problems I might cause you?"

"Is she one of your southern belles who thinks her money can buy her anything she wants?" Ellen asked her brother in a rude tone.

The wagon master's eyes went wide at the gleam of gold on his table. "I think it will do just fine," he said, glaring at his wife before snatching up the coins and dropping them into his vest pocket. "Do you have all the provisions you'll need for the journey?"

"Enough to get us started." Zack glanced at Charlie. "I assume we'll be passing through settlements along the way where we can buy provisions, should we run short."

Morgan coughed to clear his throat. "Best to get what you need here rather than pay the outlandish prices at posts along the trail. I'd suggest you stock up on bacon, dry beans, and root vegetables here, along with flour and meal if you have room for it. The man at the mercantile in town has my list of recommended provisions."

He smiled at Charlie. "I'd also suggest another barrel for water. We'll be going through some arid country, and it's best to have the extra barrels to fill when we come to a good supply of water, so you and your animals don't suffer."

Charlie nodded. "I'll go to the mercantile once I have a chance to go through our provisions and take better stock of what we have."

"Our provisions?" Ellen said to Zack. "Are you traveling as man and wife, brother? That sort of behavior will not be tolerated on this train."

"Mr. Drake is a gentleman, ma'am, and our agreement is that I will supply him with his meals if he would escort me to Oregon." She turned to Morgan. "If that isn't something you approve of, then we can end our agreement now that we've arrived here. I'm perfectly capable of tending to my animals myself."

Morgan smiled and nodded. "You can line up behind the last wagon, ma'am."

"When will we be leaving?" she asked as another group of six wagons arrived, and dust filled the air around them.

"I'd hoped to leave in the morning," he said and blew his nose, "but it looks as though we have a few more stragglers."

A striking redhead dressed in the latest fashions came strolling up to the table with a man about her age at her side. "I'm Jolene Bennett," she said with a thick southern drawl, "and this is Lance Bennett. We have seven wagons in our group and would like to join this train to Oregon."

Morgan examined the newly arrived group. "I only count six wagons, ma'am," he said with a grin at the pretty woman.

She rolled her big green eyes. "I have two more cousins who are supposed to meet us here," she stated, her eyes studying the line of wagons already assembled. "Robert and Thomas Davis," she said with an exaggerated sigh of frustration. "I'd have expected them to beat us here. They left Memphis a week before we did."

Morgan ran a finger down his roster of names. "I don't have any Davises here," he said.

"That old horse of theirs probably gave up the ghost on 'em," Lance said. "I told them to shoot the damned old thing and get a new one before they took off."

"I'm certain they'll be along soon," Jolene cooed to the wagon master. "Can you give them a few more days, sir?"

Morgan glanced at his long line of waiting wagons. "I'm afraid not, ma'am. If we don't get moving, we risk getting caught in snows in the mountains."

"Oh, please, good sir," she begged with mock tears in her eyes. "Bob and Tom are family, and we can't leave without them."

"I'll give them one more day," Morgan said, relenting to the pretty woman's charms, "but this train crosses on the ferry first thing day after tomorrow."

"Oh, thank you, sir," Jolene responded, oozing southern charm. "You are such an understandin' gentleman. I'm certain Bob and Tom will be along very soon."

Charlie clutched Zack's sleeve. "I think I know who she's talking about, don't you?"

He gave her a nervous frown. "Yeah, I do, and if she's waiting for them to show up here, it's gonna be a long one."

"I gotta go," she said and trotted back toward the wagon with a hand over her mouth.

Charlie's stomach grumbled, and then her breakfast rushed back up her gullet. She clutched at the wagon's wheel for support as her head spun, and she spewed the meal onto the weedy ground behind the wagon. After heaving until nothing came up but air, Charlie wiped her sweaty brow, stumbled to a fallen log nearby, and dropped onto it. She trembled from weakness and needed to catch her breath.

Had the meat they'd eaten for supper last night been bad? If that were the case, Charlie knew she'd have been spewing it out from both ends, and she wasn't. The only times she'd ever vomited like that after breakfast had been when she was … Charlotte closed her eyes and hung her head, trying to think back to when she'd bled last.

It had come while she was on her knees in the strawberry patch back on the farm. That had been three weeks before Clive and his sons arrived, knocked her unconscious, and had their ways with her. Tears stung Charlie's eyes, and they slid down her sunburned cheeks.

She couldn't be pregnant—not by one of those pieces of Davis filth. What sort of child would it be? Charlie dashed the tears from her cheeks. Maybe it would be a good child. They were Davis men, and that made them kin to her husband, and her husband had been a very good man. Maybe this was her way to have a piece of him to hold on to after all.

How was she going to explain this to Zack? She'd told him her husband was dead in the war, and the war had been over for almost five years. Her stomach lurched again, and she heaved up dry air. What was she going to do?

Clinging to that tiny spark of hope that this Davis child in her belly could be one final connection to her lost husband, Charlie stood and hobbled back to the wagon. She wished she could lie down for a spell to regain her strength and ponder what she would do next, but Charlie needed to get the wagon in line with the others and straighten out things inside. She had hours of work ahead of her and no time to ponder this.

By her reckoning, she was two months along. Charlie ran a hand over her flat belly. She wouldn't begin to show for another two or perhaps three months. They would be well into their trip north by then. Perhaps almost to Oregon.

Charlie released a long sigh. She'd never carried one of Davis's children more than three months before the terrible cramping came, and she expelled it in a painful gush of water and blood. Would she feel the same sense of agony and regret if she lost this one in the same fashion? Charlie thought not.

Families outside laughed and fussed as they loaded their wagons for the journey. Most of these people were honest, God-fearing folks. What would they do when they found they had a pregnant, unmarried woman in their midst? Would they deny her and cast her out?

Memories of her mother and Reverend Tally flooded Charlie's mind. Would they call her a trollop and whore to be shunned? Would Zack? The memories of going into town with Grandmother Byrde and watching women and girls she'd known all her life in Fern Hollow turn their backs on her in the street still stung Charlie when she thought about it. Could she go through that again? Could she deal with Zack feeling that way about her?

Charlie ran her fingers through the hair Zach had cut short like a boy's. The baggy men's clothes she wore would help to hide a swelling belly too. Maybe she could pull it off after all. No one had called her on her deception yet, and she thought it wouldn't be difficult to keep her distance from folks here. All she had to do was stay with the wagon and the animals.

Charlie climbed up onto the bench of the wagon and dropped her shorn head into her hands. Did she want this child born a bastard with all that entailed? Davis had been born a bastard and had lived with the snickering behind his back throughout his childhood. Had it not been for his grand-parents' place in society, it would have been much worse. Did Charlie want that for this child?

Davis had also been a half-breed Cherokee, and this child wouldn't have that to deal with, but nonetheless, other chil-dren and some adults would be cruel to a fatherless child. Charlie didn't want that for her child. She caressed her abdomen again. She was already thinking about this little spark of life as a child—the child she could never give her beloved Davis.

Should she tell this child Davis Byrde was his or her father and show him or her the tintype photo of the handsome young man in uniform? No, she was intelligent, and she hoped the child would be intelligent and figure out soon enough that a man killed in the war couldn't be the father.

Charlie fretted some more. She knew her body was changing with the child in it and with that, her moods. It had been the same before. She'd become irrationally emotional, crying for the least little thing. Charlie knew she couldn't do that now.

She needed to talk to Zack. Maybe he'd marry her, and then she could go back to being a woman in the dresses she loved. She needed to explain everything to him that had happened to her. Would he understand why she'd really killed Floyd and Vernon?

It bothered her that she hadn't been completely honest with the man. Now she would have to come clean and tell him the truth. She'd been savagely abused, and now she carried one of those horrid men's child in her belly. Would he think that child was going to be horrid too and not want to have anything to do with it—or her?

As Charlie sat in the sun, a thought came to her. Perhaps she could find a bottle of whiskey somewhere. She could get Zach drunk and put him in her bed to sleep it off, and when he woke, she could give him the impression they'd coupled. Then after a month or so, she could say she was with child and that it had to be his. He'd be obliged to marry her then.

Charlie sat up straight on the wagon's bench seat and ran her hands through her hair. She couldn't do that to the man who'd been so kind and helpful to her. She was an honest person, not a lying cheat. Tears ran from her eyes again. She wasn't that kind of woman. She wouldn't use deceit to get a husband and father for a child that wasn't his.

Zach wasn't a stupid man either. He'd know when she delivered a fully formed and healthy child months less than those required that she'd tricked him, and he'd hate her and the child. Charlie couldn't do that to either of them. It just wasn't right. Charlotte McCleod Byrde wasn't that sort of woman.

Charlie let her head fall back. She wept in silence as she moved the wagon into the line where Morgan had told her to put it.

❧ 10 ❧

The woman with the striking green eyes and red hair was unbelievably beautiful, but Zack smelled nothing but trouble coming from her.

"You travelin' with this train too, handsome?" Jolene purred at Zack as Morgan filled out paperwork for the new additions.

"I'm working as an outsider for the train," he said uneasily, "while I travel with my young cousin, Charlie, to Oregon."

Jolene took a paper from the bag on her wrist and unfolded it to show Zack. "Have you happened to have come across this woman?" she asked and moved the poster beneath Zack's nose.

"I don't think so," he said, giving a copy of the same poster Tom had in his possession a quick look. "Who is she, and what did she do?"

"She's a murderess, and she's gonna be our stake in the Oregon Territory if we can find her and turn her over to Jolene's Uncle Clive," Lance explained when he joined them and put an arm around Jolene's shoulder.

"Clive Davis is a member of my family," Jolene said, "and

this woman killed his two boys and burned down his family farm in Tennessee."

"Burned his farm?" Zack asked with interest as he studied the poster.

"She was squattin' on it," Lance said. "Claimed to have been married to the former owner's illegitimate half-breed grandson and was trying to claim it for herself."

"And she killed his sons?"

"Uncle Clive wanted to make an honest woman of the bitch," he said, "by marryin' her to him or one of his boys, but she slit the boys' throats in their sleep while he was off after a preacher and then burned down the house and barn out of nothin' but damned spite."

"That's terrible," Zack murmured with a shake of the head, "but what makes you think she's gone north?"

"Word has it her daddy and brother ran off from her and her mama to Oregon some years ago," Jolene said. "Clive figures she's headed there to find them."

Zack nodded. "That makes sense, I suppose."

"You married, Mr. Drake?" Jolene asked, batting her eyes in a flirty manner.

"No." He turned back to Morgan who was finishing with the final member of Jolene's troop. "I'm gonna go check on Charlie if you don't need me for anything here, Cap."

Morgan waved him off, and Zack headed for the wagon with Jolene, staring after him. Charlie needed to know about this woman and her connection to Clive Davis and his family. When he got back to the wagon, he heard retching and peeked around to see Charlie hunched over the bushes with the reins of two mules in her hand.

"Are you all right?" he asked as he took the mules in hand. "Do you have a fever, or did you eat something that didn't agree with you?"

Charlie stood up and wiped her mouth on her sleeve.

"Think that meat may have been off last night," she said quietly. "How are you feeling?"

"Come to think on it," he replied, "my bowels were a bit loose this morning."

"Sorry about that," Charlie said as she headed to the wagon.

"Whatever you do," Zack warned, "don't let that bunch that just came in get wind that you're a female."

Charlie stopped in her tracks and turned to face him. "Because they're related to those two we buried in the field?" she asked, her face growing paler.

"That, and they're showing that poster around."

Charlie dropped on the step leading up into the wagon. "Oh, good Lord," she mumbled as she ran trembling fingers through her hair. "Maybe I should just forget about this trip with the wagon train and try to make my way on my own."

Zack went to her side. "Don't be ridiculous, Charlie." He patted her hand. "Just keep to the wagon, and don't let nobody see ya without your clothes."

Charlie chuckled as she glanced up at the canvas covering the rusty metal ribs. "I suppose that will be easier now with the ribs and all."

"Of course, it will," Zack said, trying to sound supportive. "Now, let's get in there and try to put things in some sort of order."

Charlie rolled her eyes. "I fear that's going to be a bigger job than you think."

"I'll start unloading all the kitchen items to transfer into the utility cabinet on the outside since we'll be doin' all our cookin' over the fire rather than on a stove."

"The meat and foodstuffs should stay inside the wagon to keep animals from being tempted to them," she said, putting her mind to the task at hand and getting to her feet.

"Yeah," Zack sighed. "The two-legged as well as the four."

"You think people would try to steal our supplies?" she asked, turning to stare wide-eyed at Zack.

"When folks are hungry," he said with a shrug, "they'll do about anything, so it's best to keep our foodstuffs in the wagon where they're safe, and we can look after 'em."

Charlie nodded and began to hand crates out of the wagon to Zack. He made room in the utility cabinet that the original settlers headed to Tennessee had used to store small tools, bits of wire, and other things needed for work around the farm and a workbench. Now it would become a makeshift kitchen cupboard and food-prep area as they traveled. Charlie suspected that had been its original purpose ninety years ago when the family had traveled in the wagon from Carolina.

After three hours, Charlie had moved the kitchen to the utility box outside and set up a makeshift bed atop trunks and crates. Grandmother Byrde's favorite chair sat in one corner and could be turned for use at the small vanity. Barrels of flour and other dry goods took the place of side tables, and Zack had hung an oil lamp from one of the metal ribs to light the space at night.

"Just remember to blow it out before you undress," he warned, "or you'll be givin' the other wagons a peep show."

Charlie felt her cheeks burn with embarrassment. She hadn't thought about that. "I'll keep that in mind," she mumbled. "Thanks, Zack."

The wagon smelled of smoked meat and onions, but Charlie thought she'd be comfortable in the small space. She'd taken more of Davis' things from the trunk and had them folded on the vanity. Tearing apart the bed every time she wanted to change clothes didn't make much sense to her, and there wasn't room for such foolishness either.

"This looks comfy," Zack said when he peeked in for a final look at her day's work. "What's your take on our stores?" he asked as he dropped into the chair.

Charlie pointed to the floor. "I think there will be plenty of room for you to bed down in here if we run into bad weather."

"I'll be fine beneath the wagon or beside the fire," he told her. "Besides, I'll probably be riding security most nights. It's what Morgan hired me for." He grinned. "Now, how about those stores? We don't want to get caught short along the trail."

"I think we have plenty of sugar and salt." She studied the small barrels. "But we could do with more flour, meal, another side of bacon, and a bag of dried beans."

"How about coffee?" he asked with a grin. "I know you like your tea, but I'm a coffee man myself."

"I suppose we'd best find that mercantile then," Charlie giggled.

Zack saddled his horse. "You can ride up behind me," he said, "and we'll take one of the mules to haul back what we need from the mercantile."

Charlie got on the horse and wrapped her arms around Zack's waist to secure herself. He reeked of man-sweat and trail dust, but Charlie thought he smelled divine. She'd missed the smell of a man.

"Don't hold me like a woman holds a man," Zack snapped, and Charlie loosened her hold.

"Sorry." She lowered her hands to grasp the saddle for support.

"Goin' in for some supplies, Cap," Zack called when they neared Morgan's wagon. "You and Ellen have need of anything?"

Morgan waved. "No, we're good."

"Your sister doesn't like me," Charlie said.

"Ellen is bitter about what my parents have done with my former intended, Penny and her new husband Doug," Zack said, "and she's very protective of Morgan and his reputation. She'll like you well enough once she gets to know you."

They found the mercantile, and Zack got down from the horse. He offered his hand to Charlie, but she ignored it and slid off on her own.

"You don't need to be that way about it. I just didn't want you drawin' attention to us with your arms around me in an unnatural fashion for two male cousins," Zack said as he followed Charlie into the store.

The Independence Mercantile smelled like any other Charlie had ever been in. She caught a whiff of the sweets in glass jars near the door and the overpowering aroma of kerosene coming from somewhere near the back. In between were the scents of strong soap and smoked meat. A woman stood near the door. She wore the black dress and the black linen cap of a widow.

"What can I do for you fellas today?" a skinny man standing behind the counter asked.

"We're with Cap Morgan's train leaving in the next day or so," Zack replied, "and we're in need of a few more supplies."

The widow walked up to Charlie and Zack. "I'm traveling on the train to Oregon too," she said in a voice heavy with recently shed tears. "My husband died two days ago from a snakebite."

"I'm so very sorry to hear that, ma'am," Zack said with an uneasy glance at Charlie.

The woman was shorter than Charlie, several years older, and pudgy. "I could use some help with supplies," she stated. "My husband had made arrangements to work for supplies, but now that he's gone," she said, wiping tears from her eyes, "I find myself stuck and in need of help from strangers."

"What do you need, ma'am?" Charlie asked with a glance at Zack, who seemed to shake his head.

"I have family waiting for me in Salem," the woman said, "but I'm going to need people to help me with my supplies until I can get there to them."

"I've got Mr. Morgan's recommended list of supplies right

here," the man at the counter said and lifted a piece of paper with a supply list printed on it. "Why don't we have a look and see how you fare?"

Charlie walked away from the woman and took the list from the man. She could see the proprietor had considerably inflated the amount of goods on the list. She was a tea drinker but knew she wouldn't have need of five pounds of tea for a trip that would take a few months.

"We'll take ten pounds of ground coffee beans," she told the man, "a side of bacon, a twenty-pound sack each of flour and meal, ten pounds of dried beans, and a bushel of potatoes."

"We also need an empty water barrel," Zack added as he began to wander down one of the aisles.

"You two vagabonds have the coin to pay for a big order like this?" the man asked in a rude tone.

Charlie took her pouch from her pocket and dropped it on the counter with a loud, heavy clink. "We pay our way," she hissed at the man. She dug into the pouch, brought out a twenty-dollar gold eagle, and handed it to the widow. "I hope this will help you get the supplies you need, ma'am."

The woman's mouth fell open, and her eyes went wide. "It will, young man, thank you so much."

Zack returned to the counter with his arms loaded down and frowned when he saw the widow clutching the gold coin. "I don't think that was a good idea, Charlie. That woman has probably been out there collecting coins for weeks, using the excuse that she'd lost her husband."

He shook his head. "Your fancy dishes won't work well on the trail." He dropped two blue enameled plates and cups, along with a matching coffee pot, onto the counter. "Your bar of soap was getting thin too," he advised, and Charlie saw a large yellow bar of soap with the other things on the counter. "You need yeast for bread?"

Charlie glared at the man scurrying around to collect their order. "We can make do with biscuits and cornbread when I run out of yeast."

The bell at the door rang to announce new customers, and Charlie turned her head to see Jolene and Lance Bennett enter together. She walked toward the back of the store to avoid them.

"Well, hello, darlin'," Charlie heard Jolene coo to Zack in that too sweet voice. "You and your boy stockin' up?"

Lance added with a chuckle, "We saw y'all workin' on that old wagon all mornin'. Do ya really think it will make it all the way over the mountains to Oregon?"

"It's made it this far," Zack answered matter-of-factly.

Charlie returned to the counter with a crock of vinegar, some vanilla extract, and a ball of lavender-scented soap.

Jolene picked up the soap and sniffed it. "Lavender is the scent of love," she said with a grin as she studied the other items on the counter.

"It's also a scent that keeps lice and other bodily pests away," Charlie said. "You'd best do well to stock up as I reckon bath houses will be few and far between out there on the trail."

"Well, I never," Jolene gasped in mock indignation. "You need to teach your boy some manners, Mr. Drake."

"He's my cousin," Zack said with a smile tugging at his lips, "not my boy, and he speaks the truth. We'll be out in the wilds, and critters like lice and chiggers will make a meal of us if they can."

"Damnit," Jolene hissed under her breath as she stared at the ball of lavender soap, "go find us some of that girlie soap, Lance."

"Are you traveling on the wagon train, too?" the widow asked, approaching Lance as he went for the soap.

"I told you she was a professional mooch," Zack whispered into Charlie's ear. "Bet she don't get nothin' from them, though."

"We'll need a jug of lamp oil too," Charlie told the proprietor, who'd returned with a large slab of bacon. "Do you have any with Tansy in it to burn against mosquitoes?"

The man nodded and left again. "You're making friends left and right, Charlie," Zack chuckled. "Do we have everything we need here?"

"I noticed on that list," she said, indicating the list of supplies on the counter, "we should have some medical supplies. Do you think there is an apothecary here in town?"

"You don't think they'd have it here?" Zack asked, his eyes darting toward the aisle Jolene had disappeared down.

Charlie didn't know why the redhead bothered her the way she did. "I'd rather spend my money at an apothecary if I'm buying medical supplies."

The proprietor returned with the lamp oil. "Will this be all for you?"

"I believe so," Charlie said, "and would you mind itemizing the bill?"

The skinny man glared at her as he began scratching on a pad of paper with a pencil he'd taken from behind his ear. "Mouthy brat, isn't he?" the man asked Zack.

"He minds the money," Zack said with a grin at Charlie.

"They gotta learn sometime, I reckon," the man muttered as he totaled the figures on the paper. "That'll be five dollars and twenty-one cents."

Charlie nodded and fished a Quarter Gold and a two-bit silver piece from her pouch. "Thank you for your time," she said in a cordial voice. "Is there an apothecary in town?"

"Up the boardwalk, just past the barbershop." He nodded to the north end of the street, away from the river.

They carried their purchases outside, and Zack tied them to the mule.

"I'll walk down to the apothecary and make my purchases," Charlie told him.

"Don't buy over much," Zack warned, "we don't want to weigh the wagon down too much."

"Or lighten my pouch," Charlie said as she patted her pocket.

"That too," he said. "We may require it later."

Charlie entered the apothecary shop, and the pungent and medicinal smells of astringents and other medications overcame her. "May I help you, young man?" a balding man with spectacles asked.

"We're leaving on the next wagon train to Oregon," Charlie said, "and I thought we should have some medical supplies on the wagon, in case of emergencies."

"Very wise notion on your part," the man said. "What did you have in mind?"

Charlie thought for a minute. "Willow bark tea for pain and swelling if you have it, yarrow salve for scrapes and bruises, and a roll of gauze bandages."

The man nodded in appreciation of Charlie's knowledge. "Excellent choices, young man, but might I also suggest a bottle of wood alcohol and another of iodine to clean cuts and scrapes? Doctors during the war found them invaluable for stemming infection and the loss of limbs due to it." He smiled when Charlie nodded her approval. "Laudanum is also good to have on hand for pain the willow bark can't handle."

"I'm not familiar with that," she stated. "Do you have any reading material that might give instructions for its use?"

"You read?" the man asked, his eyes wide.

"Regularly," Charlie said with a grin at the man's surprise as she began to peruse the rack of dime novels. She chose four and took them to the counter. On a shelf behind the man, Charlie saw a leather-bound book titled *Medical Discoveries of This Century*. "Is that book for sale?"

The man smiled and rolled his eyes. "That book costs three dollars, young man. I seriously doubt you have that kind of money to spend on a book you'd hardly underst—"

"I'll take it," Charlie said and took her pouch of coins from her pocket.

While the man gathered her order, Charlie wandered around the small shop and stopped when a bright bonnet caught her eye. She fingered the satin ribbon and velvet trim while she admired the rows of lace and satin flowers decorating it.

"Not quite your style," the man called with a chuckle, and Charlie stepped away from the fancy bonnet.

"My mother would have loved it," she said. "She had a fondness for pretty things like that."

"Most women do," he said knowingly. "It's why I keep a few in stock all the time."

Charlie smiled. "Wise man," she complimented him. "How much do I owe you?"

"Four dollars and ten cents," he said as he put things into a white cloth sack for her to carry.

Charlie took the coins from her pouch and handed them over. "I appreciate your time."

"I hope you get something from that book, young man, though it's written for the professional medical mind and not a simple layman."

Charlie smiled. "I think you might be surprised what some simple laymen can comprehend, sir." She took the sack and left the store without waiting for a reply.

"Did you get what you need?" Zack asked when she joined him at the horse. The widow had returned to the porch but had no supplies in hand.

"That I did," she said and climbed up onto the horse without his assistance.

"Damnit, Charlie," Zack hissed as he climbed up in front of her, "I didn't mean to make you mad earlier."

"You didn't," she said. "You were right. I need to keep in mind that I'm a boy and your cousin."

Zack let out a long breath. In his experience, when a woman told you that you were right about something, it never boded well.

❧ 11 ❧

S upper that night was catfish.

As they rode back to the wagon, Zack and Charlie encountered two young Negro boys returning from the river. Both carried stringers heavy with shiny, black catfish.

"Looks like you fellas had a good day," Zack called down to them as he slowed.

"They was bitin' at everthin', mister," the older of the two said with a broad smile.

"What you gonna do with all those fish?" Charlie asked.

"Mama's gonna cook 'em up, and we's gonna eat 'em," the younger one answered, giving Charlie a look as though she must be daft if she didn't know what they intended to do with the fish.

"Would you consider selling us some?" Charlie asked and slid off the horse.

The younger boy looked from his stringer to his brother and then back to Charlie. "Sell my fishes to you?"

The older boy tugged on, the younger's arm. "Come on, Tully, we'd best be gettin' home, or Mama's gonna whoop our butts." He glanced up at Charlie. "You know she don't like us consortin' with white folk."

"I don't want to buy them all," Charlie said, "just four or five for our supper tonight."

"These little niggers givin' you trouble, boy?" Lance Bennett called as he and Jolene came upon them.

"Nah," Zack said, "we're just negotiating for some catfish for our supper."

Lance slid off his horse. "Didn't they teach you fellas nothin' about niggers up north where you come from?" He stalked by to loom over the two small boys who now crouched together on the side of the dirt track. "You don't negotiate with 'em." He laughed maniacally and reached for the stringer, the youngest one held. "You just take from 'em as they probably stole 'em from a white man anyhow."

Charlie stepped between Lance and the boy. "These boys caught the fish in the river, sir, and they belong to them."

Lance glared down at her. "You Yankees are all alike," he snarled, shaking his uncombed blond hair. "Niggers got no minds like us and need to be owned and told what to do so they don't get themselves into trouble. They're no better than that mule there and should be treated like one." He began to unbuckle his belt. "I bet if I strapped their black hides good, they'd be more forthcomin' with those fish."

"We are quite capable of negotiating our own price for our supper," Charlie said, still between Lance and the shivering boys. "If they want to sell their fish, they will name a price. If they don't want to sell their fish, they are free to go on their way with them."

"Come, Lance," Jolene ordered with a pinched nose from the horse she rode upon side-saddle. "The boy seems determined to eat fish handled by filthy little nigger boys. Let's leave him to it and be on our way. I'm certain Millie has our supper near to ready."

"Ignorant Yankee scum." Lance spat as he heeded Jolene's call and turned back to his horse. "All y'all ruined this country with your meddlin' in Southern affairs." He returned to his saddle, and the couple rode off toward the wagons.

"This trip is going to be a pure joy if you keep making friends like that," Zack said with a grin on his handsome face. "Ignorant scum like him are who cost us the war."

"We're sorry about that," Charlie said, turning to the two boys.

"C'mon, Tully," the older boy urged, tugging on the other's frayed cotton shirt. "Mama's gonna tan our hides when she hears about this."

The younger boy stared up at Charlie. "How much you pay for my stringer of fishes, ma'am?"

Charlie smiled. "Whatever you think they're worth, young man." She winked. "But I really like catfish and would pay about anything to have a mess for my skillet tonight."

The boy smiled, and Charlie was taken by how his big brown eyes lit up his face. "Me an' Lester been at it since daylight," he grinned. "I'd reckon I've earned a day's wages for all this work. Our Mama gets a dollar a day for takin' in washin'."

Charlie dug into her pocket and pulled out a shiny silver dollar. "I'd reckon you've earned the same for your hard work," she said and offered the coin to the wide-eyed boy.

Tully handed over his stringer of fish and snatched the coin from Charlie's fingers. "Now, you give your mama that dollar, Tully. She may have to go to the store and buy your supper now," Charlie told him.

The boy clutched the coin to his chest. "But this is mine. I earned it, and I should get to keep it."

"You were going to give your mama the fish, weren't you?" Charlie chided. "It's only fair that you give her the dollar since you no longer have the fish to give her."

His brother laughed as Tully considered her words. "I 'spose you're right, ma'am," the boy finally said. "Thank y'all for the dollar." He and his brother began to run down the road toward town.

Charlie turned toward Zack with the stringer in her hand. "He called me ma'am."

Zack began to laugh. "I guess you can't fool everybody with your disguise, Charlie." He reached for the stringer. "Give me those, and I'll take 'em down to the river to clean."

Charlie walked back to camp with the mule in tow while Zack took the fish to clean. She unloaded the supplies, except for the heavy barrel, and put things away before gathering stones for a fire ring and some dry branches she broke up for kindling. She'd wait for Zack to return to start the fire as he had the flint in his bag.

She hoped he didn't have too much trouble cleaning the catfish. They could be a booger to skin without a pair of plyers. As Charlie scooped white lard from a tin stored in the wagon, she heard him return.

"Is that boy a good cook?" she heard Jolene coo, and Charlie's breath caught in her throat. Was she going to have to put up with that redheaded cow traipsing into their camp uninvited all the time?

"Charlie is a great cook," Zack said.

"Well, if you ever want to taste real fine southern cookin'," Jolene continued in her sweetest southern drawl, "come down to our camp some time. Our girl Millie is a great cook. Her mama trained her well in our kitchen before the war."

"She was a slave?" Zack asked with nervous hesitation.

"Millie knows her place," Jolene stated. "She'll attend to all your appetites if she's told to."

Charlie rolled her eyes and got to her feet. This woman had some nerve, making offers like that. She stepped outside with the pot of lard in her hand. "I set the fire," Charlie announced as she jumped to the ground, "but you have the flint, so I couldn't light it."

"Millie would be happy to see to your boy's needs as well .

. . for the price she paid for those fish." Jolene smiled coyly. "She'd make a man of him in a night. I have no doubt."

Charlie pushed past the grinning woman. "I seriously doubt that," she growled as she moved toward the fire pit with the kettle of lard and set it on a flat rock to await the flames.

She took the stringer of skinned fish Zack had left the heads on and began getting them ready to fry. She cut off the heads and rolled the fleshy bodies in salted meal. There were six broad-bodied fish, and Charlie looked forward to a hardy meal. While Zack tended to the fire, Charlie returned to the wagon for some potatoes to peel, an onion to chop, and a skillet.

Jolene walked to where Zack knelt and ran her hand across his broad shoulders. "Don't forget my offer," she said before turning to saunter away.

"Does your husband know you go about making offers to strange men?" Charlie couldn't stop herself from asking.

"Lance isn't my husband, darlin'," she said with a grin on her pink lips. "He's my younger brother and," she said, glaring at Charlie, "as head of the Bennett clan, I'm free to make any offers I see fit."

"How lucky for you." Charlie seethed with an urge to toss a potato into her smirking face. "Why are you and your clan headed to Oregon?"

"Gold, darlin'," she said and turned back toward her wagons. "They've struck gold in the hills around Baker City, and I intend to go collect my share."

"By pimping out poor Millie, I bet," Charlie mumbled under her breath as she peeled and chopped the onion on the workspace of the utility cabinet-turned kitchen.

Zack hung the kettle of lard over the fire and turned to watch Jolene's swaying behind as she walked away. "That's one beautiful woman," he said with a deep sigh.

"Maybe on the outside," Charlie hissed, "but she's rotten as a bruised apple on the inside."

"Most men won't look much deeper than that creamy skin and pretty red hair," he noted.

"She just tried to sell the services of her poor maid to warm your bed, Zack," Charlie snapped. "She's going to Oregon to be a mistress of whores in the goldfields."

Zack shrugged. "The war forced a lot of women to make unfortunate choices with their lives."

"As I see it, she's not giving that Millie any choices at all." Charlie sliced the potatoes and added them to the onions and lard in the skillet. She took them to the fire ring and set them to cook. The lard in the kettle had melted and bubbled. Charlie took the plate of coated fish and dropped them one-by-one into the hot fat.

Zack watered the animals while Charlie minced more onion and mixed up stiff dough for hushpuppies. She inhaled the aroma of wood smoke and frying onions as she turned the potatoes and rolled the fish in the kettle of hot lard with a fork. When the potatoes were soft and browned, Charlie set the skillet aside and forked off a piece of flaky white fish to test for doneness.

Once she'd made room in the kettle, Charlie added spoons of the hushpuppy dough and watched them brown and float to the top of the bubbling lard. She filled their cups with cool water from their barrel and loaded the new enameled plates from the mercantile with fried catfish, potatoes, and hush-puppies.

"Supper's ready," she called to Zack, who was bedding down the animals for the night in a stand of lush grass and weeds.

"It sure smells good," he said when he came to sit by the fire and take his plate.

They ate in silence as they listened to the noises of the camps around them. They heard the voices of adults talking and laughing, the sounds of children playing, and music. A harmonica played a sad tune from one camp and from another, a fiddle played something more lively.

"Music with supper is nice for a change," Zack said with a grin. "This is really good, Charlie. I haven't had catfish in a coon's age." He bit into a hushpuppy. "And I've never had these before."

Charlie's brow furrowed in surprise. "You've *never* had hushpuppies before?"

"That's what they're called?" He popped the last of one into his mouth and chewed. "Must be a Tennessee thing. Never had 'em in Indiana."

They finished their meal, and Charlie washed the dishes while Zack laid out his bedroll beside the fire. The camp grew quiet with only the sound of the occasional boat on the nearby river to disturb them.

"I have to patrol the camp in a couple of hours," Zack told her as he settled into his bedroll, "so I'm gonna try to catch a few minutes of sleep before then."

"I'm going to read for a while," she said. "I'll wake you if you haven't gotten up by then."

"Thanks and supper was really good. I'm glad you stopped those two little fellas today."

"I'm glad you liked it. We probably won't get the opportunity for catfish much once we travel north. They're more of a warm water fish."

He grinned up at her. "Yeah, but trout are good too, and they like cold water, I hear."

"I'm sure we'll have the opportunity to sample many different things as we travel north."

"As long as it's not poisonous snakes and wild Indians, I'm good," Zack said before closing his eyes.

"From your mouth to the angels' ears," Charlie said with a sigh as she climbed into the wagon.

She lit a lamp, kicked off her boots, and poured some water from her pitcher into her washbowl on the vanity.

Remembering Zack's warning, Charlie dimmed the lamp before lathering her washcloth with the ball of lavender soap and scrubbing her face, underarms, and crotch.

She washed her hair, brightened the lamp again, and crawled into bed with her book on modern medicine. Contrary to what the man at the apothecary said, Charlie had little difficulty understanding the language of the medical text. When something confused her, she referred to the pictures and figured it out.

Her mother had been a wise woman in the Hallow, and Charlie had learned a good bit from her about treating illnesses, stitching wounds, and setting broken bones. She knew about herbs and midwifery as well.

Charlie put a hand to her belly. If she could find some pennyroyal, she could rid herself of this child, but she wasn't certain she wanted to be rid of it. In a way, she had come to think of it as a part of Davis. Clive and his boys were Davis kin. Could she destroy the only thing that might bring him back to her, if only just a little?

Tears burned her eyes. The way it got in her belly wasn't the babe's fault. Had Davis's mother blamed him for his violent conception and destroyed him before he could draw a breath, Charlie would never have met the only man she'd ever loved. If she destroyed this child, she might be denying another person the love of their life. She didn't think she could do that.

Charlie caressed the cool, smooth skin of her abdomen. "I won't kill you, little one," she whispered. "It's like as not my body will reject you as it did all the others before you anyhow."

Tears trickled down her cheeks as she remembered Davis' strong arms around her as she'd wept after each loss. Things would have been so different if she'd delivered even one of those children, and it had been a boy. Clive would have had no claim on the farm, and maybe Davis wouldn't have gone off to war.

She wiped her eyes when she heard Zack moving around outside in the dark. She rolled off the bed and stuck her head out of the opening in the canvas. "You heading out?" she asked softly.

The camp was quiet, and Charlie could hear the sound of the river and night birds' calls. The air was cool and smelled of wood smoke and the honeysuckle growing in the brush.

Zack walked over and kissed her cheek. "I have a four-hour shift," he said and moved his kiss closer to her lips. "Stay in the wagon and tie the flaps up secure before you go to sleep. You don't want any of these yahoos creepin' in on ya in the night."

Their lips met, and Charlie leaned into the kiss, parting her lips for his tongue to enter.

"I have a chamber pot in here under my bed," she said with a grin, "so I've no reason to venture out."

"Good. I'll ride by from time to time just to check and make certain. You checked that front flap to make sure it's tied up tight?"

Charlie rolled her eyes. "I did, but I'll check it again before I turn off the lamp."

"Good," he said again with a nod. "I'll see ya in the mornin', Charlie. Have a good night." He tipped his hat and rode away into the darkness.

"You as well, Mr. Drake," she whispered as she tied the flap to cover the rear opening of her canvas enclosure. Then she went to the front to make certain her knots were tight and the flap secure against intruders.

Charlie sighed and turned off the lamp. In the darkness, she pulled out the chamber pot and relieved herself for the night. After returning the lid to the pot and sliding it back beneath her bed, Charlie crawled beneath her blanket and made herself comfortable for the night.

She tossed and turned for a few minutes, listening to the sounds of the dark camp and thinking about Zack's warm lips on hers. It surprised her how uneasy she felt without him nearby. As she neared sleep, a baby began to cry from somewhere in the camp, and Charlie found her hand protectively holding her belly again. "It's all right, little one," she crooned softly, "you're perfectly safe where you are.

❧ 12 ❧

They ferried across the Missouri River two days after arriving in Independence.

Jolene's cousins never arrived, and Cap Morgan, with Ellen standing nearby, resisted the redhead's charms when she begged for a few more days.

"Your cousins can join the train if they catch up with us later, Mrs. Bennett." Jolene had never informed the wagon master that Lance was her brother and not her husband. "I can't hold this train any longer. We're already late in the season as it is and will likely hit foul weather in the mountains, which could prove disastrous."

The big ferry took four wagons and their teams at a time across the wide river. Charlie enjoyed the cool breeze on the water, but the mules didn't like the swaying motion of the trip, and she had to stand between the two leads with her hands holding their halters while she cooed softly to them that everything would be all right in a few minutes.

It took over seven hours to transport the entire train across the river on the ferry and, by then, all they could do was make camp and wait for morning to continue.

"Is it going to be like this all the way to Oregon?" Charlie asked in frustration as she served Zack a supper of pork chops, biscuits, and gravy that night.

"I hear tell there are a lot of rivers to cross between here and there," he said with a grin.

"Oh my goodness." Charlie sighed. "I don't suppose I'm the most patient of souls."

"A good cook, though." He bit into a hot, juicy pork chop before forking up a mouth full of biscuits covered in cream gravy.

"Men." Charlie rolled her eyes and huffed, "as long as your bellies are attended to, you're happy."

The following morning, they began the trip in earnest. The rolling hills and bluffs of Missouri became flat prairie covered in nothing but knee-high grass as far as the eye could see. Years of travel by wagons headed to Oregon had rutted a trail easy to follow to Charlie's amazement. Piles of furnishings and personal possessions dumped from wagons to lighten their weight dotted the route.

Charlie was astounded to see beautiful highboys and rosewood dining tables now bereft of their fine veneers due to exposure to the wind and rain. People passing by had pilfered through the items, taken some, and left others.

They stopped for the night near one of those piles and something caught Charlie's eye. A tall wardrobe lay on its side with one of the heavy doors thrown open. Fabric fluttered in the breeze, and Charlie couldn't resist exploring. While Zack tended to the animals and got the fire ready for the night, Charlie wandered over to the once fine piece of furniture. The large oval mirror set into the door was cracked and broken. Charlie had to be careful not to cut herself on the glass.

Inside the abandoned cabinet, she found a woman's entire wardrobe, and she wondered what would have enticed the owner of the fine clothes to simply push them off the wagon and go on her way. The piece of cloth to catch Charlie's eye belonged to a dress's skirt—one of the sweeping hooped-skirted dresses worn by women before the War. The fabric was terracotta and white plaid taffeta highlighted by lines of gold woven into the pattern. Charlie imagined it had been breathtaking when worn with bright white lace trim on the skirt, collar, and cuffs.

"Not a practical dress for farming in Oregon," Zack said from behind her as Charlie studied the garment in her hand.

"No," she had to admit, "but it would make a nice party dress."

"You're a boy now," Zack whispered into her ear with a chuckle, "and shouldn't be interested in party dresses and such."

Charlie had owned plenty of pretty dresses when she'd lived with Davis and his grandmother on the farm. Taffeta fabric had always been one of her favorites, and this dress, though years out of fashion now, could be taken apart and used to fashion something more up to date.

Her shoulders fell as she held the voluminous dress in her arms. Zack was right. She was supposed to be a boy now, and what boy would be spending his evenings snipping the seams of a dress to recover the fabric? Charlie stood admiring the gold lines in the plaid and made her decision. What she did in the evenings in the privacy of her wagon was her business, and the others in the train didn't need to know what it was. She rolled the dress with its bright-white taffeta underskirt into a tight ball and turned to wade through the tall grass back to the wagon.

"You're gonna give yourself away, Charlie," Zack laughed. "I'm gonna go check on the stock while you make supper."

"What ya find pilferin' through that old wardrobe?" Jolene asked as Charlie neared their wagon with the roll of fabric clutched to her chest.

"Nothin' you'd be interested in," Charlie said as she turned toward her and Zack's camp, trying to avoid further conversation with the annoying redhead.

"You one of those boys who likes to dress up in women's clothes?" Jolene asked with her brow arched and a grin on her powdered face. She reached out to touch Charlie's sunburned cheek. "Are you one of those Nancy boys who'd rather dress in women's clothes and take a woman's place in the household? I've noticed you do all the cookin' here." She laughed softly. "I could make a place for you in my establishment in Oregon. There are men who'd rather be with a Nancy than a real woman, and I bet you'd clean up real pretty."

Charlie jerked away from Jolene's touch. "You're disgusting, madam."

"I'm a businesswoman who sees all the angles, young man," Jolene said with a shrug. "You'd do well to keep that in mind."

"To keep what in mind?" Zack asked as he joined them.

Jolene fluttered her long lashes Charlie knew she darkened with kohl powder. "I was just makin' your cousin here an offer to come work for me once we reach Oregon, and I get myself established in Baker City."

"She thinks I'd make a good boy whore," Charlie said in disgust.

"I beg your pardon?" Zack gasped, his cheeks turning pinker than the sunburn already there.

"It's obvious he is already inclined in that direction," Jolene said with a breathy sigh. "I was simply offering the boy an alternative that could be monetarily beneficial to both of us."

"Go fix supper, Charlie," Zack said and motioned her toward their wagon.

"You see," Jolene said with a sneer, "he takes orders from a man like a good woman would. I could make a good Nancy out of him in my establishment."

"Miss Bennett, my cousin, has no inclination in that way, and I'd appreciate you remembering that," Zack declared, lashing out verbally at the offensive woman.

Jolene stared at Zack for a minute before answering. "Perhaps I misread you, Mr. Drake, and you and your cousin are both Nancy boys traveling together and sharing your disgusting turn in the dark here amongst us good people. Perhaps I should have a talk with the wagon master and see if he condones such depravity in his train." Jolene turned and stormed away before Zack could answer.

"That's certainly not the kind of shit we need here," Zack grumbled under his breath as he stomped back to their fire and dropped to the ground. "That bitch is gonna cause us trouble if she can."

"You think?" Charlie hissed as she sliced a sweet potato into a skillet with some strips of bacon and set it in the fire. "She's a whore mistress, and I called her on it."

"You should have left that dress where you found it," Zack snapped. "Now she's going to Morgan with a story that the two of us are Nancy boys traveling together."

Charlie stared at him with her eyes wide before she began to laugh. "He's going to know that's not the case. He knows I'm not a damned boy and that you were engaged, so you obviously prefer women. She'll look like a trouble-making busy-body and nothing more ."

Zack's face lightened with a relieved smile. "Oh, yeah, I forgot about that."

The bacon began to sizzle in the skillet, and Charlie used her fork to turn it and the potatoes. As she was taking the skillet off the fire, a child's scream ripped through the night. Charlie and Zack both got to their feet and began running toward the sound. It came from a wagon behind theirs in Jolene's camp.

"What happened?" Zack demanded of the people gathered around a man and woman holding a screaming little girl in their arms.

"Jenny fell off the wagon," a woman who Charlie

suspected was the child's mother said as she tried to calm the child. "I think her arm is broken."

Charlie stepped forward to inspect the awkwardly bent limb of the screaming, thrashing six-year-old. "It's definitely broken," she confirmed, taking charge of the situation. "Zack, will you get my bag from beneath my bed and bring one of those small crates to break up for splint material?"

The man beside the distraught mother stepped between Charlie and the woman with the child. "Who the hell are you, and what do you think you're doing?"

"I'm Charlie McCleod, and I'm going to set this little girl's arm so that it will grow straight again." Charlie reached for the child. "Who are you?"

"I'm Jenny's dad, Jim Willard," he said, putting a gentle hand on the screaming child's sweat-soaked brown curls, "and this is my wife, Emma."

Tears of fear and distress for her child slid down Emma's cheeks as she tried to calm the thrashing little girl in her arms. "Can you help my baby?" Emma asked, staring at the unknown boy attempting to take her child from her arms.

"I can," Charlie replied confidently.

"Here's your bag," Zack said, returning with her black leather satchel where she kept herbs for healing. "I brought that new book you bought in town too." He handed her the leather-bound book from the apothecary.

"Thank you." She took the book and opened it to a page she'd turned down and ran her finger down the page before returning to her bag and removing the bottle of laudanum. "I need a small cup of clean water," she told Emma. "This will help stop her pain and settle her down some so I can set her bone."

Jolene and Lance came running into the camp. "What the hell is going on here?" Jolene demanded when she saw Charlie administering to the screaming child. "What's this boy doing in our camp?"

"Charlie knows medicine," Zack said, stepping between Charlie and the redhead. "His mama spent time in a doctor's family and taught him how to tend to wounds and set broken bones."

"Just because his mother was some doctor's whore," Lance hissed, "doesn't mean he's qualified to tend our children."

Zack held up the book he'd brought from the wagon. "He reads and understands books like this. Can any of you say the same?"

Jim returned with a small cup of water and handed it to Charlie, who measured out laudanum from the bottle and mixed it with the water. "Can you get her to drink this?" she asked Emma and handed her the cup. "It will ease her pain."

The child fussed and refused to drink at first, but Emma eventually got her to take the infusion after adding a little sugar to the mix. Within minutes of swallowing the liquid, Jenny calmed and rested quietly in her mother's arms.

Charlie took the opportunity and went to work straightening the broken limb and setting it back into place. Zack broke up the wooden crate and offered two short, flat pieces Charlie used to bind onto Jenny's arm with strips of gauze.

"Do your best to keep those on her arm," Charlie instructed Emma. "The bone should heal enough to remove it in about six weeks." She took some packets of willow bark tea from her bag and handed them to Emma. "Make her drink this three times a day to help with the pain and swelling. You'll probably need to doctor it with sugar to get her to drink it because it's bitter as hell."

Emma looked up from her sleeping daughter's face. "When will she wake up?" she asked nervously.

"The laudanum should make her sleep through the night," Charlie replied. "If she wakes up in pain and fusses, make her some of the willow tea. Too much laudanum isn't good, so I wouldn't recommend any more for her, and if the willow bark doesn't seem to be enough, give her a little warmed whiskey with sugar in it."

"That's what my mama always gave us if we had a pain," Lance said with a confirming glance at Jolene.

"Maybe you're good for more than cookin' and sewin', Nancy boy," Jolene muttered to Charlie before saying her good-byes to Jim and Emma and leaving the camp with Lance.

"I'll check back in on her in the morning," Charlie told the sleeping child's parents.

Emma wrapped her arms around Charlie's neck. "I don't know how to thank you, young man. You've saved my little girl's arm."

"And maybe her life," Jim added. "I've seen men lose their arms from breaks and then their lives if the corruption sets in." He hugged Charlie too. "Thank you, son." He wiped a tear from his cheek.

"I'll check on Jenny in the morning," Charlie repeated. "It was good to meet both of you, though I wish it had been under better circumstances."

Charlie and Zack returned to their camp.

"Maybe that will temper that bitch's threats for a while," Zack said as he glanced toward Jolene's wagon. "The Willards seem like nice folks."

"I wonder how they hooked up with the likes of Lance and Jolene."

Zack shrugged. "They were all probably just traveling in the same direction at the same time, like us," he said with a yawn as he settled himself by the fire. "I'm not looking forward to the watch tonight. It's been a long day."

"When are you supposed to go out?"

"In two hours." He stretched out on his blankets. "Can you wake me if I oversleep?"

Charlie thought about the plaid taffeta dress and smiled. "Yeah. I was going to be up for a bit longer tonight, anyhow."

"I thought you probably were," he said with a wink. "I'll see you in a couple of hours."

Charlie climbed into the wagon, returned her medical bag to its spot beneath the bed, and shook out the plaid dress. She lit the lamp over her head and found her scissors. Charlie spread the plaid taffeta dress over her knees with a sense of satisfaction and began snipping the tread of the hem in the skirt. Pre-war dresses were made with skirts that could contain as much as eleven yards of fabric. The styles today could be made from six or seven, and Charlie smiled at the possibilities.

Her face fell when she wondered where or when she'd ever wear a dress again, and especially a taffeta party dress. Well, she wouldn't be hiding herself as a boy forever. When she got to Oregon, she'd be free to be Charlotte again and wear dresses if she wanted to.

For the first time in a long time, she wondered what she was going to do with her future. She touched her belly. Would she have a child in her future to raise alone? Could she do that? What would Zack say when he learned the truth? Would he call her a whore and refuse to have anything to do with her?

That thought made Charlie sad. She'd become attached to Zack more than she thought she could become attached to another man. She didn't want him to think badly of her.

Charlie sat snipping the threads holding the garment's seams and thought about the dress she would make from it. This dress had been put together some time ago by an expert seamstress. The stitches were uniform and tight, and the thread was of good quality. Even after its exposure to time and the elements, the thread held firm, and Charlie almost hated to cut it.

The wardrobe had been lined with cedar, and Charlie could still smell the fragrant, pest-repelling wood in the fabric. The area of the skirt that had been flapping in the breeze was faded some and stiff with dirt, but it only amounted to a yard or two of the fabric, and Charlie thought she could cut it out easy enough and still have plenty to work with.

She watched the small mantel clock, and after two hours without hearing Zack outside, Charlie climbed out of the wagon to wake him for his patrol shift.

She shook his shoulder and called his name. "It's time to wake up, Zack."

He rolled, grabbed her, and pulled her down to him. "I've missed you, sweetheart." He tugged Charlie close for a passionate kiss.

Charlie pulled away and slapped him. "Zachary Drake," she spat, "what the hell do you think you're doing?"

Zack sprang up with a shocked look on his face. "What the hell, Charlie?"

"It's time for your shift on the watch," she said and fled back to the wagon. *Sweetheart?* Had he been talking to her, or had he been dreaming about his lost love in Indiana? Charlie suddenly felt a surge of jealousy toward the woman Zack had professed to love once and obviously still had feelings for if he was dreaming about her.

❧ 13 ❧

Clive Davis arrived in camp a week after they'd crossed from Kansas into Nebraska. To Zack and Charlie's amazement, he rode in the wagon they'd left behind belonging to Bob and Tom. A different horse pulled the old rig, but it was the same wagon with a tarp stretched tight across the top.

"Where do you think he came up with that?" Zack asked Charlie as they watched Clive pull up beside Morgan's wagon and stop.

"There's only one place he could have gotten it," Charlie said with a shiver of fear in her voice.

They watched as Jolene and Lance ran up to join Clive at Morgan's wagon. She wrapped her arms around his neck and greeted him with enthusiasm.

"This isn't going to be good for me," Charlie said. "That bastard wants me dead at the end of a rope."

Zack took her hand. "I won't let him hurt you, Charlie. I promise you that."

Clive conducted his business with Morgan and then walked back through the camp with Jolene and Lance at his side.

Charlie busied herself, making their supper, and kept her

face turned away from Clive Davis. "Who's the fella with Jolene and Lance?" Jim Willard asked as he and Emma walked up with little Jenny, who was recovering nicely.

Zack shrugged. "Looks like a newcomer to the train. Maybe it's the cousin she was expecting in Independence."

"I think those were brothers," Emma said as she set Jenny on the ground beside the fire. "I don't recall her mentioning anybody else she was expecting to join us." She smiled at Charlie. "What can I do to help with supper?"

The Willards had become regular visitors to their camp since Jenny's injury. As Zack had speculated, the family had joined Jolene's troop because they were all headed to Independence from Memphis at the same time, and traveling as a group sounded safer than traveling alone. The Willards didn't feel comfortable with the Bennetts or their plans for a house of ill-repute in Baker City and were happy to have an alternative place to spend their evenings. They'd even moved their wagon behind Zack and Charlie in line.

"This here is our Uncle Clive Davis," Lance said by way of introduction as they were passing. "He'll be joining us as we travel to Oregon since that murdering bitch killed his boys in Tennessee and burned his farm."

"Lots of folks lost family and farms in the war," Jim said. "We lost everything, and I'm moving my law practice from Tennessee to Oregon for a fresh start."

"Nobody seems to have seen her, Uncle Clive," Lance said, "but we're keepin' our eyes open for her as we travel and passin' round those posters to the local authorities."

"She'll be easy to spot with that head of gold hair," Clive said, "and she's as crafty as any whore, flauntin' that curvy body to get a man's attention and then killin' him when he does."

Charlie felt her gorge rise into her throat as she kept her head low and listened to the man rant. She swallowed hard to keep from throwing up into the fire pit as she sliced ham into the skillet. She put a hand protectively over her belly, then drew it away and rushed to the wagon for potatoes to peel and fry.

"Are you all right?" Emma asked when Charlie returned to the fire with the potatoes and an onion.

"I'm fine," she said. "I'm just not certain I care much for that man."

Emma snorted. "Me and Jimmy don't care much for any of that Bennett clan. Do you know what they plan to do when they get to Oregon?"

Charlie nodded. "She's a whore mistress and plans to peddle flesh to the miners there."

Emma nodded. "And she's been sellin' the services of that poor little gal she keeps in her wagon to anyone who'll pay her a dollar." Her eyes widened. "She even offered her to Jimmy. Said I looked as I could use a night's rest from his affections. Can you believe the nerve?"

"I believe Miss Bennett and all her ilk are out to do no good," Charlie said with a deep frown.

"Miss Bennett?" Emma said with a raised brow, "Don't you mean Mrs. Bennett?"

"Lance is her brother and not her husband," Charlie said. "I heard her tell Zack. I think she thought he might want to court her if he knew she wasn't married."

"Why that sneaky little tart," Emma gasped. "The wagon master assured us this was a wholesome and respectable train with only married women and single young women in the company of their families in attendance."

"He doesn't know either," Charlie said in the man's defense. "She told him Lance was her husband and not her brother."

"Well, we'll see about that." Emma jumped to her feet. "I have a young daughter to think of here, and I don't want her subjected to that sort of thing." She smiled down at Charlie. "Can you look after Jenny for a bit?"

"Certainly."

Emma grabbed her husband's arm and yanked him up. "Come on, James Willard. We need to go have a chat with the wagon master of this travelin' whore train."

"What the hell was that all about?" Zack asked as he watched Jim being led away toward the head wagon.

"It seems Jolene's been offering Millie's services around a bit too freely."

"Oh, boy," Zack said with a grin. "Morgan's not gonna be happy about that, and Ellen takes special exception to whores."

"I'm certain he won't be happy at all when Emma gets done with him." Charlie took their supper off the fire and set it on a rock to keep warm until Jim and Emma returned. "I'll make a fresh pot of coffee. I'm sure we're all gonna need a cup."

Emma and her husband returned with frowns on their faces.

"I gather things didn't go well with the wagon master," Charlie said as she filled cups with coffee.

"He reminded me," Jim said, "that as a lawyer, I should understand that a person is innocent until proven guilty and that since she paid her fees to travel on this train, he couldn't ask her to leave for no good reason."

"But he's putting Millie off the train at Fort Kearny," Emma said. "He's had other complaints that she's been offered for the beds of men."

"But that poor girl isn't the one doin' the offerin'," Charlie protested angrily. "Jolene is."

"The wagon master said he plans to make some announcements in the mornin' at Sunday Services." Emma glanced around the camp. "Where's Jenny?" she asked with sudden desperation in her tone.

"I fed her," Charlie replied as she filled plates with smoky ham and fried potatoes, "and she was getting sleepy, so I put her to bed in your wagon." Her eyes shot from Emma to Jimmy. "I hope that was all right."

"Of course, it was all right." Emma sighed with relief as she rose to go check on her child.

"Jen probably gorged herself on this," Jimmy said as he tore off a bite of ham with his teeth. "She loves ham and fried potatoes with onion."

"She especially enjoyed making the skillet pies with the dried cherries I got in Independence," Charlie grinned.

"You made cherry pie in a skillet?" Jimmy said, his eyes searching the fire pit area.

Zack began to chuckle. "Jenny was right when she said her daddy would be so happy. He loves cherry pie, she told us."

Jimmy chuckled, and his cheeks flamed red with embarrassment. "She's right," he admitted. "I am rather fond."

"Fond of what, my love?" Emma asked when she returned and took a seat beside her husband on a bench Zack had made from wood he'd collected from one of the piles of discarded furnishings along the trail.

"Cherry pie," Zack said as he handed Emma a plate. "Jenny and Charlie made cherry pies in the skillet while you two were gone."

Emma grinned at Charlie. "You're teaching my girl how to cook?"

Charlie smiled. "She's pretty handy with that rolling pin even with only one good arm." She winked at Emma. "Jenny wanted to make a special pie just for her daddy, but she made one for her mama too."

Jimmy stared at his plate for a minute before setting it aside on the bench and smiled at Charlie. "Would it offend you any if I asked to have the pie my little girl made for me now rather than later?"

"Not at all." Charlie got to her feet and went to the open utility cabinet and took china plates from the open door, which was folded down and used as a workstation. She carried one to each of Jenny's parents. "She put a lot of love into these."

Jimmy used his sleeve to brush a tear from his suntanned cheek as he stared at the half-moon-shaped pie. "My little girl made this for me?"

"I think it was her third try," Zack said with a chuckle. "She burned the first two a little, but we ate them to hide the evidence."

Jimmy and Emma laughed as they cut into their pie with a fork and savored every bite. "This is really good filling," Emma said as she chewed. "I recognize the spice but can't quite place it."

"Ginger," Charlie said. "Ginger enhances the flavor of the cherries."

Emma studied the young man by the fire. "I'll keep that in mind."

"You'd better," Jimmy chuckled, "or our daughter is gonna be beatin' you out of those blue ribbons at the county fair."

They all laughed.

"Smells mighty good," a male voice said from behind the group. "You wouldn't happen to have an extra plate for a hungry new neighbor?"

Charlie's heart began to race at the sight of Clive Davis at her campfire, and she couldn't reply.

"Our supplies are limited, mister, and we weren't expecting more company," Zack said as he stepped forward with his hand extended. "Zack Drake . . . and you are?"

"Clive." He took Zack's hand. "Clive Davis."

"And you're with the Bennett outfit?" Jimmy asked. "We're the Willards, Jim, and Emma."

Clive eyed the group with his eyes on the plate of food by the fire. "All y'all are Tennessee folk? Tennessee folk are always the most hospitable to strangers in need."

"Murfreesboro," Jim said.

"Southern Indiana and Illinois," Zack offered.

"I smell coffee," Clive said with his eyes on the pot, "and did I hear mention of pie?"

Charlie rolled her eyes. It was obvious Clive had no intention of leaving until someone fed him. She remembered the last time the man sat at her table and ate her food. He'd taken so much more that evening. She put a hand to her belly. He'd given as well.

She bent and picked up the plate she no longer had the appetite to eat and handed it to the stubble-faced man. Charlie then poured him a cup of coffee. She hated that she had to use Grandmother Byrde's good china, but it was all she had aside from the two tin cups she and Zack were using.

Clive studied the delicate cup before putting it to his lips. He then began to devour the food on the plate, stuffing his mouth full like a man who hadn't eaten a meal in weeks. His cheeks were gaunt, and his eyes sunken. Perhaps he truly hadn't eaten in a while.

"And how about that pie?" he asked when he'd scraped the last bite of potato from the plate. "Some more coffee too, boy," he demanded of Charlie.

Charlie gave her pie to the man and refilled his coffee cup. "You the cook here, boy?" Clive asked as Charlie refilled the cups of the people she'd actually invited to share her food and fire. "He a mute or somethin'?" Clive asked when she didn't respond.

"My cousin," Zack said casually, "is shy in front of newcomers and, yes, he does most of the cookin' around here."

Clive grinned. "I reckon havin' a Nancy about comes in handy for a fella on a long trip like this."

Emma gasped at the man's rudeness and stood. "I'd stay and help you with the dishes, Charlie, but," she gave Clive a quick fretful glance, "I'm feelin' a need to check on Jenny."

"It's all right, Emma," she said, "I can attend to the dishes once Mr. Davis has finished."

"You have a greater tolerance for small-minded fools than I, young man," Emma said, glaring at Clive, who seemed oblivious to her words before she turned toward her wagon. "I'll see you at services in the morning, where I believe the wagon master is going to make some important announcements."

"Good night, Emma," Charlie smiled.

Jim followed his wife to their wagon. "Good night, y'all," he said before climbing in after her.

"Seem like nice folks," Clive said as he handed Charlie his empty plate and cup. "I s'pose I'll be headed back to my niece's wagon." He turned to Zack with a grin. "Lena, don't cook, but she's offered me her little nigger bitch to warm my bed durin' my stay." He squeezed his crotch when Charlie turned away and then left the camp.

"Can you believe that man?" Charlie hissed.

"He's certainly a piece of work," Zack stated. "Do you think he'll be back in the mornin', expecting breakfast?"

Charlie snorted. "I wouldn't doubt it."

She warmed a pot of water and washed up the dishes as a cool breeze blew through the quieting camp. A fiddler had played lively Celtic tunes all evening, but the musician had recently put his instrument to bed. Now, all Charlie heard was the braying of a milk cow, the distant yipping of coyotes, and the occasional yelp of pain Charlie assumed came from poor Millie as she warmed Clive's bed in the back of his old wagon. The poor girl would definitely be better off in Fort Kearny than in the hands of Jolene and Clive.

Zack left camp to take up his night duties, and Charlie retired to her wagon, where she continued to take apart the old taffeta dress. She separated the petticoat from the skirt and set it aside to make into a set of underthings for herself and imagined the day she could dress as a woman again.

The men's clothes were much more practical for traveling like this, but Charlie longed for skirts and petticoats again. She ran a hand through her hair and longed to have that back as well. She wondered what Zack would think when he saw her in the plaid taffeta dress, she planned to make.

Charlie put a hand to her abdomen. It was getting bigger. She no longer wanted to throw up her breakfast every morning, and she expected the horrible cramps to come any day now to herald the end of the pregnancy. She still didn't know how she felt about that. The other pregnancies had been Davis', and she'd wanted those children with all her heart. This pregnancy had been the result of an assault by men she hadn't known so they could take her and her property, but she couldn't blame the child for the acts of its father. It had been guiltless, but could she love it the way it deserved to be loved? Would she be able to look into its face without seeing the face of its father?

When her eyes began to blur, Charlie turned off the lamp, used the chamber pot, and crawled into her bed to snuggle beneath the warm quilt she'd added. They were farther north now, and the August evenings were cooler. Soon they would be leaving the flat Platte River Basin and turn west toward the towering mountains of Wyoming.

Charlie had never seen real mountains before, and she had to admit she looked forward to it. She fell asleep to the sound of raindrops splattering canvas over her head, and she hoped Zack had a rain slicker in his saddlebags.

As the first raindrops splattered upon the ground around him, Zack's mind went to thoughts of Charlotte Byrde and the sweet kisses he stole from her every evening. If he was honest, Charlotte filled his mind with thoughts of her most of his waking hours.

He'd never known a woman like her. She was bright, funny, and more intelligent than any woman he'd ever known. Compared to Charlotte, Penny was a silly cow, and he never knew what he'd seen in her.

The fat, cold raindrops pummeled him and Tess, driving them to the shelter of a stand of trees, where they tried to wait out the worst of the deluge. Zack seriously doubted any varmints, human or animal, would be out in search of mischief in this weather, and his thoughts returned to Charlotte safe, warm, and dry in her cozy wagon. How he longed to be snuggled beside her.

❧ 14 ❧

The wagon master officiated at services on Sunday mornings. He never preached a sermon like preachers Charlie had heard in church, and he certainly was nothing like Reverend Tally.

He opened with a prayer and a few hymns and then made announcements about the trip before ending with another prayer and more hymns. Afterward, the train enjoyed a community dinner to which every woman made an offering.

That cloudy morning Charlie had been awakened by shouting from Jolene's camp as the wagon master's men collected Millie and her things. Rain had pelted the canvas throughout the night, and Charlie had found it calming. This morning it was dreary and the sky gray with clouds.

"That girl is gonna be better off," Emma said. "Did you hear the poor thing squealing all night? I don't know what that horrid man was doing to her, but I don't think she was enjoying it any."

Charlie nodded as she filled the coffee pot with water, added the grounds, and set it on the fire Zack had built in the small smoke tent to keep from the rain. "I heard, and I'm *certain* she wasn't enjoying it."

Zack returned to camp a few minutes later, looking tired.

"Didn't you sleep at all last night?" Charlie asked with concern.

"Cap wanted us all on duty to take that girl into custody," he said with a deep sigh, "and there's been something picking off small animals as we travel. Cap thinks it's a pack of coyotes and wants us to start trailing the train to see if we can spot 'em."

"Picking off small animals?" Emma gasped.

"Yeah, keep Jenny in the wagon or close by unless you or Jimmy are with her." He yawned. "Cap is gonna make an announcement about it at the services this morning."

Zack didn't make it to the services. Charlie had insisted he get some sleep inside the wagon and put him to bed on a pallet on the floor. He refused to sleep in her bed. Most everyone else on the train joined the community for the service.

A young Negro girl in a worn and tattered dress sat huddled nearby with her eyes swollen and red from crying. Charlie shuddered to see the bruises on her face. She assumed this must be Millie and was shocked to realize she was nothing more than a child in her mid to late teens, at best.

How could Jolene have subjected a child to such treatment? Charlie's blood ran cold, remembering the pitiful cries she'd heard the night before, and she wanted to strangle the redhead who stood scowling in the crowd with Lance and Clive at her side.

"As I'm sure all of you have been made aware," the wagon master announced in a loud, firm voice, "Miss Millie here has been removed from the … eh … service of Mrs. Bennett and will be relocated to the Buffalo Soldiers' family camp at Fort Kearny when we arrive there in a week or so."

"You got no right takin' my girl," Jolene declared, stepping toward Morgan. "She's my property and has been since she was born."

Charlie heard gasps from the crowd.

"Ma'am," Morgan said with a frown on his sunburned face, "we just fought a war in this country, and this young woman was freed. We don't own folks in this country anymore."

"But the silly little cow won't know how to take care of herself," Jolene protested. "I take care of her."

"By selling her body to any man who'll pay you the dollar for it?" Emma called out with a snarl. "Are you going to allow this disreputable mistress of whores to continue traveling in our company, sir?" she yelled at Morgan, and other female voices joined in.

Morgan cleared his throat to quiet the crowd. "As Mrs. Bennett will have nobody in her company to pander," he said, glancing down at Millie, "I don't see that she will be a problem."

He raised his hands. "We are moving into the Platte River basin now, and there are precautions we need to take."

"What sorta precautions?" someone called out.

"Unless the water in a stream or river is running at a good pace, don't drink it," he cautioned. "Cholera is rampant in these stagnant streams and pools along the Platte, and I'm sure you all know what cholera can do if it's set loose in a community."

Fearful murmurs erupted. Cholera was one of the most deadly diseases anyone knew, and it gave cause to fear. "I want everyone to fill their water barrels from the first fast-moving water source we encounter and keep them topped off when we come to any others," Morgan instructed, with his voice firm and commanding. "Bathe only in running water or in the privacy of your wagons with water you know is good, and you mothers keep your children out of the stagnant pools along the way."

Emma grabbed Charlie's arm. "I'm so glad Jenny is still too small to run about with the other children."

"I'll help you keep an eye on her, ma'am," Charlie said. "I can't have her goin' and gettin' sick with the cholera after I put all that work into mendin' her arm."

Emma gave her a compassionate smile and patted her shoulder. "You're a good boy, Charlie McCleod," she whispered. "Your mama would be proud of you."

Charlie didn't know about that. Rebecca McCleod had been a strong advocate of telling the truth. Charlie suspected her mama would be sorely disappointed in her what with this silly disguise and her delicate condition.

The service ended with a prayer from Morgan, another warning about the water and the possibilities of coyotes on their trail, and a loud, off-key hymn. Everyone returned to their wagons and enjoyed the quiet Sunday without travel. Charlie and Emma baked bread for the upcoming week and did laundry in the nearby creek. When he woke, Zack filled their water barrels and tended to the animals, giving them a good currying and checking their hooves for stones and loose shoes.

Jimmy went hunting and returned with a brace of prairie chickens Charlie and Emma fried for a nice supper along with mashed potatoes and poke greens they found along the creek. Charlie and Jenny made skillet pies from a jar of apples in Charlie's stores, and they managed to get in a meal without Clive Davis inviting himself to their table.

After washing the dishes and cleaning up after supper, Charlie snuck off in the evening light to enjoy a bath in the narrow, waist-deep creek. She'd found a secluded spot on the fast-moving water shaded by the overhanging limbs of a willow and thought it would be an excellent spot for a much-needed bath.

The water was cold, but Charlie sat in it nonetheless and enjoyed the feel of the water on her body. She scrubbed with a cloth and the ball of lavender soap until she felt clean again and then attended to her greasy hair.

As she stood and reached for a linen towel she'd draped over a limb, Charlie heard a gasp. She jerked her head up to see Emma on the bank with her eyes wide and her mouth in a 'o' of surprise.

"You're a girl," Emma exclaimed, "and you're—" She pointed at Charlie's round belly.

"I'm with child," Charlie confirmed, finishing the woman's sentence as she wrapped the towel around her naked body and stepped onto the bank.

"You're as much a lying whore as that awful redhead," Emma gasped, her eyes narrowed in anger, "and I can't believe I allowed you to touch my innocent girl after you've been living in sin with Zack all this time."

"It's not Zack's baby," Charlie said with tears of shame stinging her eyes. "He doesn't even know I'm pregnant yet." Charlie used the towel to wipe her face. "It's a long story, Emma, but I can explain how I came to be in this condition."

Emma snorted. "I'm more than aware of the mechanics for getting into your condition, young lady and—"

"I was raped," Charlie finally said, quieting the other woman. "I was knocked unconscious and then raped by three men."

"Three men?" Emma gasped again. "Then, you don't even know who the father of this unfortunate child is."

"Two of them are dead now," Charlie said. "I killed them."

Emma swallowed hard, and her face paled as she watched Charlie dress in the trousers and shirt. "Maybe you'd better explain everything after all."

Charlie went on to explain everything. She told her about her mother's murder, her rescue by Davis, her marriage, her widowhood, and then the arrival of Clive Davis and his boys at the farm that fateful Sunday evening.

"Oh, my Lord, girl," Emma sighed deeply, "and now you

have to deal with having the horrid man at your fire every time you cook a meal."

"I was surprised he didn't wander over today, when he smelled the chicken frying," Charlie frowned.

"Maybe he's layin' low after what happened with Millie," Emma said with a soft chuckle. "Did you see how bruised that poor thing was?"

"I carried the same bruises for a week," Charlie said quietly. "Luckily, I was unconscious when he took his pleasure with me and don't remember what he did."

"It included a good bit of punching, slapping, and poking his cock in places other than the spot necessary to induce your condition," Emma said as she rolled her big brown eyes and her cheeks turned a deep shade of pink. "His wagon was parked beside ours last night, and we couldn't help but hear the goin's on, even with the rain. The man is depraved beyond reason."

"I'm sure he is." Charlie ran a hand through her hair to release the tangles.

"So, you're the blonde whore he says murdered his sons and burned his farm?"

"Is self-defense murder?" Charlie asked. "And it was my farm, not his."

"That's a question for Jimmy," she said. "He's the lawyer." Emma smiled at Charlie. "I'm gonna make a suggestion, though."

"What?"

"Add a vest to your attire." She pointed to Charlie's chest.

Charlie glanced down and pulled the front of her shirt out to see two small round wet spots where her breasts poked forward.

"You're beginning to weep milk already," Emma said with a grin. "How far along do you reckon you are?"

Charlie thought about it. "It happened on the third Sunday in March," she said.

"And this is the third Sunday in August," Emma said, doing a mental tally of the weeks. "That puts you at about five months along. That's better than halfway along." She smiled wryly. "You'll be havin' that child in Oregon."

Charlie put her hand to her belly. "Five months?" she gasped. "I never carried a child past three months before."

"Looks as though this one has decided to take," Emma declared. "I'd suggest you have a talk with Zack about this before the child makes itself more pronounced." She pointed at Charlie's belly. "I was as big as Lookout Mountain when I delivered Jenny. Have you felt it startin' to squirm yet?"

"I thought it was gas," Charlie said, her eyes wide.

Emma began to laugh. "I thought it was gas when my labor started, too, but eleven hours later, I had a sweet little girl in my arms."

"I know the first one can take a long time," Charlie confirmed. "I helped my mama with midwifing before she died."

Emma put a hand to her own belly and grinned. "I'm hopin' this one slides out in a hurry."

"You're with child *too*?"

"Three months, I'd reckon," Emma said with a quick smile. "I just told Jimmy last night."

"Is he happy?" Charlie asked, wondering what Zack would say when she told him about her condition.

"Over the moon," Emma replied with a broad smile on her pretty face. "Hopin' for a boy this time, though. He says Oregon is gonna need lawyers, and he thinks Willard and Sons will be a good start."

"And what if Jenny wants to be a lawyer?" Charlie asked.

Emma grinned. "Thanks to you, all my girl wants to be is a cook and make skillet pies for her daddy."

Charlie clutched at Emma's arm. "Please don't tell anybody about this," she begged. "I can't have Clive Davis finding out who I am or that I'm carrying this child."

"You mean his child *or* grandchild," Emma said with a deep frown as she shook her head. "Your secret is safe with me, Charlie McCleod."

"This is my child." Charlie breathed a sigh of relief, her arms wrapped around her abdomen. "And I hope it's a girl who can't inherit land in Tennessee."

"Well, thankfully, we're not in Tennessee anymore," Emma said with a reassuring smile as she patted Charlie's belly. "And maybe she and Jenny will open the first female law firm in Oregon."

"Or a pie shop," Charlie said as she stood. "I'll be happy with whatever she decides to do with her life, so long as it's her decision and not some foolish man's."

Emma took her arm in hers. "I couldn't agree more, Miss McCleod. Oregon is going to be a land of opportunity and promise for all of us."

"I certainly hope so," Charlie said as they made their way back to the wagons, where Zack was getting ready to go out on his night patrol and Jimmy was putting Jenny to bed.

"Thanks for the use of your wagon today," he told her. "I haven't slept that well in weeks."

"That big puddle beneath the wagon might have made sleeping a little uncomfortable, too," Charlie said with a grin.

He looked around to see who might be gazing their way and then bent to whisper in Charlie's ear. "I wish I could steal another kiss."

Charlie smiled up at him. "It's not stealing if I give it freely."

"We're gonna have to talk about this situation soon," he stated.

A shiver ran down Charlie's spine. Did he know about her condition? Had he figured it out? "What situation?" she asked in a meek voice as thunder rolled in the distance and lightning flashed.

He squeezed her upper arm and smiled. "I think you

know exactly what I'm talking about, Charlie McCleod." He walked toward his horse with a big grin.

Charlie climbed into the wagon and readied herself for bed. What situation was Zack referring to? She tossed and turned with the thunder and rain. The wind picked up and whipped the canvas cover on the wagon. Charlie got up to secure the ties and wondered what Zack and Tess were doing in this deluge.

The wind rocked the wagon, and Charlie heard people outside. She suspected they were tying things down or collecting items left out in the inclement weather. Charlie frowned. The only thing she had outside was Zack, and she wished with all her heart that he was in here with her. She remembered rainy nights when she and Davis snuggled together beneath the blankets. Those had been such wonderful times. Could she have that with Zack?

A group of men left to hunt for fresh meat the following morning. It eased Charlie some that Clive Davis was amongst them and would be away from the camp for a time. The rain had left the ground saturated, and Morgan had decided the train would stay put for another day for some of the water to drain away.

The train would make its way toward Fort Kearny, and Charlie spent the day taking inventory of their supplies. In the months since leaving Independence, she'd used up a good portion of the flour and meal. Her smoked meat was nearly used up, her ball of soap was almost gone, and she had a list of sewing notions she wanted to purchase for the dress she wanted to make.

Jolene had an extensive wardrobe and strutted about in a different skirt, blouse, or dress every day. Charlie wondered who was laundering the clothes now that poor Millie was riding with old Mr. and Mrs. Bradshaw in their wagon. Jolene could still be heard griping that Millie was her nigger, and she intended to pursue it in court once they reached Fort Kearny before the wagon master could turn the girl over to the Buffalo Soldier population there.

"Will you look what she's wearin' today," Emma said when Jolene came strutting through camp in a tight-fitting bodice with a long apron on the front and rear, trimmed with lace and fringe. "I've never seen anything like it. Is it a long blouse or a very short dress over a flounced petticoat?"

"It's called a polonaise," Charlie explained, "and it's a bit of both."

"I've never seen anything quite like it in person or in the periodicals," Emma said as they watched Jolene pass by, laughing with the men.

"It's something that originated in Europe—Poland, I think," Charlie said, "about a hundred years ago and the style has become popular again with the introduction of bustled dresses and aprons."

Emma snorted. "I can't fathom a woman wanting to wear one of those damned things. My ass looks big enough without the addition of a metal cage to make it look even bigger."

Charlie smiled. It was nice to have somebody to talk with about clothes and such again. She hadn't realized how much she'd missed it. Since finding her at the creek, Emma had become her confidant, and someone Charlie could again be a woman with.

They cooked together, laughed together, and looked after Jenny. They gossiped about their husbands, the other women on the train and their husbands, and their hopes for the future in Oregon with their children. For the first time in a long time, Charlie thought about the future.

She no longer had Davis, but she had this baby in her belly, and that was something. She didn't have the farm in Tennessee, but she knew how to farm and could put that knowledge to good use in Oregon, where the land was said to be rich and plentiful and there for the taking.

Charlie opened the cask of salt and poured it into her large mixing bowl. Along with the salt tumbled gold and silver coins she and Grandmother Byrde had collected for their crops. She didn't have a husband or a farm, but Charlie had Grandmother Byrde's money, and that money would buy them a future in Oregon. Charlie had seen that people with money to spend were seldom ridiculed or treated poorly. She could buy her child's future with this money, and she would.

As she was returning the salt to the keg, Charlie heard loud voices. She went to the front of the wagon, where Zack was shoeing one of the mules and stuck her head out.

"What do you think is going on?" she asked.

"Looks like Perry and the hunting party is back already," he replied, straining his eyes to get a look at the returning men on horseback.

A few minutes later, Morgan came jogging up with a sour look. "We need that boy of yours, Zack," he said out of breath from his exertion, "it looks like the boys came back with cholera."

"Oh, my Lord." Charlie gasped and grabbed her bag.

After Morgan's warnings at the Sunday service, Charlie had found the entry in her medical book referring to cholera and read everything it had to offer, which wasn't much. Doctors during the war had struggled with the disease that wiped out whole units of both the northern and southern armies. They attributed the disease to poor sanitary situations, where men's fecal matter contaminated drinking water supplies, or drinking from stagnant pools.

Morgan had warned them all against doing just that, and Charlie wondered if these men had ignored his warning and taken water from a stagnant pool along the Platte.

Charlie ran with Morgan and Zack to the Perrys' wagon, where they found Mr. Perry on a pallet by the fire with his wife and daughters, Becky and Mary, ministering to him. He was gaunt and his eyes sunken into his head. Charlie had never seen a sickness take a person so quickly. He shivered on the pallet and stunk to high heaven from the watery shit he'd spewed into his drawers as he rode back to the camp.

"Get him out of those filthy clothes," Charlie ordered, "and burn them. You'll have to burn everything he touches while he's ill."

Martha Perry was trying to force water down her husband's throat without much success. "I know you're supposed to force fluids on a cholera victim," she said as she tried to keep her husband from batting away the cup.

"Boil a potato with the skin on," Charlie told one of the weeping girls. "And if you have a galvanized nail, throw it in the water too. When it cools, get as much of it down his throat as you possibly can."

"That's an odd stew," Morgan said, his face screwed up in confusion.

"According to my book," Charlie said, "the skin of the potato has a mineral called potassium in it, and the galvanized nail has something called zinc. When the body tries to flush out the disease in the shit," she explained, "it loses those minerals, and they must be replaced somehow, or that loss contributes to the death of the patient."

Morgan nodded but didn't look convinced. "I told you Charlie understands this medical stuff, Morgan. She'll get the men through this if anybody can."

Charlie glanced around to see if anyone else had noted his use of the feminine pronoun, but everyone around the Perry camp was in action, cutting potatoes to boil and searching for nails.

"I'll go round to the other wagons and tell them what you said, Charlie," Morgan said before trotting away.

"We should really isolate the sick, sir," she said. "Move their wagons away from the others to avoid contamination because of the close quarters."

"I'll see to it," Zack said.

An hour later, four wagons sat off by themselves with a fire in the center, and women tending to the men as they groaned, passing watery stool and vomiting. They wore pieces of white linen penned like babies' diapers, which Charlie told them to leave untended until the men either recovered or passed away. Then they were to be removed and burned.

The only man unaccounted for was Clive Davis. Charlie wondered if he'd avoided contracting the illness somehow.

"Didn't Clive go out with the hunting party?" Charlie asked Zack when she had a free moment.

"I think so." He rolled his eyes. "I'll go over to their camp and check on him."

A half an hour later, Jolene came storming into the camp of sick men. "Get your ass over to my uncle's wagon, boy," she demanded in a shrill voice, "and tend to him the way you're tendin' to these fellas."

"Bring him and his wagon over here, ma'am," Charlie requested. "This is the sick camp now. I can't be runnin' back and forth for just one man."

Jolene's eyes narrowed. "Are you refusin' to tend to my uncle, boy?"

"Tend to your uncle like we're tending to our family," Mrs. Perry snapped. "Or bring his wagon here the way the others did. We don't have time to listen to you whine, *madam*." She stressed the title to let Jolene know it wasn't meant as anything but an insult.

"My uncle is worth ten of these damned dirt farmers; boy, now come on over and tend to him." She glared at Charlie. "I thought doctors took some sort of oath to tend sick folks."

"I know some doctorin'," Charlie said with a sigh, "but I'm no doctor, and I took no oath." She told Jolene to boil potatoes with a nail and force Clive to drink. "I'll look in on him when I can."

Jolene snorted in resignation and pointed a finger at Charlie. "If my uncle dies because you refused to tend him, boy, I'll see you hung for murder."

"Get in line with the rest of your damned family," Charlie

muttered to herself as she strode over to kneel beside Mr. Perry, who was gasping for breath.

They lost him a few minutes later, along with one of the others. Before dawn, Mrs. Perry and one of her daughters also succumbed. Charlie learned cholera could take a body within hours of contamination, and it wasn't a pretty passing.

"Where are you going?" Zack asked when Charlie walked out of camp after Mrs. Perry took her final breath.

"I guess I'd best go and see to Clive if he's not gone already."

"You sure you want to do that?" Zack asked with concern in his voice. "They should have brought him over here."

"It's all right," she said. "I need to get away from here for a bit anyhow. I think Travis and Pete are gonna make it. They're sleepin' easy now, their color is better, and the cramps in their legs have eased up."

"I'll walk over with you in case that shrew tries to give you any trouble." Zack squeezed her hand.

His touch was comforting, and Charlie relaxed a bit for the first time in hours. As she settled, the baby flipped over in her belly, and Charlie smiled. Did it respond to Zack's touch the same way she did? She knew she was going to have to tell him soon. Davis' shirts and vest weren't going to hide things for much longer.

When they neared the camp, they heard the hoarse cries of Clive Davis as the cramping in his lower limbs pained him. They went to the only wagon with a lamp and climbed inside. Clive writhed and groaned on a thin pallet while Jolene and Lance knelt at his side.

"So, the good doctor has finally decided to grace us with his presence," Lance snarled when he saw them.

"Did you make the water I told you to?" Charlie asked Jolene.

She nodded and stared down at her uncle with genuine

concern. "But I couldn't get much of it into him. He slapped the cup away when I tried."

"That seems to be the general experience," she said. "How are the two of you feeling? Any discomfort in your bellies or pain behind your eyes?"

"Now she's worried about us," Lance hissed as he attempted to pour water down his uncle's throat.

"We just lost Mrs. Perry and one of her daughters to the disease after they were tending Mr. Perry for some hours," Zack informed them. "You should both probably drink some of that potato water."

When Lance moved to put the cup he'd been using on his uncle to his lips, Zack stopped him and added, "From *clean* cups. This cholera is catchin' fast, so you'd both best burn the clothes you've been wearin' while tendin' your uncle." He nodded and left.

Charlie knelt at Clive's side and studied the straining muscles in his legs and wrists. She put a hand to her throat to keep from gagging at the rancid stench wafting up from his pallet, brown with the loose stool he'd spewed onto it.

"He's gonna die, ain't he?" Lance asked angrily.

"Most likely," Charlie said. "This appears to be a particularly potent strain of the disease. Go out and drink something, Mr. Bennett. It's the best thing you can do for yourself now."

Lance left the wagon and Charlie found herself alone with Clive Davis for the first time. He reached up with a trembling hand and grasped her face. "I know you," he mumbled, and his eyes went wide. "You're her—the bitch who killed my boys."

Charlie tried to move back, but Clive grabbed the tail of her shirt and yanked. Buttons popped loose, and the garment fell open to reveal her protruding swollen bosoms and round, firm belly.

He pointed and grinned. "We done it, didn't we? We got you with child. That farm is mine now, and you can't deny me, woman," he cackled. "That's a Davis farm, and a Davis man is gonna run it again now."

He coughed and cried out as another spasm of muscle cramps overtook him. "Me and you are takin' that babe back to Tennessee to claim that farm," he grunted and lifted his head in an effort to sit up. "And then I'll see you hang for what you done to my boys, bitch."

Charlie yanked the pillow from beneath his head, pushed the weakened man back down onto the pallet, and covered his face with the pillow. "You aren't going anywhere with me or my baby, Clive," she said in a harsh whisper as she pressed the pillow into the wretched man's face, "because you're gonna be dead from the cholera in about another minute."

As Clive struggled beneath her, Charlie glanced outside to see Jolene, Lance, and Zack occupied around the fire. Clive's struggling ended, and Charlie took the pillow from his face. She returned it to the spot beneath his head and stood on trembling legs. She'd just killed another man. That made five from the same family in so many months.

Charlie stared down at the man who could very well be the father of the child she carried and closed up her shirt. She went to the door and climbed out of the foul-smelling wagon.

"He's gone," she told the group by the fire. "I'd recommend burning the wagon with him in it, along with the clothes you wore while tending him." She turned to walk back to her wagon.

Charlie heard Jolene weeping. "He wouldn't have died if that boy would have come to tend to him earlier. He murdered my uncle with his heartless neglect, and I'll see him hang for it."

"I murdered your damned uncle with a pillow, bitch," Charlie mumbled to herself as she neared her wagon, "and I'd do it again if I could."

"What's going on out there?" Jim called as she approached.

"Stay in your wagon, Jimmy," she called back. "I've been tending to cholera patients, and I need to bathe and burn these clothes before you can come close to me."

"How many dead?" he asked from the safety of his wagon.

"Mr. Perry, his wife, and daughter, Bekka, when I left the sick camp," she answered, "and just now Clive Davis in his wagon. I think the other two fellas are gonna pull through, though."

"That's good to hear," he said. "How are you and Zack doing?"

"All right, I think," she answered wearily. "Neither of us are showing symptoms, and I kept Zack away from the sick as much as I could. He's tending to the disposal of the bodies now."

"I should go see if I can help," Jim said and made to put a foot out of the wagon.

"You stay put, Jim Willard," Charlie ordered. "You have a family to think of. Zack and the men without families can handle the buryin' and burnin'."

"Yes, Doctor McCleod," Jim said and pulled himself back inside his wagon.

"Thank you, Charlie," she heard Emma call.

Charlie stripped off her clothes in the dark beside the fire. She didn't want to take them inside her wagon and possibly contaminate her living space. She filled a pot with water to boil and would wash outside.

As she stood naked beside the fire pit feeding her clothing to the flames, Jolene walked up with Zack. "Oh, my God," the redhead gasped. "You're not a Nancy boy, after all. You're a damned girl." She pointed at Charlie's belly. "And you're with child."

Jolene yanked her arm away from Zack's. "You've been playin' house with this little tramp the whole time," she yelled in an accusing tone, "and she's havin' your baby? I can't believe you'd lead me on like that when you've been couplin' with this little harlot under all our noses."

"I haven't been . . ." Zack went silent, staring at Charlie, who stood quietly in the shadows of the wagon. "You're with child?"

Charlie opened her mouth to explain but couldn't make the words.

"Does the wagon master know about this?" Jolene demanded. "Well, he's sure as hell gonna know about it now." The redhead stomped toward Morgan's wagon.

"What in hell's name is goin' on out there?" Jimmy yelled.

"I'll explain everything, sweetheart," Charlie heard Emma tell her husband, followed by a hushed conversation.

"*She* knows about this?" Zack asked, staring at Charlie's belly. "How did it happen? When?"

"It's a long story," she said, trembling naked in the dark. "Do you mind if I bathe and dress first?"

"Of course." He turned toward the fire. "I'll get your water for you."

"Thanks," Charlie said uneasily and stepped further into the shadows of the wagon. "I have fresh clothes laid out on my bed. Would you get them for me? I don't want to carry this sickness into the wagon. You should wash and burn your clothes too, after you finish with the burying."

❧ 16 ❧

Charlie woke to the sound of loud, angry female voices outside her wagon. She dressed and stepped outside to find a horde of women standing around.

"Is there something I can do for you, ladies?" Charlie asked. "Have more folks fallen ill in the camp?"

"None who'd want a harlot like you tendin' to 'em," one woman called out. "You and your bastard need to separate yourselves from this train in Fort Kearny, you tramp. The decent women here don't want none of your like here to corrupt our young."

Charlie's heart began to race. What was going on?

"We know what you're up to," another woman cried out. "You think you'll be able to trap one of our good boys into a marriage to support you and that filthy little bastard in your belly."

"Well, it's not gonna happen," another yelled. "You can spread your legs in one of the brothels at the fort and make your way like any other filthy harlot, but we don't want you here with us."

Charlie's cheeks burned with rage and shame. She glanced

up to see Jolene standing at the rear of the fray, grinning with delight at Charlie's discomfort.

"Go back to your husbands and sons, ladies," Charlie called out. "I have no interest or need for any of them." She put a hand on her belly. "My baby and I are going to Oregon, where we will claim land and build a farm."

She turned back to her wagon and climbed inside.

"That's not likely," someone called out. "No community is going to welcome a harlot and her damned bastard, and no land board is going to give her a farm either."

Was that true? Would land agents deny her a farm because she was a single woman with a child? She thought of the gold and silver coins in the salt cask and smiled. If they wouldn't let her homestead, then she would simply purchase land that had already been established.

Charlie pulled the hat from her head and ran fingers through the hair Zack had cut. She stared at the plaid dress she'd been working on in the evenings and smiled. Maybe it was time for Charlotte McCleod Byrde to return to the world.

Charlie closed the canvas flap behind her, peeled off the pants and shirt, and replaced them with a taffeta petticoat and camisole she'd made from the underskirt of the old dress from the wardrobe. Over that she slipped the plaid polonaise she'd constructed and trimmed with bright-white lace. The garment hugged her upper body and fell in shimmering waves over her backside and swelling belly. Atop her growing blonde curls, Charlie placed a small teardrop bonnet decorated with the plaid taffeta, white lace, and satin ribbon salvaged from the old garment.

She twirled around and smiled at her reflection in the cracked mirror of the vanity. It felt good to be a woman again. Charlie slipped on her boots and stepped out of the wagon. The crowd of grumbling women had gone and Zack stood by the fire with Emma, Jimmy, and Jenny.

"Good morning," she said. "Is the coffee ready?"

Zack turned with the others at the sound of her voice, and his mouth fell open in shock at her appearance. "Charlie?" He gasped, his eyes wide. "Is that really you?"

Charlie stepped down and twirled around for them all to see. "In the flesh," she said. "Now how about that coffee?"

Zack filled a china cup and handed it to Charlie. "You're beautiful," he said. "I think that dress makes you glow."

Jimmy chuckled. "It's not the dress, my friend. It's the babe." He pulled Emma close. "Isn't my Emma glowing too?"

Zack's mouth fell open. "You're with child too?"

"Must be all this fresh northern air," she said with a wink at Charlie.

Jenny went to her mother without taking her eyes off the transformed Charlie. "Who's that lady in the pretty dress, Mama?" she asked, her brown eyes wide.

"It's me, Charlie," she replied, "and I have a present for you, Miss Jenny."

"A present for me?" Jenny smiled smile as Charlie went back into her wagon and returned carrying another dress and petticoat in her arms, but much smaller than her own. "I had to guess at the sizing," she said and handed the dress to Emma, who held it up to examine it more closely.

"It's beautiful, Charlie," she said with tears in her eyes, "and these seams look professionally done."

"Children tend to be a little rougher on their frocks as I recall," she grinned. "So I tried to make them extra tight."

"Can I wear it today, Mama?" Jenny begged as she held the dress up to her body. "It's so pretty."

"You can wear it to Sunday service, I suppose," Emma said and smiled at Charlie.

"Today might not be the best day for that." Charlie brushed her hands over the skirt of her dress. "There might be some upset there today after the fuss I saw here this morning."

Emma grinned. "Good. This trip was beginning to get

boring." She stood and took Charlie by the arm. "Let's go and raise some hell at Sunday service, Miss Charlie."

They dressed Jenny in the new petticoat and dress. The little girl giggled and ran her hands over the luxurious fabric as she twirled. "I feel just like a princess, Mama. It's so pretty with all the lace and ribbon." She looked up at Charlie. "You look pretty too, Charlie—much prettier than when you were a boy."

Charlie smiled down at the beaming child. "Thank you, Jenny. I appreciate that." She glanced over at Zack, who stood beside Jimmy, his eyes wide.

"And thank you for making this dress for me," Jenny said as she continued to dance around the clearing between the wagons.

"I'm just glad it fits," Charlie said. "It taxed my brain with all the math involved."

The little girl stopped and frowned. "You have to know math to sew dresses?"

Charlie grinned. "Almost as much as you need it to cook."

"Then I reckon I'll never learn to sew or cook," the little girl said with a deepening frown, "'cause I hate doing sums."

"That she does," Emma groaned. "She vexes me to no end when I set her to doin' 'em."

"Aw," Charlie said with her arm around the girl's shoulder, "it's easier than you think. I'll show you when we make that cake we were talking about."

"Cake?" Jimmy asked eagerly, bursting into a big smile.

"For your birthday, Daddy," Jenny said. "Charlie promised to help me make one when she was still a boy."

The sound of old Miss Hirsh's off-key piano rang out in a hymn along with Morgan's deep voice and those of the other members of the train.

"Well," Charlie said with a sigh, "I suppose I'd best go and face the music."

Zack stepped up and took her hand. "I'm here to help and

support you, Charlie," he whispered into her ear. "I hope you know that."

The warm breath on her neck made Charlie shiver and warmed her in places that hadn't been warmed in quite some time. She leaned into him and smiled.

"We all do," Jimmy added as he took Emma's hand. "You've helped our Jenny like nobody else on this train, and me and Em appreciate that more than you'll ever know."

"That's good to know, Jim," Charlie said, "because I think I may require a good lawyer."

Jim glanced at her, his face screwed up in confusion. "I'll do whatever I can, but what would you need a lawyer for out here in the middle of nowhere, Nebraska?"

Emma smiled at Charlie and patted her husband's hand. "I'll explain it to you later, sweetheart."

Jimmy rolled his eyes. "Another one of those secret woman things, huh?"

Zack chuckled and squeezed Charlie's hand in his.

They walked into the Sunday service, and everyone went quiet. The faces of the women were stern as they stared at the group, and the faces of the men showed amazement when they saw Charlie in the dress.

"I'm sure it's all about to become perfectly clear," Charlie whispered.

Jolene stepped forward. She wore a black mourning dress and bonnet. Charlie assumed that was for Clive, and another shiver overtook her.

"You have a lot of nerve showing your face here, wearing a fancy dress, *harlot*," Jolene hissed, her rouged nails pointing at Charlie as other women in the gathering joined in to agree with the redhead.

"That would be rather like the pot calling the kettle black, would it not, Jolene?" Charlie countered.

"You've got no right to call this woman a harlot," Jimmy called out, "when you've made statements more than once in the presence of witnesses about what you plan to do when you reach Oregon, Miss Bennett."

"You mean Mrs. Bennett," someone called out to correct Jim. "A lawyer like yourself should know to address a lady properly and give a married woman the respect due her."

"Not unless they've made marrying your brother legal in this country and never let me know about it," he called back to gasps in the crowd.

"All right, all right now folks," Morgan yelled to quiet the crowd as he stood with Ellen at his side. "It seems we have us some woman troubles here to sort out."

He glared down at Zack while Ellen scowled at Charlie. In the many weeks of travel, the woman hadn't spoken more than a handful of words to her, and those had been curt and cold.

"I want to know what your name is," Jolene demanded, marching up to Charlie, "since it obviously isn't Charlie like you told everyone when you were prancin' around makin' everyone think you were a Nancy boy."

Charlie heard more gasps and stepped forward to the sound of the taffeta skirts swishing along as she walked. "My Daddy and my brother called me Charlie," she said in a loud, firm voice for all to hear, "but my Mama always called me by the name she gave me at birth, Charlotte—Charlotte Louise McCleod."

Charlie stepped closer to the woman dressed in black. "And when I married," she continued, "it became Charlotte Louise McCleod Byrde, but Davis and his grandmother still called me Charlie."

Jolene's rouged lips parted, and her mouth fell open in a gasp. "You're the Charlotte Byrde my uncle Clive was huntin' for? The whore who killed his sons and burned his farm?" She stepped forward and delivered a slap to Charlie's face. "And you murdered him last night as he lay in his sickbed," she yelled, "when he recognized you for the murderin' whore you are."

Lance stepped between his sister and Charlie. "I'm takin' you back to Tennessee to hang, woman," he spat as he grabbed Charlie, "and claim that farm as the only livin' male Davis heir."

Emma leaned into her gaping husband. "Now you know the reason she thought she might need a lawyer," she whispered above the noise of the buzzing crowd.

17

Jim Willard stepped forward to come to Charlie's defense. "There's no need to drag this poor woman back to Tennessee," he declared. "I'm a member of the Tennessee Bar Association and can defend her in a trial here with some of you good people sworn in as the jury to hear the case, and the wagon master sitting as a judge."

"Just hang the damned slut," one female voice Charlie thought she recognized called out, with others cheering along.

Charlie glanced into the crowd to see the widow from the mercantile staring at her with narrowed eyes and a smirk. The woman had come to her wagon to beg supplies a few weeks after leaving Independence, and Charlie had turned her away. The widow had yelled at her and told her she owed her more supplies because she hadn't given her enough money in the mercantile to outfit her properly. Now she owed her more or she'd starve before reaching Oregon. She'd finally relented and given the woman some bacon, meal, and beans. Why would this woman call for her death now when Charlie had been generous to her with her money and supplies? She would never understand people.

Charlie put a protective hand over her belly. "What about

my babe?" she cried. "It's innocent and if you hang me, you'll be killing my baby too."

"There'll be no hanging of pregnant women on my train," Morgan shouted to quiet the crowd. "This sort of trial would be seen as legal and binding?" he asked Jimmy.

"As legal and binding as any court in the land, sir. A wagon train falls under the same laws as a ship at sea, and the wagon master is like to the captain. Your judgment is final and binding in all matters."

Morgan, with a grimace, continued. "Then I suppose we're gonna have ourselves a trial."

"And the hangin' of the murderin' slut and her bastard at the end," the voice of the widow called out.

"Now," Morgan declared in a loud, firm voice, "let me make this perfectly clear. Any man who takes the oath to sit on this jury will promise to listen to all the testimony given and render a verdict based on that testimony." He glared down at the woman who'd called for the hanging. "This will not be a mock proceeding, and if I get the feeling that it is, I will render a verdict directly from the bench as is the right of any judge." He stared at Jim. "Is that not true, counselor?"

"It is, sir," Jim nodded.

"Mr. Bennett," Morgan said, "I suggest you act as the prosecution as this trial has more to do with you and your family than anyone else."

"I would see it as my duty and an honor, sir," Lance said with an elegant bow to Morgan.

Except those closely associated with those participating in the trial, every man put their names into Morgan's hat and twelve names were drawn for the jury. Charlie was unfamiliar with any of them, and she suspected that it was a good thing.

She met with Jimmy by the fire at their wagons and gave him papers she thought might be useful to the proceedings.

"I'm not going to try to fool you, Charlie," he said gravely, "this isn't going to be easy. Jolene has gone around, poisoning the minds of women and men in this camp against you."

"But Charlie has done nothing but good in this camp," Zack said firmly. "She's tended the sick and injured on many occasions and purchased supplies for them that couldn't afford them. Did you know that?"

Jimmy shook his head. "No, I didn't, and if any of those folks are sitting on the jury, I'm sure it will help, but folks are bored on this train, and a good hanging gets everyone excited."

"So, killing my baby and I will just be a break in the monotony?"

"Morgan's not gonna let them kill your baby, Charlie," Zack said. "He made that plenty clear at the outset."

Ellen came storming into their camp with a scowl on her face. "I hope you're happy, Zackary," she scolded her brother. "Your little tart here is probably going to cost Morgan his business when word gets around about all of this."

"What are you talking about, Ellen?" Zack demanded.

Zack's sister rolled her eyes. "These trains run on reputation, Zackary," she hissed. "No good families are going to want to sign up to travel on a train that the wagon master allows murderesses and harlots to join up." She pointed a finger at her brother. "You're determined to ruin my family, just like you ruined Mama's and Daddy's," she spat, "and I'll not stand by and let that happen." She turned and stormed away again.

"Your sister *really* doesn't like me," Charlie said with a frown.

"Yeah, but Morgan does, and he won't let anything happen to you while you're carrying that babe." Zack put an arm around her shoulder and pulled her close.

"I know," Charlie said with a deep sigh and stepped out of his arms, "but I can't help but worry."

"Maybe you should have thought of that before you went

storming into services this morning," Zack snapped, "lookin' for a fight."

Charlie's mouth fell open, and tears slid from her eyes. "Guess I found one, huh?"

"And I hope for you and that poor child's sake you can win it." He stared for a minute at Charlie's belly before turning and walking back to the fire to pour another cup of coffee.

Emma put her arm around Charlie's waist. "Jimmy's the best damned lawyer to ever come out of Tennessee." She kissed Charlie's tear-streaked cheek. "If anyone can win this fight, it's him."

They returned to the area set up as the makeshift courtroom where people sat on benches and chairs dragged up; the twelve jurors were seated to one side, and Morgan sat up on the back of his wagon, elevated above everyone else.

Morgan used a regular hammer for a gavel and pounded it on his table to bring the crowd to order. "Are the two parties ready to get this show on the road?"

Jimmy had given Morgan a general layout of a trial with opening statements, the witness statements, and then closing arguments by both sides.

Jimmy stood. "The defense is ready, Your Honor," he said in a formal tone.

Lance stood as well. "I'm ready to send this murderin' bitch to hell."

Morgan pounded his hammer to quiet the crowd, who all seemed to favor hanging the murdering bitch as far as Charlie could tell. What foolishness had she gotten herself into now?

"Mr. Bennett, would you care to stand and address the court with your opening statement?" Morgan asked.

Lance stood but looked stunned with his mouth opening and closing and no words coming forth.

"Perhaps we should allow Mr. Willard to begin so Mr. Bennett can get an idea of what's expected of him," Morgan offered.

Jimmy stood and rolled his eyes. "It's out of order, Your Honor, but I get your meanin'."

He stood and walked over to face the men of the jury. "Gentlemen," he began, "I intend to show you that Mrs. Byrde had no plans to murder anyone. She was in her home when three men came and demanded she turn the home over to them. They made lurid requests, and when she asked them to leave, they resorted to the unthinkable, leaving her in the condition we find her today."

There were gasps from the women in the crowd as Jimmy ended his statement and returned to his seat.

"Are you ready to make your opening statement now, Mr. Bennett?" Morgan asked.

Jolene sat beside Lance and whispered in his ear. He finally stood. "I'm ready, sir," he said and walked to the jury.

"You're gonna hear nothin', but bald-faced lies come from this thievin' bitch," he said angrily. "She's done nothin' but lie to y'all since joining' this train, and that should be all y'all need to know about the character of the bitch you're dealin' with here. Did y'all know her mama was hanged and burned as a witch?"

There were gasps from the crowd.

"She was," Lance continued. "Her mama used black magic to kill babies in their mama's bellies. That's the line of women she comes from, and ya shouldn't show her or her bastard anything less than what them folks shoed her evil mama back then. Then she went and married a half-breed bastard in order to come into control of the rightful Davis family property Clive Davis was attempting to reclaim. She's a liar, a whore who spread her legs for a filthy half-breed, and a murderer of good family men."

Morgan had to pound his hammer again to quiet the crowd after Lance's salacious rant. "If you folks can't keep quiet, I'll send you back to your wagons," he warned. "And,

Mr. Bennett, let's keep the foul language in front of the ladies to a minimum."

He cleared his throat again when Lance said nothing more. "I suppose we are ready for our witness testimony now. Mr. Willard, you may begin."

"I call Charlotte Louise Byrde to the stand," Jimmy announced.

It was the first time Charlie had heard herself called by that name in a long time, and she smiled as she stood and walked to the chair set aside for the witness seat. She took the oath to tell the truth with her hand upon the Bible, though it meant little to her. The Bible was a Christian book, and Charlie had never considered herself amongst them, though Grandmother Byrde had taken her to the big church in town and had her head sprinkled with water by her priest and told her she was now a child of the Christ.

"Mrs. Byrde," Jimmy began, "can you clarify for us the prosecutor's statements about your mother?"

"My mother," Charlie said, "was murdered back in Tennessee by a man calling himself a preacher."

"Why?" he asked, clearly uncomfortable with this line of questioning.

"He said she was a witch."

"And was she?" Jimmy asked as gasps could be heard in the group behind him.

"She was a cut wife and practiced country medicine."

"A cut wife?" Jimmy asked. "What exactly is that?"

"She was a midwife who would also help a woman or girl rid herself of an unwanted child." Charlie put her hand on her belly.

"I see," Jimmy said, "and this preacher killed her for that?"

"Because his young wife went to my mother to rid herself of his unwanted get, and the girl died of complications soon after."

"I see, and what of his allegations about your husband, Mr. Byrde? Was he an Indian?"

"He was half Indian," Charlie replied. "His mother was attacked and assaulted by some Cherokee while out picking berries, and they left her with Davis in her belly."

"But he wasn't raised by his father's people?"

Charlie snorted a laugh. "He was raised in a nice house on a nice farm by his grandmother as his mother passed in birthing him. I'd have to say Davis Byrde was probably raised whiter than many of you."

There were a few insulted gasps from the crowd.

"Grandmother Byrde served her Sunday suppers on a table set with white linen cloth and porcelain China plates. Her meals were served with sauces and not gravy, and Davis said his prayers from a psalter every night before going to bed."

"And he was an educated man?"

"He attended University in Nashville and graduated with honors from the School of Agriculture."

"And did you live with him out of wedlock, Mrs. Byrde, as Mr. Bennett has eluded?"

"I was twelve years old when Davis rescued me from Preacher Talley, and I lived in the home of Davis's grandmother in my own room until we were married when I was sixteen and Davis was twenty."

"Now, I come to a delicate subject, Mrs. Byrde. Can you tell the court what transpired between you and the Davis men?"

"You mean how they insinuated themselves into my home, saying they were kin to my husband and his grandmother, knocked me unconscious when I asked them to leave after they'd eaten my food, and did things to me to leave me in this condition?" She pointed to her belly, and there were gasps from the women in the crowd.

"I know it may be disconcerting, Mrs. Byrde," Jimmy said

solemnly, "but yes, please tell the court everything that happened that day to your best recollection."

Charlie took a deep breath and then went on to recite the events of that Sunday afternoon and Monday morning.

"So, you do not deny killing Vernon and Floyd Davis?"

"I was defending myself against further violation," Charlie said with tears trickling down her cheeks.

"And you burned the house?"

"The barn as well," she confirmed, "after I'd turned out the animals."

"And why did you do that, Mrs. Byrde?"

"Because I didn't want to cause harm to innocent creatures."

Jimmy smiled. "No, Mrs. Byrde, I mean, why did you burn the house and barn?"

Charlie shrugged. "Because they were mine to do with as I pleased, and I knew Grandmother Byrde wouldn't want the likes of Clive Davis and his ilk dirtying up her fine home."

"I have here the will of Sandra Davis Byrde, who bequeathed the before mentioned farm to her grandson Davis Byrde and his wife, Charlotte. Where is your husband, Mrs. Byrde?"

"Buried in a battlefield grave somewhere around Vicksburg," Charlie said as she wiped tears from her eyes.

Jimmy winked at Charlie before returning to his seat. "Your witness, Mr. Bennett."

❧ 18 ❦

Lance Bennett stormed toward Charlie with a snarl on his face.

When he got to her, he drew back his hand and slapped her in the face with such force, it knocked her from the chair. "You're a lyin' bitch, Mrs. Byrde, and we all know it."

Jimmy jumped to his feet and yelled, "Your Honor, I object to this vile treatment of the witness." He rushed forward to help Charlie back to her feet and right the chair.

"Mr. Bennett, you've been given a good bit of leeway in this court, but striking a witness, especially a pregnant woman, is beyond acceptable behavior," Morgan thundered. "I've a good mind to call this in favor of Mrs. Byrde and hang *you* instead."

"I'm sorry, sir," Lance said flatly, "but this woman's filthy lies about the good men of the Davis Family—my good family —were more than I could bear. Please forgive me."

"Can you control yourself enough to continue?" Morgan asked, peering down from his high seat.

"I can, sir," he replied and approached Charlie again. "So, you admit you're the daughter of a witch who murdered babies?"

"I admit nothing of the kind," Charlie snapped. "My mother was murdered by a man who *called* her a witch. She practiced country medicine and helped women and girls to rid themselves of unwanted children."

"Children given to them by God," Lance said with a smug grin.

"Children given to them by men like the Davis men, who gave this one to me."

"Yet you didn't try to rid yourself of this one," he pointed out, "though you obviously possess the knowledge of how to go about it," he added snidely.

"She's a good woman who did everything she could to save my family!"

The voice belonged to a young woman Charlie recognized as the youngest Perry daughter, Mary. She called out to the jury from the gallery. "This trial is a mockery of the justice system!"

"Thank you for your opinion, young woman," Morgan said, "but you should sit down and allow things to continue."

"Yes, sir." Mary sat back down.

"You were saying, Mrs. Byrde?" Morgan prompted.

"Like my husband's mother," Charlie said in a strong, clear voice, "I didn't see its father's failings as a man to be the child's fault."

"And you don't deny murdering my cousins, Vern and Floyd Davis? How about my uncle, Clive? Will you admit murdering him too because he failed as a man in your estimations?"

"I don't admit to murdering anybody," Charlie snapped. "I shot Floyd and Vern to save myself from being attacked by them again. Clive Davis died of cholera," she said calmly, staring Lance in the face. "I had nothing to do with that."

"That's a lie," Jolene screamed as she jumped to her feet and pointed at Charlie. "You denied him aid that could have saved him. Those other two fellas lived because you tended to them with your country witch medicine. If you'd come and tended to Uncle Clive, he'd have lived too."

"I asked you to bring his wagon to sit with the others in the sick camp, Jolene, so I could look after him the way I was looking after the others, but you refused. I told you what to do for him—the same things we were doing for the folks in the sick camp—and I came to check on him as soon as I could, but it was too late for him by then. There's nothing more I could have done for him, Jolene."

Charlie took another deep breath. "Clive Davis died of cholera. I had nothing to do with it."

Lance stood, staring at his sister and then back at Charlie.

"Do you have any more questions for this witness, Mr. Bennett?" Morgan asked with a bored expression.

"No," he retorted, "I've heard enough of this bitch's lies. I'm done with her."

"Do you have any other witnesses, Mr. Willard?"

"Yes, I'd like to call Mr. Zackary Drake at this time."

Zack stood, swore the oath, and took the witness chair.

"You are familiar with Mrs. Byrde?" Jimmy asked.

"I am," Zack stated. "I met her in Illinois on my way to Independence."

"And how was she dressed when you met her?"

"She was wearing a dress like any woman."

"And the two of you decided to travel together?"

Zack shrugged. "We were both going to the same place, and she's a damned good cook."

People on the benches in the gallery laughed.

"And who's idea was it for Mrs. Byrde to dress as a man and cut off her hair?"

"It was my idea," Zack replied. "I knew she wouldn't be safe on the trail as a pretty woman, and the wagon master demanded she hide her identity as a female in order to travel on the train."

Jimmy stared up at the wagon master. "Is that true, sir?

Did you know Mrs. Byrde was a female and ask that she conceal it from everyone as she traveled with us?"

Morgan rolled his eyes and released a breath. "I did, sir. Having a woman traveling alone on a wagon train can . . ."

He glanced at the crowd of scowling women. "It can cause trouble amongst the other females, as evidenced by the caterwauling I heard this morning outside Mrs. Byrde's wagon."

The women continued to scowl while the men laughed.

Jimmy returned to his seat. "He's your witness, Mr. Bennett."

Lance stood after, having his sister whisper something into his ear. "You say she's a good cook, Mr. Drake?"

"She is," Zack nodded.

"What else is she good at, Mr. Drake?" Lance asked with a sneer.

"I expect she's good at lots of things," Zack said with a confused look.

"She's good at things in bed, isn't she, Mr. Drake?" Lance demanded as Jolene grinned. "That child in her belly is really yours, isn't it, Mr. Drake? You made her your whore when you met up with her in Illinois, did you not, sir, and her lies about my family are just that? She murdered those good men for no reason whatsoever except to keep them from recovering the property she'd stolen from them by way of marrying a half-breed bastard who had no right to the property either."

"Mrs. Byrde and I have never had any sort of romantic relationship, Mr. Bennett, and that you should suggest it is disgusting. She's a good and respectable woman, sir."

"She's an admitted killer, Mr. Drake, and probably a whore who found herself with child by way of her misdeeds and is looking for another good man to pin it on."

"Then she certainly wouldn't have chosen one of the Davis men," Zack sneered.

Lance's face turned a deeper shade of red as he scowled.

"Are you finished with this witness, Mr. Bennett?" Morgan asked.

"I'm done with this liar too. He's obviously coupling with the whore and lying for her." He glanced up at the jury. "The jury should completely disregard the testimony from this man." He stormed back to his seat.

"Then, I suppose, we can hear your closing statements before I turn this over to the jury." Morgan turned to Jimmy. "Mr. Willard, let's hear from you first as Mr. Bennett seems to be in need of a good example here."

Lance scowled up at Morgan and started to speak, but Jolene stopped him with a touch of her hand on his arm.

Jimmy patted Charlie's hand reassuringly before he stood and walked to the jury. "While the prosecution, in this case, has made many disparaging claims against my client, he has presented no proof whatsoever of those claims. Mrs. Byrde was attacked in her home by men presenting themselves as family in order to force her into an unwanted and unsolicited marriage. They planned to impregnate her and use her embarrassment over the situation to force her into wedlock with one of them in order to lay claim to her legally inherited property.

"She killed those men, and she's never denied that to keep herself from being ravaged by them yet again, and then she burned her farm to the ground, as was her right to do because she owned the property—the house and the barn.

"Clive Davis died in this camp of cholera, as everyone here is aware. He returned from a hunting trip with the illness, and my client did everything in her power to assist his family. She has no culpability in that man's death though, and I say to you all," he said forcefully, "that she had every cause to do so . . . had she turned her back on the horrid creature completely, and denied him her aid in any way, which she *did* not.

"Charlotte Byrde hid her identity as a female, not to hide her identity as a killer, but to save herself from being ravaged yet again by some other male. Furthermore, she did that at the behest of our wagon master. A woman on her own is not safe in this wild west, as can certainly be attested to by Mrs. Byrde."

Jimmy returned to his seat.

"You may speak now, Mr. Bennett," Morgan instructed.

Lance stood and approached the jury. He pointed at Charlie. "That woman may not have killed my uncle Clive, but she admits to killing my poor cousins after she let them and my uncle couple with her multiple times over the night. This coupling may have caused her pregnancy, but I believe the whore coupled with Zackary Drake, and he's the one who fathered her bastard. She's lied to everyone on this train about her identity and her circumstances. I submit that she's a lying whore who is guilty of murdering my cousins and deserves to hang along with her little bastard." He spun and strode to his seat beside Jolene.

Morgan stood. "I will tell you all again," he said sternly. "No pregnant woman will be hanged on my train. If you find this woman guilty of the charges leveled against her, she'll be housed in comfort at Fort Kearny until the birth of her child, and then the authorities there will carry out her sentence."

Jimmy took Charlie's hand and squeezed it. "It's gonna be all right, Charlie," he whispered. "Your babe will be safe no matter what happens here today, and Emma and I will see to its upbringing."

Tears of relief slipped from Charlie's eyes. She trembled with nervous fear as she studied the faces of the men sitting in judgment of her. Did they see her as a lying whore who murdered men?

"I'll poll the jury where they sit," Morgan announced. "Each of you stand in turn and have your say one way or the other as to Mrs. Byrde's guilt or innocence."

The first three men stood and said "innocent" to both sighs and groans from those sitting in the gallery.

The fourth man stood and stared at Morgan. "I vote innocent, Your Honor, sir," he proclaimed, "but I know that bloodthirsty shrew I'm wed to wanted her found guilty."

There was a yelp from a female, followed by some laughter.

"Should I be found dead in my bed in the mornin'," he continued, "then just get right to her hangin' and forgo any trials." He turned to smile at Charlie. "Had those bastards done that to my little girl, I wouldn't have expected anything less from her than to have blown their damned brains all over the walls too."

Charlie was surprised to hear agreement voiced from others in the gallery.

The rest of the jury voted not guilty, and Morgan told Charlie she was free to go. "Everybody be ready to travel at first light in the morning," the wagon master bellowed to everyone. "We've got miles to make tomorrow if we plan to roll into Ft. Kearny this week."

Charlie stood on shaky legs. "I had Mr. Willard prepare something," she said, and the crowd quieted. "I have no need for the property in Tennessee now. It's five hundred acres of cleared farmland in the Tennessee River valley."

She took a sheet of paper from Jimmy and turned to Lance. "Here's the deed if you want it, Mr. Bennett," she said and offered it to Clive's nephew.

Lance reached for the deed. "You're just givin' it to me?"

Charlie shrugged. "It's you, or some other squatter will likely move in on it."

Before Lance could take the deed, Jolene swept in, thumped her brother on the head with something heavy, and sent him to the floor. "I'm the oldest in the clan," she declared as she snatched the deed from Jim Willard, "and if anyone is going to take possession of that property, it's gonna be me."

She glared down at Charlie. "It should be obvious to everyone that the only ones with any brains in the Davis clan are the females." She stepped over Lance. "When my fool brother wakes up, tell him to catch up with us. We're headed back home, now that we have a home to go back to." Jolene held up the deed, turned, and marched away with others from her clan following behind.

"Well, if I never," Morgan said, his eyes wide as coins as he watched her go. "Let's say a prayer of thanks to our Lord and then call it a day, folks."

Everyone stood, and Zack rushed over to stand beside Charlie. "I'm so glad this is over." He took her hand.

Charlie leaned her head onto his shoulder. "Me too," she whispered as the baby kicked and rolled in her belly, and she gasped, throwing a hand to her abdomen in surprise. With a broad smile, she said, "But I think it's really just beginning."

Morgan ended his prayer, but before they could leave, he strode up with Millie at his side. "I have a favor to ask of you, Mrs. Byrde."

"What can I do for you, sir?" Charlie asked with hesitation as Zack left to speak to his sister.

"Millie here has been keeping company with old Mrs. Bradshaw and her husband." He glanced down at the girl fidgeting at his side, "but she—Mrs. Bradshaw—got it in her head the old man was lusting after her and sent her back to me."

"That old man was puttin' his dirty hands on me every chance he got when the ol' bitty wasn't lookin'," Millie spat. "I couldn't take a pee without him followin' to watch me hike my skirts and squat."

Charlie grinned when she saw Morgan's cheeks flame red at the girl's words. "So, you want her to move into my wagon?"

"Well, you *are* a single woman traveling alone," he said, "and she's closer to your age and all. I thought she could ride with you until we got her to Fort Kearny and the Negro settlement there."

Charlie studied the big-eyed, dark-skinned girl who appeared to be in her late teens or early twenties. Her dress was old, tattered, and faded, and she wore no shoes on her dusty feet. Her black hair was brushed back and coiled into a bun. She carried a flour sack in one hand filled with her few possessions, and Charlie felt sorrow for the girl who was as alone in this world as she was. "What do you want, Millie?"

The girl looked up at Charlie in surprise. "Ma'am?"

"What do you want to do? Do you want to go to Fort Kearny to live with your own people there?"

Millie glanced up at Morgan. "They're not my people," she said, and her eyes went to Jolene's wagons, leaving the train. "Them there are the only people I ever had."

"Did you want to return to Jolene?" Charlie asked.

"No, ma'am," she answered, her brow furrowed. "Miss Jolene is an evil woman. I was glad to be taken out of her service, ma'am."

"Then, what's your wish for your life?" Charlie asked with a kind smile.

"Nobody's never asked me that before," the girl said, her eyes wide. "I don't rightly know."

Charlie, suddenly feeling maternal, wrapped an arm around the girl. "Then, we'll just have to figure it out on our way to Oregon. I hope you don't mind sharing a bed because I only have one." Charlie chuckled. "But I reckon it will be getting colder pretty soon, and we'll be glad of the body heat."

Millie's mouth fell open, and she gasped. "You'd share your bed with the likes of me?"

"I told you Mrs. Byrde was a good woman, Millie," Morgan said with a smile.

"Thank you, sir," Charlie said, returning his smile. "Millie is more than welcome to join my wagon for as long as she wants to stay."

"I'm glad to hear you say that," Morgan stated, "but I have one more favor to ask."

He glanced over his shoulder, motioned with his arm to someone, and Mary Perry stepped forward.

"We had to burn the Perry wagon, and poor Mary has nowhere to stay."

"I could stay with the Bradshaws now, sir," Mary said with an uneasy glance at Charlie.

Millie spoke up. "That filthy old man would be on a pretty white gal like stink on a skunk, Captain. Don't you dare," she said in a fearsome tone to Morgan, "set that gal to livin' with them Bradshaws . . . to be pinched and prodded by that old man and ordered about by that old woman who wants her coffee on the saucer just so."

"I'll ask you like I asked Millie, Mary," Charlie said solemnly. "What do *you* want to do?"

"I want to go to my aunt's in Oregon and find a husband," she replied shyly. "Aunt Edith wrote to Father in Illinois and told him there were plenty of men there with the need of a wife. That's why we were going." She burst into tears. "Father wanted to find a good husband for my sister, who had productive farms, and one for me."

"Well," Charlie said, "let's get you to your aunt's and see where it goes from there."

❧ 19 ❧

Zack was shocked to find three young women sitting around his fire when he returned from his camp rounds for his supper.

"What's going on here, Charlie?" he asked when he strolled over to the fire to pour himself a cup of coffee. The rich aroma of venison stew filled the encampment. He looked around for Jim Willard, but their wagon was dark, and the small family gone. Fiddle music and laughter filtered in from somewhere in the camp. They must be dining with another wagon tonight and enjoying some dancing.

"My wagon has been deemed the single women's wagon by Morgan," Charlie said with a frown as she stirred the pot of stew.

"We was just sayin'," Millie offered with a giggle, "that we could be one of them cat wagons Miss Jolene was always goin' on about."

"What?" Zack spat coffee through his nose with a cough.

All three young women laughed at his sudden discomfort, and Charlie took his hand. "You should see your face," she said as she laughed.

"That wasn't funny," he scowled. "After what went on

today, I'd have thought you'd try to keep a lower profile around here."

"Hey," Charlie chided as she buttered biscuits to add to his plate, "this was Morgan's idea, not mine."

"Morgan's?" he said, his brow furrowed. "What the hell was he thinkin'?"

"He was thinkin'," Millie offered, "that me and Miss Mary would be in better company here with Miss Charlie than in the hands of that nasty old Mr. Bradshaw and his sour old wife who was just lookin' for a maidservant."

"That wasn't workin' out for you?" he asked as he took a plate of stew from Charlie piled high with three freshly buttered biscuits.

Millie snorted as she forked up a gravy-coated potato from her plate. "That old bastard had his hands on me every chance he got and followed me around like a pup after its mama's teat."

Zack raised an incredulous brow. "Ain't he about sixty?"

"Closer to seventy," Mary Perry said with a grin as she chewed. "He's always given me the willies." She gave them an exaggerated shudder and took a swallow of coffee.

"Don't mean his post won't still stand straight," Millie said with a long sigh. "And that wife of his ain't inclined to bring it down for him no more."

All three women began to giggle again as Zack's cheeks flamed red with embarrassment. Was this how women talked amongst themselves all the time? He swallowed a mouth full of hot coffee as he pondered their conversation. This was going to be a long trip. What was Morgan thinking? And what were people going to say about him sleeping in the same camp with three young single women?

"Hey, buddy," Jimmy said cheerfully as he slapped Zack on the back, "what do you think about our new arrivals? Don't they brighten up this dreary camp?"

Zack glanced at Emma, who'd taken a seat beside Charlie, but was not quite as cheerful as her husband.

"This is going to be so great," Little Jenny said when she joined the group. "Millie and Charlie will teach me to cook, and Mary is going to teach me to embroider and sew."

"Sounds like they are going to turn you into prime wife material, Jen," Zack said sunnily. "Some man is going to be very lucky someday."

The little girl's face darkened with a frown. "You're going to teach me to ride a horse and shoot a rifle, Zack. Remember? I'm going to be a rancher in Oregon, not a silly housewife."

"Oh, my," Zack said with a quick glance at Emma, who scowled at him from her seat. "Where were you all off to tonight?"

"The wagon master and his wife invited us to supper," Emma replied with a quick glance at Charlie. "They wanted to explain their decision to put the girls with Charlie . . . eh . . . rather than . . . another wagon."

Jimmy began to chuckle as he poured himself coffee. "It seems the Widow Patton had requested to take in the girls."

Millie snorted. "That fat, whiny little shrew wanted herself some slave labor, and I'd wager she'd not have fed us, unless we had the coin to pay for the rations and then cooked it too." Millie laughed, but Mary looked horrified.

"I have no funds to contribute to this trip now," Mary said to Charlie. "All of Daddy's cash was hid in the wagon somewhere, and I couldn't bring myself to go back in there and look for it before they . . ."

She began to sob, and Millie, who sat beside her, wrapped the young woman in her arms. Zack felt for the girl who'd screamed and sobbed when they'd put the torch to her family's wagon the night before with her parents and sister dead inside. He still couldn't get that stench of their burning bodies out of his nose.

He smiled when he saw Charlie rise and go to the sobbing girl. She was a good woman, and Zack thought Mary and Millie were lucky to have landed in her care. Morgan was a wise man, and Zack made a mental note to thank him for his kindness.

He thought back on the laughter he'd listened to them sharing when he'd arrived in camp. Charlie needed these gals' company now as much as they needed her.

"You don't have to worry about that, Mary," Charlie informed her. "Neither of you do. I have plenty of supplies, and I'm set to purchase anything else we might need along the way, so don't worry about that."

Millie jerked up her head and scanned the surroundings. "Don't you go sayin' stuff like that where folks might be hearin' it, ma'am," she scolded. "There are those about who'd be lookin' to come in your wagon and filch what ya have if they thought it worth their time."

"Yes, I'm certain there are," Charlie sighed, "but I think the majority of those left with Jolene this morning."

Millie grinned. "You probably right on that account."

Everyone around the fire laughed.

"My daddy's white daughter was a thieving bitch, if I ever knowed one."

"Your daddy's—" Charlie began, but Zack cut her off.

"I don't think you need fret on that, Miss Millie," Zack said as he emptied his cup. "Everyone on the train knows I work security and that I sleep with this wagon."

"And," Jenny added in her loud child's voice, "they know Charlie wears those two big guns and can use them to blow the heads off men out to do no good." She turned to Charlie. "You could teach me to shoot and cook too, Charlie."

Everyone laughed except Emma. "I think it's time you were in bed, young lady," She glanced uneasily at Charlie. "The wagon master wants us to get an early start in the morning."

"Aw, Mama," Jenny whined.

Emma stood and pointed to their wagon. "Bed, young lady, *now*," she said sternly, and Jenny got up without further fuss.

They watched the two go in silence.

"I'm gonna try and catch a few winks before my night rounds." Zack got up to go for his saddle and bedroll. "I'll bed down by Tess while you folks enjoy the fire."

Jimmy stood. "No, buddy," he called to Zack as he stood and tossed the remaining coffee in his cup into the fire, "I'm gonna join my girls in the wagon."

"Mary, Millie, and I will retire to our wagon as well," Charlie announced. "I'll clean up these dishes in the morning when I make breakfast." She motioned to Zack. "Come on back here by the fire, Zack, and I'll wake you. At midnight, right?"

"Right," he said and returned to the low fire with his saddle and bedroll. "Thanks." He kissed Charlie's cheek. "These little kisses are gonna be harder to steal now," he said with a soft chuckle.

She glanced around at the empty camp and then turned to brush her lips upon his. "But well worth it," she said softly before breaking away to return to the wagon, where the two other young women waited.

Charlie and the women had spent the afternoon tearing the wagon apart and rearranging things to make room for the additions. She dug more bedding from one of her trunks and made space on the floor for a pallet Millie insisted she sleep upon, while Charlie and Marry shared the raised bed.

"Ain't proper for no white gals to sleep on the floor or share their bed with a nigger like me," she'd said as they moved furniture and crates of supplies in the wagon.

"You're a human being like the rest of us," Mary had said. "You and I can take turns on the pallet, but Charlie should always have the bed, as she's with child and all."

"Sounds fair to me," Millie had finally agreed with a shrug, "if it's all right with Miss Charlie."

Charlie had grinned. "It's going to be nice to have company. I've missed having other women about to talk to, and I don't mind in the least sharing my space."

Millie snorted. "I had to share a ten-by-ten slave cabin with my mama, two sisters, and three brothers." She motioned around the cramped wagon. "This is gonna be just like home."

"Where is your family now?" Mary asked as she folded a quilt that smelled of cedar and camphor.

"Dead in the war, I reckon," Millie said as she picked up the chamber pot to carry out and dump. "Mama died before the war, and my sisters was sold off young to men who fancied pretty little black gals in their beds."

A frown creased her pretty face. "Miss Jolene came by her notions about sellin' women from her daddy—my daddy too. He run a brothel by the river in Memphis. The boys run off after the fightin' started to join the Blue bellies when they come close, but I was left stuck with Jolene and Lance."

"You worked in a brothel?" Mary gasped. "How horrible for you."

Millie shrugged. "Weren't so bad after the first few times," she said. "Most was gentle like, but some, like Mr. Clive, got their enjoyment from causin' pain to a gal."

Mary's face paled. "How old were you then . . ." Her eyes darted around, and she finally asked, "The first time you were with a man?"

"Not much older than little Jenny," Millie said, and Mary gasped. "Some men fancy youngins and will pay a premium price to be a gal's first."

Mary dropped into the chair, piled with bedding. "I have a lot to learn about men."

Millie grinned at Charlie. "Then, you landed in the right wagon, Miss Mary."

They spent the remainder of the afternoon getting comfortable with one another. Millie had a wicked sense of humor and giggled every time she made Mary blush with one of her pronouncements about men. Charlie noted the other girl grew a thicker skin soon enough, and her blushes came fewer and farther between.

Charlie smiled and thought this must be what it would have been like had she had sisters. Their first night together in the wagon was cramped but comfortable. They took turns using the chamber pot, and Charlie had to step over a softly snoring Millie to creep outside to wake Zack for his night rounds.

"I didn't think you three were ever gonna quiet down," Zack said when she finally roused him. "Sounds as though Morgan made a good call putting the three of you together." He raised up on his elbow and, with his other arm, pulled Charlie down for a kiss. When he did so, the baby decided to deliver a kick and Zack jumped in surprise. "What the hell was that?"

Charlie put a hand to her abdomen. "It gets excited when we touch. I don't really understand why."

"Must be a boy," Zack said as he struggled to his feet and pulled her into his arms. "You certainly excite me."

Charlie felt her cheeks flush and whispered, "A few stolen kisses are one thing, Zack, but I don't think we should take it any further than that."

Zack dropped his arms and stepped away. "I'm sorry. I meant no offense, and I certainly didn't intend to take liberties, Mrs. Byrde." He snatched up his blanket and saddle before storming off to Tess.

Tears stung Charlie's eyes as she climbed back into the wagon.

"Don't worry yourself none," Millie whispered as she rolled out of Charlie's way. "That man is sweet on you, and he'll get hisself straightened back out about it soon enough."

"He's very handsome," Mary added with a yawn and rolled to face Charlie and Millie. "I hope I can find a man as handsome as Zackary Drake when I get to Oregon."

"Pretty white gal like you, Miss Mary, ain't gonna have no trouble findin' a man to marry up with." Millie rolled over and tightened the quilt around her body. "I'm the dirty nigger whore ain't no good man gonna want."

"Don't talk like that, Millie," Charlie said as she crawled back into bed. "You're a beautiful girl, and I bet you'll have no end of suitors once we get to Oregon."

Millie snorted. "If I had money, I'd wager on that."

✣ 20 ✣

The train slogged through mud and flooded streams as they made their way toward Fort Kearny.

All the water barrels were topped off in several fast-moving tributaries of the Platte, and only a few wagons got bogged down at crossings because of the high water and steep, slick banks.

The train suffered no more cholera cases, and they arrived on the outskirts of Fort Kearny a week and a day of hard travel after Charlie's trial. Zack remained distant and had begun taking more of his meals with the wagon master and his wife.

"We'll be getting into the mountains once we cross into Wyoming," Mary said as they dressed to walk into the fort for supplies. "I've never seen real mountains before. Those we went through in Missouri were only really hills. I hear tell the mountains in the west are so tall, they have snow on the tops all year round."

"Well, let's hope we don't have to cross over any of those," Charlie said. "I don't have any cold-weather clothes, and I don't relish traveling through the snow in this poor old rig."

She made a mental note to check the supply of heavy

stockings and flannel fabric at Fort Kearny's mercantile while they were there.

"Y'all ready to go?" Jenny called from outside the wagon. "Mama wants to get her shopping done so she can get bread baked today while we're sittin'."

Charlie, Mary, and Millie joined Jenny and Emma outside, and they began the trek up the muddy track into the fort for supplies. Charlie took the reins of one of the mules, which would carry back the parcels she knew they'd be loaded down with. She needed more flour, and she suspected Emma did as well. Jimmy enjoyed biscuits with every meal.

"Well, I see you have your girls all dolled up, Mrs. Byrde," the widow Patton sneered when she joined them along with some of the other women from the train. "I don't suppose you've taken the same notion as our recently departed Mrs. Bennett and are taking them into town to entice the lonely gentlemen of the fort for a profit?"

Mary and Millie wore clothes from one of Charlie's trunks. Neither of them had clothes of their own any longer, and Charlie's dresses fit them well enough. She was dressed as a woman now as well and enjoyed the swish of petticoats beneath her skirt.

"You got a foul mouth on you, *Missus*," Millie spat. "Mrs. Byrde is a respectable woman who's given Miss Mary and me a place to stay and clothes to wear out of the goodness of her heart. You got no call talkin' to her in that fashion."

"There's nothing respectable about that." The widow pointed to Charlie's belly. "I can't fathom the wagon master and his good wife allowin' the likes of any of you stayin' amongst us." She pushed through to lead the group toward the stone walls of the fort.

"Go on," Millie called after the woman who strutted ahead of them in her black widow's garb splattered with gray mud. "Find a good moochin' spot on the steps of the mercantile. Did you bring a cup for the alms you hope to collect as well?"

Millie shook her head as some of the other women laughed at the woman ahead of them, who was almost running now. "Damned beggar's got no pride." She took Charlie's hand and squeezed it. "Don't let nothin' that worthless sow has to say break your spirit, Miss Charlie. She ain't worth it."

Mary brushed at the green poplin skirt she wore and straightened the blouse made of green and purple plaid and trimmed in narrow white lace at the collar and cuffs. It had been one of Charlie's favorite outfits and looked lovely on Mary. "I feel like a beggar myself now," she said, brushing a tear from her pale cheek. "I should go back to the wagon and not be traipsing around the fort in your nice clothes, Charlie."

"Don't be ridiculous, Miss Perry," Ellen Morgan said from behind Charlie. "Mrs. Byrde's other young charge is correct. Mrs. Patton's words are of no consequence to any of us on this train. You and the others in the wagon with you," she said grudgingly and took a quick breath, "are members in good standing of our little community and due the respect of any other woman here."

Charlie saw nods and heard sighs of agreement, though she thought they came with reluctance from some.

As they neared the mercantile, they saw Mrs. Patton on the porch with her gloved hands cupped in front of her. "Help for a poor widow who's lost her husband to snakebite on her way to Oregon," she said to a group of soldiers and their wives as they entered the building.

"Can you believe the gall of that woman?" Mary hissed as they neared the porch. "She begged flour and sugar from my mama on more than one occasion, and Mama always gave it to her. I can't believe she'd call me a whore after that."

"I gave her twenty dollars in gold while we were in Independence," Charlie said as she tied the mule to the hitching post in front of the mercantile, "and I believe hers was one of the loudest voices in the crowd at my trial, calling for my hanging."

"She'd be one I'd worry about pilfering your wagon if she could, Miss Charlie," Millie declared as she glared at the woman collecting coins from the military men and their women.

"I wouldn't doubt that in the least." Charlie dropped a copper penny into the woman's outstretched hands, which gained her a sour look from the widow. "I know you have more than that in your leather sack," Charlie heard the woman mutter, "Ill-got, no doubt."

"Morgan has Zack and some others patrolling the camp while we're in town for supplies today," Ellen said in a loud, clear voice. "The wagons should be safe from pilferers today." She, too, dropped a small coin into the widow's hands but received a smile rather than a scowl.

Inside the large well-stocked mercantile, Charlie and her friends found everything they needed and then some. Charlie would return to camp with the mule loaded with sacks of flour, meal, coffee, and dried beans. She also bought a large bag of grain for the stock and some bolts of flannel for warmer clothes. She spent more than she'd intended but had purchased nothing frivolous aside from some more dime novels and a bag of rock candy for Jenny.

"Will you take a look at that," Millie said with a sigh as a group of Negro men wearing uniforms walked into the building as Charlie paid for her purchases.

One of them was very tall, had a muscular build with a light complexion, and Charlie had to admit was quite handsome.

"You certain you don't want us to take you to that Buffalo Soldiers' Camp after all?" Charlie asked with a giggle.

Millie stared wide-eyed at the man as the group walked by. "I might be rethinkin' that decision," she mumbled.

The big man spoke for a minute with a man working in the mercantile, stocking the shelves, and turned back to them. "You ladies with that wagon train outside town?" he asked in a very respectful tone.

"We is," Millie replied.

"Any of you know the man leading it?"

Ellen stepped forward, holding her son's hand. "My husband is the wagon master."

The man tipped his hat. "Ma'am. Some of my men and I are about to be released from service and have been contemplating travel to Oregon to seek our fortunes." He glanced at the group of Negro soldiers around him. "We're all seasoned fighting men and could be an asset on your journey. Do you think your husband would consider having us join up?"

"Maybe I ain't gonna need to rethink that after all," Millie whispered with glee. "Maybe the Buffalo Soldier Camp is gonna be joinin' up with us instead."

"The wagon master is a good and open-minded man, sir," Millie said, stepping forward. "He's treated me with nothin' but kindness and respect."

The big man smiled, flashing a mouth filled with straight, white teeth. "That's good to hear, Miss." He doffed his hat and turned back to Ellen. "Do you think your husband would be willing to meet and talk with me, ma'am?"

Ellen smiled graciously. "If you and your folk have the wagons, supplies, and coin to pay for the journey, I'm certain Morgan would be open to speaking with you, sir."

"I'll visit your camp after our evening drills are complete then," he said with an almost formal bow. "I'm Sergeant Nathan Stone."

Another group of men entered the store, laughing and joking. Charlie saw Millie's head jerk up as she stared at the men. One of them said something, and Millie tore away from the counter toward the group. Charlie and Mary scooped up several paper-wrapped parcels and followed. The man from the mercantile carried out their heavier purchases to tie on the mule.

Millie put her hand on the shoulder of a man who'd turned down an aisle. "Luther?" she asked softly. "Luther Swann?"

The man turned, and when he did, Mary gasped in horror. Where his eyes had once been were a mass of scars that extended down his chin on the left side of his face and pulled down his lips.

"Ma'am?" he said as he turned. "Yeah, I'm Luther Swann. Who's askin'?"

Millie put a hand to his scarred face, and Charlie saw tears welling in the girl's eyes. "It's Millicent, Luther. Your sister Millie."

"Millie?" he gasped, and his hands reached out to touch her. "Dat really you, Mill?" His hands found her face and began to touch her cheeks, nose, and lips. His scarred mouth pulled into a broad smile. "You just as pretty as ever, girl."

He ran his hands over her wiry raven hair before pulling Millie into his arms.

"What happened to you, Luther?" she asked.

The man in a faded uniform shrugged. "You knows how it is, Mill," he said with a sigh. "We nigger boys joined up to fight the rebs, and the white captains put us on the front lines as cannon fodder."

"Simon and Monty?" she asked, her eyes scanning the faces of the men who were staring around her for one she might recognize.

Luther's face fell. "Both lost in the first month after we joined up."

"Oh, Luther." Millie threw her arms around the man's neck as she sobbed.

"What's going on here, private?" the big man asked when he came upon them.

"Sorry, sarg," Luther said. "This here's my sister Millie and I just told her about Simon and Monty, sir."

"Well," the sergeant said solemnly, "let's get to it. You have that list of supplies and the cash we collected from the troops?"

"I do, Sarg." Luther moved Millie aside. "I'm in charge of the supplies for our trip to Oregon," he told his sister.

"But you're blind," Millie gasped in surprise.

"Private Swann is the best supply clerk this unit has ever had," the sergeant said with a wide smile and pointed a finger at his temple. "Keeps everything up here down to the last pickle in the jar."

Millie smiled. "Luther was always good like that. Daddy taught him to count cards when he was just a runt."

"Where is our dear daddy now, Millie?" Luther asked, his mouth drawn into a stern frown.

"Shot dead in a poker game when he tried to cheat some Yankees." She stared around uneasily at the men in blue uniforms, who began to laugh.

Luther grinned. "That sounds like Daddy. What happened to the house?"

"Jolene and Lance tried to run it after the Yankees was done with it; they used it as a hospital and cut legs and such off in Daddy's fancy study," Millie explained, "but they lost it to carpetbaggers when they wouldn't pay the taxes they demanded."

"Neither of them two had the sense God gave a piss-ant," Luther said with a shake of his head. "Where they at now?"

"Jolene wanted to go up to Oregon and open a whore-house in Baker City," she said, "but her and Lance are on their way back to Tennessee now to try their hand at farmin'."

"Farmin'? Them two lazy nitwits?" Luther began to laugh. "Our daddy birthed some amazin' children." His scarred mouth twisted in mirth. "But when he put them two in his wife's belly, somethin' went terrible wrong."

"Can you come to supper tonight, Luther?" Millie asked.

"Can you still cook Mama's chicken and dumplin's?"

Millie grinned and slid her hands over the blue muslin skirt of the dress she wore. "I surely can," she answered with enthusiasm, "and poke greens with a big pan of cathead biscuits."

"That sounds like a meal no man in his right mind would want to miss," Nathan Stone said when he overheard their conversation.

"Please join us, sir," Charlie requested. "We'd be proud to have you at our fire."

"I have to see the wagon master anyhow, so I'd be pleased to." He doffed his hat and bowed again. "For now, ladies, the private and I have business to attend to here." He took Luther by the arm and led him away.

When Charlie and the women left the mercantile, they found the widow Patton picking at the parcels on the mule. "What you think you're doin' there, woman?" Millie yelled. "Get your hands off Miss Charlie's purchases."

Widow Patton glared at Millie. "Mrs. Morgan said I could add my supplies to the ones on this mule to carry back to the camp." She secured a canvas bag to the back of the skittish animal.

"That mule ain't Mrs. Morgan's to commandeer," Millie hissed at the widow. "It belongs to Mrs. Byrde, and you got no right to it."

"I've got every right, you little nigger tart, if the wagon master's wife gives me her leave," Widow Patton hissed in return.

"Ladies," Ellen called when she walked out of the busy mercantile and heard the commotion, "what's going on here?"

"This little nigger whore is trying to tell me, a respectable white woman, what I can and cannot do," Widow Patton huffed as she glared at Millie. "I was securing my purchases to this animal when she accosted me. She should be banned from our train, madam. I've a mind to go to the wagon master about it when we return to camp. Good white folk shouldn't be subjected to the likes of her."

"Did you ask Mrs. Byrde's permission to use her animal as I asked you to do?" Ellen asked with a glance at Charlie.

"I—I . . ." the widow stammered. "You said we were all using the animal to pack our goods back to camp."

Ellen rolled her eyes. "I said Mrs. Byrde had graciously offered her mule but that you should ask if there was still room for your goods as well, Mrs. Patton."

"I couldn't afford much," the widow said, her bottom lip quivering. "My one little sack of flour, meal, and beans doesn't take up much space."

"Mrs. Byrde?" Ellen asked.

"It's already tied on," Charlie said with a deep sigh. "Just leave it."

The widow Patten gave Millie an indignant sigh as she passed her to scurry away down the road back leading toward camp.

"Foul-mouthed bitch," Millie said just loud enough for the widow and those close by to hear.

Mary covered her mouth to hide a smile, and Charlie laughed out loud as she untied the reins to lead the mule back to camp.

"Why is that fat little woman so mean, Mama?" Jenny asked Emma as they walked.

"She's sad because her husband died, honey," Emma told her, "and that kind of sadness can make some people do and say mean things."

Jenny stared at the woman ahead of them. "That woman was mean before her husband got bit by that snake."

❧ 21 ❧

Zack wasn't happy about sharing supper with the Negro army officer and his men in blue uniforms, but he put his best foot forward for Millie's sake when Charlie told him one of them was her brother.

He wore a green calico shirt with a white starched collar and cuffs, a black string tie, and clean trousers. "You fellas could put up one hell of a fight as I recall," Zack said uneasily as they sat around the fire with plates of chicken and dumplings, poke greens in vinegar, and fat biscuits sweetened with some of Charlie's raspberry jam.

"You fought with the rebs?" Luther asked as he forked up a fat dumpling to pop in his mouth.

"My political sympathies fell along with those of the southern states," he said. "I believe in state's rights."

Luther nodded. "I've heard that before, and I'd almost agree, had those states not wanted to keep my people in chains." He grinned as best he could through the scars. "What's your opinion on Expansionism and Imminent Domain?"

Zack was taken aback by the question. Were his prejudices

that bad? Why shouldn't this man, though he was a Negro, have political opinions?

"Polk and Jackson had the right of it," Zack replied. "This country should be ours from the Atlantic to the Pacific." He glanced at Charlie, who sat quietly with her plate on her lap and made certain everyone had a helping of everything. She was a gracious hostess, even in this primitive situation.

"And the Indians who were here first?" Nathan Stone asked, his eyes narrowed and his chiseled face gleaming in the light of the fire.

He intimidated Zack some but was friendly enough, and Zack thought the big sergeant and his men would be an asset on the trip to come.

"Seems to me the white man has been somewhat unfair to them."

"White Europeans have always had a sense of entitlement for some reason and looked to profit off them they saw as inferior," Zack said bluntly, "but not just them."

"How's that?" Stone asked.

"Wasn't the largest plantation in Louisiana with hundreds of enslaved Negroes owned by a black woman who came up from the islands?" Zack asked with a grin, "and weren't your people sold into slavery in Africa by your own folk?" He swallowed some coffee. "When it comes to making a profit off the backs of others, the only color that seems to matter is gold."

Luther snorted with laughter. "You got the right of that, reb."

"His name is Zack," Millie scolded her brother. "And you should show him some respect at his fire while you're eatin' his food."

"Sorry, sir," Luther said. "I meant no disrespect."

"None taken, and it's Charlie's food, not mine. She's the money behind this operation. I'm just a poor soldier like y'all."

Everyone laughed.

"And fine food it is," Stone said cheerfully, trying to cut the tension that had built in the group. "If y'all eat like this every night, you might be havin' a good deal of company from here to Oregon."

"You'll be joinin' the train then?" Millie asked with a smile.

"We have twelve wagons and ten families," Luther replied, "but I'm gonna need someone to help me handle mine." He reached for his sister's hand. "Can you still wrangle a team, Millie?"

"She can handle my mules as well as anyone I've ever seen," Charlie said.

"It would be greatly appreciated if someone could keep my best stock clerk from driving his wagon off into a gorge," Stone said with a broad smile.

"You have your own wagon?" Millie asked her brother.

"Brand new with a fine team of six draft animals and stocked with provisions," Luther stated proudly.

"As our severance package from the Army," Stone said, "they set us up pretty good." He stood and handed his empty dishes to Charlie. "The wagon master has agreed to take us on. We'll be bringing our wagons out to join you in the morning."

Millie helped her brother to his feet and then wrapped her arms around his neck. "I'm glad you got room for me, Luther," she said with a grin at Charlie, "'cause Miss Charlie fidgets in the night worse than Clara or Pearl ever done when we was kids."

They bid their guests good night, and Mary and Millie retired to the wagon, leaving Zack and Charlie alone by the fire. "You aren't happy about these new additions," Charlie commented. "Is it because they're Negroes?"

Zack's eyes widened. "Do you think I hate black folk because I fought for the South?"

"Of course not. You just appear to be flustered about it."

"I'm flustered," Zack said flatly, "because we're getting ready to cross into rough country with treacherous mountains, Cheyenne, Shoshone, and Sioux."

"Then the addition of twelve wagons filled with seasoned soldiers should be a welcome thing," she said.

"That's gonna put the train over thirty wagons long. That's a lot to patrol in Indian territory."

"But the new men will be able to help."

Zack ran a hand through his hair. "I hope you're right," he said. "There's also the problem of the others to deal with when they find out."

"What do you mean?"

"Not everyone is as accepting as you are, Charlie. There will be trouble with some of the other families. I've heard harsh words regarding Morgan's decision not to put Millie off here at Fort Kearny and to keep her on the train. I fear there'll be hell to pay when they find out he's taken on twelve wagons of Negroes as well."

She took a deep breath. "I'd have expected that from a train filled with Southerners, but most of these folks come from the North. I'd have thought they'd welcome them."

Zack rolled his eyes. "Whites are whites no matter where they hail from, and most see themselves as superior to the black man. There will be trouble," he said with a loud sigh, "mark my words."

As much as he wanted to touch her, Zack kept his distance from Charlie. If she wanted more kisses, she'd have to make the first move. He didn't intend to rile her again.

"Have you made any plans yet?" he asked to make conversation.

"Plans?"

"For what you plan to do when you get to Oregon. You still gonna look for your daddy and brother?"

Charlie shrugged. "I'd like to, but the man I spoke to at Fort Kearny said it might be near to impossible unless I can find some of his trapping friends. I got some names from him and will start asking after him and Thomas once we get into the mountains. There is supposed to be a big rendezvous close to Boise when we're supposed to near there. The man told me every trapper worth his salt in the territory would be there to trade." She shrugged. "I'll ask Morgan about detouring to include it if we can."

"That's a great idea." Zack put an arm around her shoulder. "Do you mind if I hug you?"

"I've missed it," she admitted and snuggled into his shoulder. "I've missed *you*, Zack." She lifted her face and offered her lips.

Zack touched them with his. This woman drove him mad. Did she know the effect she had on a man?

He put his hand on the back of her head and pulled her face into his. She parted her lips and allowed his tongue to twine with hers, and soon Zack felt his manhood beginning to stiffen, and he pushed her away.

"I'm sorry, Mrs. Byrde. I shouldn't have done that." He jumped up and strode toward the animals, leaving Charlie beside the fire with her mouth open.

He gathered his saddle and bedroll and carried them back to the fire. When he got there, Charlie was gone, but Jimmy was there.

"Hey, buddy," Jimmy said good-naturedly. "What's your opinion on these new wagons Morgan has taken on?"

"They're all good fighters," Zack replied, "and that will be good in Indian territory, but ..."

"But?" Jimmy asked as he sipped coffee.

"But I fear there will be trouble from some in the camp."

Jimmy nodded. "I fear I have to agree."

"You're a man from Tennessee." Zack dropped his bedding. "What are your feelings on it?"

Jimmy raised a brow. "Just because I'm a Tennessee man doesn't mean I'm one of those who dresses in a white hood at night and rides about the countryside terrorizin' folks who sympathize with the Negro and have given them paid jobs."

"I didn't think you were, Jimmy," Zack said. "I only wanted your opinion on Morgan's decision to add the Buffalo Soldiers to our train."

"Their presence may very well keep the Indians at bay," he nodded. "I hear the tribes have a great deal of respect and admiration for them, but there are definitely those on this train it will rile some."

"The Carson and Mulroony outfits, I'm guessin'?" Zack poured himself a cup of coffee and squatted beside the fire to join Jimmy.

"Them, and that damned widow Patton," Jimmy added, his lip curled in disgust. "I heard her runnin' her mouth this afternoon about meetin' up with 'em at the mercantile and how they was talkin' about joinin' up with us." He shook his head. "The bitch had the gall to say they'd be a strain on our resources and would end up begging from every other wagon to support them on into Oregon."

Zack shook his head and spat into the fire. "That woman should have been left behind in Independence. She's been nothing but trouble."

"I hear she really showed herself today at the fort when the women went in for supplies."

Zack nodded and grinned. "She'd best watch herself around Charlie, or she's likely to end up with an extra hole in her forehead."

"Can't say as I'd blame her any. Did you hear that bitch at the trial, callin' for Charlie to be hung along with her babe?" Jimmy shook his head. "She's a liar, a beggar, and a trouble-maker." He emptied his cup. "She makes the train look bad every place we stop with her hand out, whining for alms. It's a pathetic sight."

"I've talked to Morgan about her, but he thinks I'm harboring a grudge against the woman because of how she acted at Charlie's trial. Maybe if you and Emma brought up her behavior to him?"

"I'll speak to Em," Jimmy responded. "I think she and Ellen have become friendly."

"Ellen's no fan of Charlie, but she's fiercely protective of Morgan's reputation as far as this train goes. If she thinks that woman's actions are doing something to tarnish it," Zack said with a mischievous grin, "the Widow Patton is likely to find herself at the bottom of a very deep mountain gorge."

Jimmy raised a brow. "Why do I suddenly find myself in fear of the women you associate yourself with, my friend?"

They both laughed, and Jimmy bid him goodnight. Zack spread out his bedroll beside the fire, added wood against the evening chill, and snuggled in for the night. It was his first night off in weeks, and he looked forward to a nice long sleep.

Thoughts of Charlie's lips upon his and her sweet-tasting tongue in his mouth roused his manhood again, and he put his hand into his trousers to take care of it. He fell asleep, wondering what it would feel like to be inside her and have her arms around him with the scent of that lavender soap filling his nostrils. Did she have the same thoughts about him? She'd been married. She knew about the pleasures between a man and a woman. Did she want to enjoy those pleasures with him?

Coyotes yipped in the distance, and wood popped in the fire. He heard the soft laughter of the women in the wagon as they settled in for the night, and Zack smiled. One of those women was Charlie, and it was nice to see her as a woman again.

❧ 2 2 ❧

The wagon train crawled into Wyoming territory, over steep mountains, and experienced the first truly cold nights on their journey.

"I can't fathom this," Charlie said as she snapped an icicle off the shelf, making up her kitchen on the old wagon. "It's only August. How can there be ice already?"

She wore a long-sleeved dress and had wrapped her body in a quilt against the morning chill as she sliced bacon for breakfast.

"We're on the top of a mountain, woman," Zack grinned. "It will warm up when the sun comes out and once we get down into the valley."

"It sure is pretty, though," Charlie said as she gazed up at the tall trees around them and breathed in the scent of pine resin. "And it smells so good."

"You got a minute, Zack?" Morgan asked, surprising both of them.

"Sure, Cap," Zack replied and poured some coffee. He handed the cup to Morgan. "What ya need this morning?"

The big man took the cup of steaming brew and said, "It's

more what the entire train needs. We're in dire need of some fresh meat." He glanced at Charlie. "I know this wagon is well set for provisions, but some of the others ain't so well off." He took a quick swallow of hot coffee. "I thought maybe you could take Stone and some of his boys out with your rifles and hunt for fresh meat."

Zack frowned at the mention of the big sergeant's name. "Stone?"

"I know you carry no fondness for the man, Zackary," Morgan said in a pleading tone, "but we're moving into Cheyenne territory, and those Indians carry a deep respect for the Buffalo Soldiers. They might turn away and give you a pass to hunt hereabouts if they see them in your company."

Zack nodded and glanced toward the Buffalo Soldiers' wagons. "I can see your point there, Cap. I'll go have a talk with Stone after I have my breakfast."

Morgan smiled at Charlie, squatting by the fire, wrapped in her quilt, and chuckled. "You might be wantin' to change back into those warmer men's clothes, Mrs. Byrde."

"I just put on an extra chemise and petticoat," she said as she turned the fat slices of bacon in the skillet.

"I hope your condition isn't painin' ya none over these mountains, ma'am," the wagon master added, "'cause these ain't nothin' compared to what we'll come to once we reach Idaho." He shook his graying head as tiny white flakes of snow began to filter down through the branches of the tall pines. "I hate that we got such a late start for the season."

"I'll get some men together for a hunt," Zack said, "but we really need to get down off this mountain before the snow sets in."

Morgan turned his head to study the gray sky. "This will pass soon enough with no accumulation to worry about, but you're right. We need to get down into the valley as quick as we can.

Charlie warmed her hands over the fire as she sliced a potato into the skillet. She was out of eggs again. Mrs. Bradshaw's hens had stopped laying with any frequency, and there were other wagons carrying families who needed the eggs worse than she and Zack did. When they reached the next settlement, she would buy a basket of fresh eggs and cream to churn into butter.

"I'm going down to have a talk with Stone while you finish breakfast," Zack said as he refilled his cup.

"Be certain to complement Millie on her new apron if she's wearin' it," Charlie told him as he stood to leave.

"Apron?" Zack asked with a furrowed brow.

"It was her latest sewing project in our little sewing circle, and she spent a good bit of time embroidering the pockets and bib under Emma's close supervision. Tell her it looks nice if she's wearing it."

"As if I'm supposed to know a new apron from an old one," Charlie heard him mumble as he walked away.

"What's he grumbling about?" Mary asked when she climbed out of the wagon, also wrapped in a blanket. "Why is it so cold?" She went to the fire and poured herself coffee.

The wagons inched into the valley, down the winding trail cut by hundreds of wagons before them, and began the trek across the rolling grasslands of Wyoming toward Fort Laramie, where they would stop for more provisions. Charlie had her list in her head for the mercantile and looked forward to the shopping trip with Mary, Emma, and Millie. The three women had grown close over the long weeks of travel together, and Charlie felt as though she finally had a family again.

The hunters rode out together in high spirits and came across a small herd of buffalo and a small band of Cheyenne. In the end, they shot and killed six of the big beasts. After some strained negotiations, using hand signals and the broken English one of the Indians could speak, the men from the train took the meat from three of the animals, and the Cheyenne took the meat from the other three, along with the hides, horns, and hooves of all six.

Charlie was excited to receive a hunk of butt meat and sliced off four steaks to fry for their supper. She set the rest aside to roast in her Dutch oven overnight with potatoes, carrots, and onions for suppers later in the week.

"Stone and his men are good hunters," Zack said as he used his knife to slice into the steak Charlie had fried for him, "and they're cool under pressure. Not a one of 'em so much as flinched when those Cheyenne rode up on us."

"I hope they leave the train alone," Mary said with a shiver. "Indians were the one thing my mama was scared of on this trip. She never gave a thought to cholera."

Charlie watched the girl brush a tear from her pale cheek. "Millie has nothing but good things to say about Mr. Stone," Charlie said with a grin, trying to lighten the mood.

"I think Miss Millie has designs upon the man." Zack chuckled as he chewed.

"Why do you say that?" Charlie asked, though she already knew. Millie Swann was utterly smitten with the big sergeant and made no secret of it during their conversations while sewing together.

"How often did she put her hair up or rouge her lips when she was stayin' in your wagon?" Zack asked with a grin on his handsome face, which needed a shave. "She looked as shiny as a new penny this morning in her pretty new apron and all done up like she was goin' out to a dance on a Saturday night when she was just makin' breakfast in camp."

Mary giggled. "Zack's got the right of it. She's sweet on him, that's for certain."

Charlie smiled. "I'm glad she's found a place for herself and some happiness."

"Luther sure seems happy to have found his sister," Zack

added a piece of wood to the low-burning fire. "I don't think it will be near as cold tonight, girls."

"I'm glad of that," Mary said, "but the bed in the wagon is plenty warm and cozy."

Zack grinned as he stared at Charlie and wondered what it would be like to snuggle beneath the blankets beside her. He shook his head to dislodge the unseemly thought. They'd shared a few kisses on occasion, but the woman still insisted upon keeping their distance from one another in public. Did she not want a proper husband and father for that child?

Jimmy, Emma, and Jenny joined the group by the fire, and Emma dropped thinly sliced beef into the skillet along with diced turnip and salt.

"I'm so glad of the fresh beef, Zack. Thank you so much," Emma said gratefully.

"It's buffalo, Mama, not beef," Jenny corrected as she watched the skillet.

Charlie grinned. "Buffalo and regular cows are close cousins, Jenny. They're near enough to the same that you won't be able to taste the difference."

Emma glanced at her daughter. "I hope that's the case," she sighed. "She's a picky eater as it is."

Zack popped the last bite of steak into his mouth. "I can't tell the difference," he said as he chewed, "but I'm bettin' Charlie could make boot leather taste good."

Charlie smiled at the handsome man across the fire. "I don't know as I'd go so far as to say that."

Emma stirred the meat and turnips. "Do you have a little cinnamon?" she asked Charlie. "I like to season my turnips with it, and my tin is empty."

"Sure." Charlie got to her feet. "I'll be right back." She hurried off toward the wagon and her cooking cupboard.

"I hope you're going to ask that woman for her hand before she pops that child into the world," Emma said to Zack.

"What?" Zack gasped and snorted coffee through his nose.

Jimmy laughed. "My wife can be as subtle as a copperhead on a flat rock, but she does have a point, Zack," he grinned. "That woman needs a husband, and that child is gonna need a daddy."

"Here's the cinnamon," Charlie said and handed Emma the small spice tin. "I brought a jug of cider too. It'll tender everything up and goes good with the cinnamon." She offered Emma the jug of cider. "Why did everyone get so quiet all of a sudden?" Charlie stared at the silent faces around the fire.

"Mama thinks Zack should marry you before your baby comes out," Jenny said in a matter-of-fact tone.

"Oh." Charlie lowered her heavy body down to the bench. Squatting on the ground was becoming more difficult as the baby grew inside her. "I see."

Three men came storming into camp and changed the direction of the conversation. "The buffalo was nice, Drake," Frank Mulroony hissed, "but don't ya think ya shoulda asked your own kind to hunt with ya rather than them black bucks?"

"My wife can't eat that meat tainted by the touch of them black fellas," Frank Turner added with a disgusted snort. "You should know better than that bein' a reb and all."

Emma added the cider to the skillet and jumped back as the steam sizzled up in her face. "In my experience," she said coolly, "hungry folk will eat almost anything and be grateful to have it. How about you, Charlie? What're your thoughts on the subject?" Emma handed the jug of cider back to her friend.

"None of us give a good goddamn about what Drake's harlot has to say on any subject," Mulrooney said as he glared at Charlie. "She don't count for nothin' in our opinion and shoulda been left to fend for herself in one of the brothels at Fort Kearny, along with that little nigger whore she buddies up with."

From her seat by the fire, with Jenny in her lap, Mary gasped with disgust.

Zack shot to his feet and turned on the men. "I'll thank you to leave our camp, Mulrooney if you can't keep a civil tongue in your head in front of women and children."

"Ain't no rule says a man has to be civil to a dirty whore," Carson Booth said as he stared at Charlie and licked his peeling and cracked lips. "How much for a turn with her, Drake? I think I could scrape up two bits for a poke, or even a suck, as she's ripe with child and all."

"Watch your language, sir," Emma hissed as she pulled Jenny close, "there's a child present."

"You seem a fit woman, Mrs. Willard," Mulrooney stated flatly, "that's why it surprises me you'd subject your innocent girl to the likes of her and them she keeps company with."

Mary shot to her feet. "And just what do you mean by that, Mr. Mulrooney?"

"I got no trouble with you, Miss Mary, but you really shouldn't be in the company of this harlot if you want to find a good man like me, or one of the other boys in my outfit, to marry ya and give ya his good name." He smiled cheerfully at the young woman. "The stain of her might not wash off that easy, ya know."

Mary's laughter sputtered forth. "Mr. Mulrooney, I'd rather marry a wild Indian than you or one of the filthy, unwashed, foul-mouthed, inbred boys in your outfit."

Mulrooney's eyes grew wide. "I fear it's done too late for you, Miss Mary." He turned and motioned for the others to join him. "Ain't nothin' in this camp but harlots and nigger lovers."

Emma scooped supper from the skillet onto three plates and popped a piece of turnip into her mouth. "You were right, Charlie," she said as she chewed. "that cider made all the difference."

Charlie sat on her bench with her hands on her belly. "Is

that really what everyone thinks of me on this train? That I'm just a harlot?"

Emma handed the plates to her husband and Jenny. "Those are small-minded men. Don't pay any attention to their blather." She motioned to Jimmy, and the three of them walked back to their wagon.

"She's right," Mary said with a hand on Charlie's shoulder, "those men are foolish and full of bull excrement. Don't pay them no mind, Charlie." She bent and kissed the top of Charlie's head. "The only opinions that really matter are those of the people here in this camp who care about you, and we think you're wonderful, kind, and gracious."

Mary marched off to the wagon.

Zack took a seat beside Charlie on the bench. "They're all right about one thing, Charlie," he said as he took her hand. "You need a husband and," he put a hand on her belly, "and that babe needs a daddy."

Charlie rested her shorn head on his shoulder and asked with a chuckle, "You volunteering?"

"I might be," he whispered. "Would it be so terrible if I were?"

Charlie jerked up her head and stared at him in dismay. "I don't need your pity, Zack. I'll be able to take care of myself and my baby when we get to Oregon."

Zack rolled his big hazel eyes. "Had you been able to take care of yourself," he said with a skeptical grin, "I doubt you'd be in this condition in the first place."

Charlie shot to her feet. "Is that so?" she snapped, tears stinging her eyes. "Well, ask Vern and his brother Floyd about that. I think I took care of them plenty good."

She whipped around to storm back to the wagon Mary had lit with the lantern while she read. "I don't need a husband, Mr. Drake, and I certainly don't want one out of pity for my situation."

Charlie hefted herself up and climbed into the wagon, leaving Zack to stare after her with his mouth open.

"I would have expected a better proposal from you, Zack," Jimmy called from his wagon with a deep chuckle. "That idiot Mulrooney could have done a better job of proposing to a woman than that."

Zack shook his head as he stood to collect his bedroll to spread out by the fire. What had he done so wrong?

❧ 23 ❧

Three days after the buffalo hunt, the wagon train had Laramie in sight.

"It's not a big town by any means," Morgan told them over coffee, "but it has a railroad station and a mail drop. It's an up and coming town, in my opinion."

Ellen patted her husband's stubbled face. "I'm hoping it has a barber who offers hot baths."

Morgan swatted away his wife's hand. "It does," he said with a roll of his eyes, "and I planned upon a visit."

"Take your son along with you," Ellen said. "While he's a few years from needing a shave, he's in sore need of hot water and a bar of soap."

Charlie giggled. "You should take Mr. Drake with you as well. Emma, Mary, and I have found it necessary to sit upwind of him during meals."

Everyone but Zack laughed.

She and Zack had been keeping their distance from one another since the night by the fire. Mary and Emma had both scolded her for not accepting his proposal and said a wedding in the camp would have been a welcome event. When she heard about it, Ellen told Zack he was a fool for proposing marriage to a woman like Charlotte Byrde and lucky she'd turned him down.

The women walked into town together, as was their routine. They wanted to visit the mercantile or dress shops while the men tended toward the barber, the livery, and the saloons. The widow Patton made certain she traveled into town ahead of them all, and the women found her in her usual place upon the steps of the mercantile, dressed in her black linen with hands out for alms.

Ellen shook her head upon seeing the crow. "Can you believe her gall?"

Emma snorted. "She should be the best provisioned amongst us, with jars filled with small coin to boot."

Charlie remembered her donation to the woman in Independence. "Not all of them were so small," she said as they strolled up the dusty street.

Charlie was so tired of dust. Her wagon traveled in the twentieth spot in line, and she had to wear a kerchief around her face most days against the fine particles of soil ground down by the hooves of the many animals and numerous wagon wheels. It coated her tongue with grit, filled her eyes, and when she washed at night, the water in her basin turned gray with the stuff she wiped away with the cloth. Charlie and most of the other women would be so glad to get to the end of this journey and never breathe dust into their lungs again.

"This seems a nice town," Emma said as they neared the steps leading onto the boardwalk near the tidy mercantile. The buildings along the front street were lopsided and painted a variety of colors. The signs of the businesses had been lettered by a professional painter and were even with proper spelling. They'd laughed together over many a supper about signage they'd seen along the trail with misspelled words and sloppy lettering.

Laramie was a railroad town now with an extensive depot, stockyards, and fancy hotels for travelers. "What I wouldn't give for a night in a place like that," Emma said with a deep sigh as they passed the Sutton, a large building with many windows displaying lace curtains. "I wager they offer hot baths in the rooms," she mused aloud wistfully, "and bring you your meals in bed."

Charlie smiled. She wasn't sure about eating a meal in bed, but a hot bath would undoubtedly be nice at this point. Charlie hadn't soaked in a tub of hot water in months. When she got one, her baths were in cold, fast-moving streams taken hastily to avoid being seen by any men who might be skulking about the waterway in hopes of seeing just such a sight. Charlie's opinion of the opposite sex had diminished a good bit over the past several months. Aside from a very few, Charlie thought men were all liars, thieves, and molesters of women.

She put a hand to her belly and hoped to heaven this child was a girl. She couldn't imagine birthing a boy child that would turn out like one of the Davis men she'd encountered or a Mulrooney. How disappointed their mothers must have been. This would be a girl child, and Charlie would raise her to be strong and independent. She would have a sound mind, and Charlie would teach her to read and love books.

"Are you going in, Mrs. Byrde?" Ellen asked as she stepped past Charlie and up onto the boardwalk, bringing her back to the here and now.

"Do you think they'll have rock candy, Charlie?" Jenny asked in an excited voice and tugged at Charlie's blue calico skirt.

Charlie smiled down at the beaming girl. "I've spoiled you with rock candy," she said and patted Jenny's head, "but I'm sure they do and, if not, then licorice for sure."

Emma rolled her big brown eyes. "Yes, you have, Mrs. Byrde."

"Or peppermint?" the little girl gushed as she followed her mother onto the boardwalk, past Widow Patton with her gloved hand extended, and into the mercantile.

"What a well-stocked store." Ellen sighed appreciatively when they stepped inside.

The big mercantile had shelves from floor to ceiling filled with all manner of goods. Charlie saw shelves stocked with china dishes, galvanized wash pans, tins of fruit, and bars of soap. In another section, she saw clothing already made. There were men's shirts, coats, and vests, women's dresses and frilly underthings, and sturdy clothing for growing children. There were bins of dry goods and barrels of dried fruit and nuts.

"This is amazing," Emma said as she popped a fat raisin into her mouth from one of the wooden casks lined up down the center of an aisle.

"Rail service gives us access to all sorts of goods we never had before," a woman in a bright white apron said as she filled a shelf with lamp chimneys from a wooden crate on the floor. "It's truly an amazing time to be alive."

"You have quite the store here," Emma told the woman as she chose another raisin.

"I'm quite proud of it," she said, "and it could only have happened in the great Wyoming Territory, where women now have the right to independently own their property."

"Are you telling us," Ellen asked with her eyes wide as she motioned around to indicate the mercantile and its goods, "that this is *yours*?"

"Lock, stock, and barrel," the woman said with a broad grin. "Deanna's Laramie Mercantile belongs to Miss Deanna Pace and nobody else."

"No husband or father looking over your shoulder and telling you what to do?" Mary asked, wide-eyed.

"Or taking the profits," Deanna stated, shaking her head. "No, this is all mine, and no man can take it or my money from me."

"But that isn't the natural way of things," Mrs. Mulrooney gasped in her Irish accent. "Men are the heads of the clans and the heads of the families. Men make the laws, and it's the place of women to serve and submit."

The woman in the apron laughed. "Doesn't she know how foolish that outdated drivel sounds?"

"Obviously not," Ellen said with a grin.

"This territory has given its women the right to vote as well *and* sit upon a jury," the woman declared proudly.

Charlie smiled to herself as she thought back to her trial only weeks before and remembered the women in the gallery calling for her hanging. She thought perhaps it was better that it had taken place in Nebraska with only men on the jury to decide her fate.

"Mrs. Sutton, who built the hotel across the street, is the widow of a big rancher and the head of the City Council here in Laramie," the woman told them with a sly grin. "She's the best businesswoman I've ever met and took those thieving railroad men for everything she could get when they came through Wyoming, grabbing land and trying to cheat the people settled here."

"But I thought you said the railroad was a boon to your town," Ellen said with a brow arched in confusion.

"Oh," Deanna said, "it is now that it's here, but those land-grabbers tried to cheat their way through the territory, and Mrs. Sutton saw right through 'em and beat 'em at their own game."

"And how did she manage that?" Ellen asked.

The woman smiled. "The railroad had men to feed, and Mrs. Sutton had herds of beef. While the railroad could steal folks' land with their Imminent Domain, they couldn't steal cattle to feed their workers."

She took the last two chimneys from the crate and placed them on the shelf. "Mrs. Sutton made a fortune from her beef and managed to acquire a prime location for her hotel near the depot along with the lumber and men to build it. She's a very astute businesswoman."

"Sounds like a no-good tart to me," Mrs. Mulrooney hissed as she motioned to the women with her. "I don't think this is the sort of place I'll spend my good man's coin in."

She and her cohorts stormed out.

The woman rolled her striking blue eyes. "It's the only mercantile for the next eighty miles," she winked as the other women laughed.

Charlie, Mary, and Emma spent an hour roaming through the mercantile, and when they'd finished, Charlie's mule was loaded down with supplies. Morgan had told them Laramie would be their last supply stop until Boise the next month.

The poor mule was loaded with sacks of flour, meal, beans, feed grain for the stock, and sundry items like soap, lamp oil, and candles. Jenny carried a supply of rock candy, fabric for a new frock Mary promised to help her make, and a heavy cookbook. She'd also chosen several dime novels with stories about outlaws in the untamed west.

"Are you certain you want your little girl reading that sort of thing?" Ellen had asked Emma when she'd seen the little girl hand the novels to Charlie.

"I'm just glad she wants to read at all," Emma had said with a smile. "Charlie has been an outstanding influence on Jenny in that regard."

Ellen rolled her eyes. "My boy is upset that she's teaching your girl to shoot and wants to know if she can teach him too." She shook her auburn head. "I don't know that teaching her gunplay is being a good influence on any young girl."

Emma grinned. "I won't have to worry about her when young men start coming to court her."

"Knowing how to shoot a gun certainly didn't help to keep Mrs. Byrde from ending up in her present condition, though, did it?" Ellen sneered as she stared at Charlie's belly.

"No," Emma replied in a lowered voice, "but the sons of bitches won't be doin' it again to another poor gal now, will they?"

Ellen cleared her throat with her cheeks pinker than normal, given Emma's use of foul language in public. "No, I don't suppose they will."

"Every woman should know how to use a gun in this wild country," Mary stated. "My daddy taught my sister and me to shoot his handgun, as well as the rifle. We could both take down a deer or rabbit when we needed to."

"Or an attacking Indian too, I'd wager," Deanna said with a grin. "Your daddy is a very wise man, young lady."

Mary gave her a sad smile. "That he was," she said before she turned and rushed away.

"Mary lost her entire family to cholera back on the trail," Charlie told the woman, who stared after Mary with her mouth open in surprise at the abrupt departure.

"I'm so sorry to hear that," she said with a shake of her head. "That cholera is a nasty business and takes a good many on the trail every season."

They paid for their goods, loaded the mule, and made ready to return to camp. A dress in a store window caught Ellen's eye, and they walked across the street to a building with a sign that read Miss Loretta's Finery. They gazed into the dressmaker's window at the creation made of China silk in a floral pattern of pinks on a beige background, trimmed with fringe and lace. The flounced skirt was made of pink eyelet that set off the colors in the flowers, and a bonnet sat atop the dress form to go along with it.

"Isn't that just the prettiest thing you've ever seen?" Ellen gasped.

"I don't know where you'd wear it," Emma said, "but it is pretty."

"I wonder how much it is," Ellen said with a deep sigh. "I haven't had a new dress in ages."

"Good afternoon, ladies." A woman stepped past the door of the shop. "Would you care to come in and have a look about?"

"We were just on our way back to our camp," Charlie replied, "and were admiring this lovely dress in the window."

Ellen broke and headed for the door. "I'd love to."

She and the other women followed her into the shop filled with tables of folded garments and dress forms hanging with all manner of lovely things.

"I haven't seen this many things in one place since we were in St. Louis," Mary gasped as she fingered a pink flannel nightdress.

"It's all so pretty, Mama," Jenny said as she stared around her in wonder. "Can you teach me to sew clothes like this, Mary?"

Mary studied one of the seams on the nightdress. "I believe these garments are constructed on one of Mr. Singer's amazing new machines." She turned to the woman who'd greeted them. "Are they not?"

The woman smiled. "They are, indeed. I'm Loretta Day, and I made everything you see in here."

"Are all the business owners in Laramie women?" Ellen asked, surprised.

Loretta grinned. "No, but there are a good many of us now."

"I hope the same can be said of Oregon once we get there," Ellen said with a sigh. "It would be nice to think a woman could have her own business and use her mind for more things than putting together a pie."

"I couldn't agree more," Charlie said. "Women have better minds for business than men and should be allowed to use them."

Loretta smiled. "You and Mrs. Sutton next door would get along well. She has a special program in place with the City Council for women who want to start businesses in Laramie."

"We're on our way to Oregon," Emma explained, "but I'd love to sit with this woman and have a discussion."

Loretta glanced at the watch she wore, hanging from a

delicate gold fob at her waist. "You can probably find her lunching in the dining room of the Sutton now."

"How much is that lovely thing in your window?" Ellen asked, gesturing.

"Four dollars, madam," Loretta told her, "and it would look remarkable on you with your coloring."

Ellen blushed at the compliment. "It's lovely, but it probably wouldn't fit."

"Oh, but it would without any alterations at all," the seamstress protested. "I construct all my garments with laces." She lifted the arm to reveal satin ribbons crisscrossing beneath the sleeve. "This dress will fit a stout woman the same as a skinny little thing like her." She pointed at Mary. "Simply by adjusting the laces."

"How amazing," Ellen gasped, stunned. "I've never heard the like."

Loretta smiled. "I read about it in a history of fashion," she said. "It was something women did in Medieval Europe so that clothes could be passed on to other family members without the need of alteration."

"You see what you can learn by reading?" Emma said to her daughter, who'd been listening to the conversation.

"I know, Mama," she said in protest. "Charlie already told me, and I read all the time now—even boring old history."

Ellen purchased the garment in the window, along with new petticoats and stockings. Charlie bought the pink nightdress for Mary, as well as one for herself in white. The flannel would be welcome on the cold nights to come.

"I'm of a mind to meet this amazing Mrs. Sutton," Ellen said after paying for her purchases, and the whole group left the shop for the hotel next door.

❧ 24 ❧

They found Mrs. Sylvia Sutton dining at her private table in the elaborate hotel's dining room.

"These women insist upon speaking with you, madam," a waiter in a crisp black suit told the woman when he led them into the dining room. "I told them you were eating, but they were quite insistent upon speaking with you."

The well-dressed matronly woman looked up from her meal to study them. "What can I do for you, ladies?" she asked in a refined accent that told Charlie the woman had been bred in a northeastern city somewhere. She motioned for them to sit, and Mary, Charlie, and Emma waited for Ellen to sit before they took seats.

"My name is Ellen Morgan, and these women are traveling with my husband and I on a wagon train to Oregon." With a sniff of her suntanned nose, she added, "My husband is the wagon master."

"I see," Mrs. Sutton said and sipped her tea. "I'd heard there was a new train outside town." She motioned for the man in the suit to pour tea for all of them. "Again," she continued with a bored expression on her powdered face, "what can I do for you?"

"We've heard wonderful things about you and your work here in Laramie," Ellen explained, "and we wanted to speak with you about doing the same in Oregon when we get there."

That seemed to spark some interest in the woman. "Is that so?" She sipped more tea. "Where in Oregon will you be settling?"

"I'm not certain yet," Ellen replied, "but Baker City has been mentioned, or we may travel on to Portland."

"Both have great potential for women with an enterprising business spirit," Mrs. Sutton said. "What businesses are you interested in starting?"

"My husband would like to build his business bringing wagon trains north," Ellen said.

"Your husband?" Sutton frowned. "Not *you?*"

"I plan to manage the operation from an office in Oregon while Morgan manages the actual day-to-day on the trail," Ellen advised.

"I see," Mrs. Sutton said with a curt nod. "And you, young lady?" she asked Mary.

"I . . . I'd like to open a dress shop like the one next door," Mary finally said with a shy grin. "Women are always in need of clothes."

"That they are, but don't forget the little ones. They'll likely need clothes along the trail too." Mrs. Sutton smiled when Mary nodded. She turned to Emma. "And you?"

"My husband is an attorney," she said proudly, "and he's going to need someone to manage his practice."

"And you, young lady?" she asked Charlie. "What business is your husband in that needs managing?"

"I don't have a husband anymore," Charlie replied. "I plan to homestead property and manage a farm for myself and my child."

"You'd be able to claim more land if you had a husband, you know."

Charlie arched her brow. "I wasn't aware of that."

"A smart woman goes in with all the information she can collect," Sutton said and turned away from Charlie, back to Ellen. "I assume this husband of yours is in agreement with this plan for you to manage his affairs?"

Ellen smiled. "Morgan hates paperwork. He had to deal with stacks of it while in the army and is more than happy to turn that part of the business over to me."

"And you are aware of how to make all of this work in your favor?" Sutton smiled slyly as she ran a perfectly filed and rouged nail around the rim of her cup.

"Morgan has to think everything was his idea, and I'm just following his directives," Ellen replied with an equally sly smile.

Sutton grinned. "You will do just fine in this man's world, madam." She sipped her tea as she studied the faces of the other women at the table. "So, we have a travel coordinator, a legal office manager, a seamstress, and a farmer here. You are all moving to Oregon and plan to settle together somewhere? Is that so?"

"We are," Emma nodded.

"Is there some way you could combine your talents into one business you could run together?"

Ellen snorted and furrowed her brow. "I don't see how. Bringing settles to Oregon has absolutely nothing to do with farming or women's clothing."

"We can put our heads together and talk about it," Charlie said in an effort to keep the woman's interest in them. "We're all intelligent women."

Mrs. Sutton pointed a finger at Charlie. "There you have it, young woman," she snapped. "Keep your thoughts on women. What do they need in the expanding west more than anything else?"

"Women?" Mary said in a hesitant voice.

"Exactly!" Sutton exclaimed and slapped her hand on the table. "Women to become wives and mothers." She pointed at

Ellen. "Mail-order brides are your hook, madam. Fill periodicals with advertisements. Advertisements in the west will garner you men who will pay for the women's transport, and advertisements in the east will garner you the women."

"And an attorney will be needed to draw up marriage contracts," Emma said with enthusiasm.

"A seamstress might offer a new husband a wardrobe for his new bride," Mary added with a timid smile.

"And a farmer?" Ellen asked with a glance at Charlie. "What might she have to offer to this endeavor?"

Charlie grinned. "Fresh and processed food for the travelers, which they would purchase directly from the transport company rather than those price-gouging mercantiles along the way."

Ellen raised a brow, giving Charlie's suggestion some thought. "I can see how that might be advantageous."

Mrs. Sutton pushed her body away from the table and stood. She wore a simple blue wool suit with a high-necked white blouse and white gloves. "You ladies have something to chew over now. I suggest you put your heads together and work out the details.

"May I offer you rooms at a reduced rate here at the Sutton for the night? I'm sure you'd all appreciate a soft bed and warm bath after your long weeks of travel in wagons."

"What would that reduced rate be, madam?" Ellen asked warily.

"Our regular rooms are a dollar a night, and the suites are five dollars, but," she said with a smile, "I'd give you suites for the one dollar rate if you planned to take more than one."

Ellen stammered, "I d-don't think we can—"

"We'll take three suites for the night," Charlie said firmly. "Where do I go to pay?"

"You can sign the register at the front desk in the lobby," Mrs. Sutton motioned.

"What are you doing, Charlie?" Mary whispered as she

followed Charlie into the ornate lobby. "I've got no money to pay for a fancy room in this hotel."

Charlie smiled and winked. "Suites come with two beds, and a bathtub with the water heated and filled by the staff."

Mary rolled her big blue eyes. "That sounds like heaven," she said with a sigh and a hand on her bosom. "I haven't enjoyed a hot soak in a tub since before we left St. Louis."

Charlie paid for the suites. One was for her and Mary, one for Emma, Jenny, and Jimmy, and one for Ellen, Morgan, and their boy. Ellen and Emma wrote notes for delivery by Ellen's boy to Jimmy and Morgan, telling them to come to the Sutton Hotel in Laramie for the night. Charlie penned one to Zack, asking him to look after their unattended wagons and that she wished she could include him on their excursion but that it would be more than unseemly to do so.

Charlie and Mary giggled like schoolgirls when they saw the elegant rooms on the hotel's top floor. Each bed was dressed in crisp white sheets, an array of feather pillows, and a heavy chenille spread with a white lace bed skirt that matched the drapes on the windows. The suite had two bedrooms with an adjoining privy closet, where a large copper tub sat along with a privy chair.

Mary ran her hand over the upholstered back of the chair. "If I ever get a husband and he builds me a house," she said wistfully, "I want a room just like this one. I don't ever want to trudge to an outhouse in the middle of winter again."

"Or squat over a damned chamber pot in the dark of night," Charlie added.

Someone tapped on the door, and Charlie answered it. A young Negro woman dressed in a black dress and white frilled apron and cap stood outside. "I'm here to fill your tub, ma'am," the girl said with a curt bob before pushing her way into the room with a large bucket of steaming water.

The girl made several trips to a room down the hall, where she told them there was a pump for water and a stove for heating it the maids used. Mrs. Sutton had designed the hotel with all the latest conveniences, and she was happy to have been given a job here.

After hot baths and much giggling, Mary and Charlie made their way back to Loretta's to browse the shop. The outfit Ellen had purchased had been changed to a black taffeta gown that shimmered in the light streaming through the big glass window.

"Isn't that something?" Mary gasped when she saw it.

"You reckon there's a theatre here in Laramie to wear it to?" Charlie asked with a snort. "Grandmother Byrde would have called that an opera gown, and I don't think there are any operas out here," she said as they left the window and entered the shop, "but it is pretty. That Loretta knows her business when it comes to trims and frills."

"And how can she help you ladies?" the woman asked when she heard them.

"We just want to look at all your pretty things, ma'am," Mary said with a sweet smile on her freshly washed face.

In her late fifties, the woman walked up with a piece of fabric and needle in her hands. She touched Mary's cheeks. "I hope to heaven you wear a hat to shade your face from the sun, child. With your fair complexion, the sun will ravage it in no time at all, and you'll wrinkle like a prune when you're my age."

Charlie watched Mary's cheeks flush with embarrassment at the woman's words. "We do our best to keep the sun and dust off," Mary said, "but it's a chore."

"As I can imagine," Loretta stated. "The apothecary here has a good cream for the face and hands. I'd recommend getting yourselves some and using it every night before you go to bed. It's called Mrs. Hagen's, and it's the best I've ever used." She touched her own soft, flush cheek and smiled. "And it's only ten cents a jar."

"We'll go down to the apothecary's and look after getting some," Charlie said.

Loretta nodded and walked away after telling them to look to their heart's content and call if they had any questions.

They wandered up and down the aisles of the small shop and fingered the dresses' delicate fabrics displayed on forms. "I could see myself with a shop like this," Mary said with a sigh.

Charlie smiled. "It all begins with an idea, and then you make a plan."

"A plan?" Mary asked, her face twisted in confusion.

"Look about." Charlie motioned the tables, shelves, and dress forms. "How much and what kinds of fabric would you need to stock a shop the way this one is stocked?"

Mary glanced around, and her face fell. "It would take a good bit of time and money to build all the stock in here."

"I'm certain Miss Loretta didn't accomplish it overnight," Charlie said as she traced a finger over the embroidery on a cotton camisole. "And maybe she had some help from friends who could sew and make a pretty trim."

Mary smiled. "She did say she had a Singer." She glanced at the curtained doorway Loretta had disappeared behind. "That would make things go a good bit quicker."

"Then put a Singer into your plan," Charlie advised with a smile.

"That and bolts of cotton, flannel, and silk," Mary said as she gazed longingly around the shop.

While Mary wandered, taking a mental inventory of Loretta's shop, Charlie admired a pink calico frock on one of the dress forms. Pink wasn't her color, but Charlie thought the dress would look lovely on Millie, and she felt bad she couldn't offer her Negro friend a night at the Sutton.

While Mrs. Sutton allowed Negro women to work as maids at the fancy hotel and change bedsheets, Charlie was confident she wouldn't allow one to sleep on those same sheets.

"Do you think Millie would like this?" she asked Mary when she wandered by.

Mary ran a hand over the soft pink fabric and smiled. "I'd wager she'd love it, Charlie. Do you think that the poor girl has ever owned a brand new dress in her whole life?"

Charlie thought back to Jolene and frowned. "I seriously doubt it."

They left the shop with the pink dress and frilly new underthings in a white box held tight with a rose-pink satin ribbon and bow. "I can't wait to see Millie's face when she opens that," Mary said with a broad smile on her pretty face.

"Let's go to that apothecary to see if we can find some of that miracle cream Miss Loretta was talking about," Charlie suggested, and they left the dress shop.

❧ 25 ❧

Z ack wadded the note from Charlie into a ball and tossed
it into the fire.

"I suppose I'm on my own for supper tonight," he
mumbled to himself. "Please watch out for the wagons,
indeed. Does she think I'm her damned employee now?"

With his young son by his side, Morgan and Jimmy walked
up to join Zack by the fire. Both had fresh haircuts and wore
clean clothes.

"It seems the ladies have opted for a night at the hotel in
town," Morgan said with a grin on his freshly shaved face.
"Can you and some of Stone's boys take the watch tonight?
I'm really not comfortable with three wagons sitting here
empty for the night."

"We're gonna sleep in fancy beds in the hotel tonight,
Uncle Zack," his ten-year-old nephew told him, "but I'd
rather stay here with you and guard the wagons."

Zack roughed the boy's hair. "Don't be silly, Tad. Go enjoy
a fine supper in the hotel dining room and think on me when
you're snuggled in that nice soft hotel bed."

"Mama's just gonna make me take another bath," the boy
whined.

"Yeah," Morgan said with a sigh as he grinned at his son, "she's probably gonna make me take another one too."

All the men laughed, and Zack wondered how all of this had come to be. Ellen had probably been enticed into the fancy hotel, but how had Charlie come to be a part of it? She and Ellen certainly could not be counted as friendly—Emma and Mary, yes, but not Ellen. His sister had a marked dislike for Charlotte Byrde and had made it known to everyone. How had she ended up at the Sutton Hotel in Laramie together with the other women?

Zack shook his head as he watched Morgan, Jimmy, and Tad walk toward town. He'd never fathom the minds of women if he lived to see a hundred. One day they were bitter enemies and, the next, they were sitting down together to supper in fancy hotel dining rooms.

Zack fried himself bacon and sliced off bread from a loaf Charlie had baked a few days before. That, and a pot of coffee, would be his supper. After his meal, Zack went to the Buffalo Soldiers' camp and collected Stone and two others for night rounds. Someone played fiddle music in the camp along with harmonica, and the aroma of fried chicken filled the air.

"Evenin', Zack," Millie said in greeting when she saw him.

She and Stone had just finished a dance and sweat beaded on her forehead from the exertion. "How ya be on this fine evenin'?" she asked, a little out of breath as she took a seat on a bench by the fire.

"In need of a little extra help tonight," he said with a glance at Stone. "Cap and Jimmy are spending the night in Laramie with their wives. Cap wants extra feet on the ground to patrol the empty wagons against intruders."

Millie snorted. "You mean against that pilferin' Widow Patton?"

"Some in this camp," Stone said as he poured coffee into a cup and offered it to Zack, "would say you need to patrol against my men and me. Are you here askin' our assistance to make certain we don't do the pilfering, Mr. Drake?"

"Mr. Stone," Zack said, anger flaring his nostrils, "the Cap and I got no call to think you and your men are anything but honest and forthright members of this train. We wouldn't be asking for your assistance if we thought anything else."

Stone smiled and offered his hand. "Thank you for your honesty, Zack. Mulrooney and his men have been giving some of us a hard time since we joined up here."

"Mulrooney and his lot are nothing but trouble," Zack said angrily. "The Cap and I don't give credence to nothin' comin' outta their mouths."

"Their camp is quiet tonight," Luther said, his blind eyes turned in the direction of the Mulrooney outfit's wagons. "You sure they're even here tonight?"

"Maybe they're in Laramie too," Millie suggested. "The wagon master said this would be the last stop we make for supplies until Boise and that we'd be pushin' hard until we got there."

"You folks all stocked up?" Zack asked. "Charlie, Ellen, and Emma went into town with the mule this morning and sent it back with Tad loaded down so heavy, the poor thing is gonna be swaybacked from the weight."

Millie chuckled. "Them gals do like to shop." She saw Zack eying the pan of chicken. "You want some supper, Mr. Drake? The fellas come upon a covey of prairie chickens today, so we have plenty."

"That would be right, welcome," Zack answered, licking his lips. "Charlie and Mary stayed in town tonight at the hotel." He hesitated before continuing. "For baths and such, I reckon."

"What I wouldn't give for a soak in a tub of hot water," Millie said with a deep sigh.

Luther snorted, then chuckled darkly. "I don't reckon they'd welcome the likes of you in their fancy hotel, sis, so you'd best settle for your baths in the washbasin in the wagon."

Millie handed Zack a plate of fried chicken with two buttered biscuits. "These heathens ate up all the beans and potatoes," she said apologetically.

"This is most welcome, Millie." Zack took the plate. "Thank you for your kindness."

"You and Miss Charlie are always welcome at our fire," Luther said, "for the kindness you showed my sister."

"How many men do you need tonight, Mr. Drake?" Sargent Stone asked as he studied Zack.

"I think three will do," Zack replied and set about emptying his plate.

The Mulrooney camp was indeed quiet, with no lights in any of the wagons when they made their rounds. "Where do you think they're off to?" Stone asked Zack when they made their patrol through the camp.

"Anywhere but here is fine by me," Zack muttered. "I'm sick to death of the foul-mouthed Irishman, and I'd wager you and your folks are too."

Stone nodded. "All their men have the impression our women are whores and make regular trips into our camp, offering money and trade for their favors."

Zack's mouth fell open, and he gasped. "I had no idea. Why haven't you reported this to Morgan? He won't stand for the like of that behavior on his train."

Stone grinned. "We take care of our own, Mr. Drake."

"I'm certain you do," Zack said as they continued on, "but Morgan needs to know about these things. It's his responsibility to keep order on this train, and he'd want to know about women being disrespected in such a manner."

"He seems to be a good man." After a few quiet minutes, the big man added, "And so do you, Zack."

"Thank you, Nathan," Zack said with a quick smile as they neared Charlie's wagon.

"You plan to wed that woman?" Stone asked.

"I asked, but she's a damned pig-headed gal and turned me down flat," Zack explained. "Says she's gonna raise that child on her own, without the assistance of any man."

"Millie said she might have a good reason not to want a man meddlin' in her life."

Zack took a deep breath. "Yeah, I reckon so."

"Didn't you say Miss Charlie was in Laramie tonight?" Stone stopped Zack and pointed at the wagon where the light of a candle inside illuminated the canvas.

Zack pulled the pistol from his holster and crept toward the wagon with it drawn.

As they drew nearer, the candle went out and a figure began to climb out of the wagon with several things in hand.

"I'd be puttin' all that down if I was you," Zack said with his pistol pointed at the figure's head.

There was a gasp as everything fell from the figure's arms and crashed on the hard ground.

"Charlie's gonna be mighty unhappy if you broke any of her grandmother's nice china," Zack said scoldingly.

৩৵৩

The next morning, the group who'd just enjoyed breakfast in the Sutton Hotel dining room came upon Zack, Nathan Stone, and some others on the trail back to camp. Zack held a rope in his hand, and tethered to it was the black-clad figure of Widow Patton, her fleshy face blotchy and her eyes red and swollen from weeping.

"What the hell is going on here, Zackary? Why is that woman trussed up like a hog bein' led to slaughter?" Morgan demanded.

"We caught her breakin' into wagons last night, Mr. Morgan," Stone said solemnly, stepping forward, "and we're takin' her into town to the sheriff."

"Can't I get a trial in the camp like she did?" Widow Patton whined and nodded to Charlie.

"Whose wagon did she break into?" Morgan asked.

"Stone and me caught her coming out of Charlie's wagon with her arms loaded down with goods," Zack said, "but when we went to her wagon later, we found evidence she'd been in others." He fished into the pocket of his coat and brought out a pair of hair combs studded with rhinestones and held them high.

Ellen gasped and bolted forward. "Those are mine!" She glared at the widow behind Zack. "Mama gave them to me for my twentieth birthday."

"I know," Zack said as he held up something more. "She had this as well."

"My good cameo," Ellen hissed. "I had that hidden in a sack of meal for safekeeping."

Widow Patton began to cackle. "You all think hidin' your valuables down in casks of dry goods is safe?" She craned her head to look up at Nathan Stone. "Tell 'em what that murderin' harlot over there had hidden down in her barrel of salt."

Zack saw Charlie jerk up her head, and her eyes grow wide. "What Mrs. Byrde carries in her wagon and how she chooses to carry it is none of anybody's business," Stone stated coolly.

"Well, I wanna know what the larcenous bitch has been concealin' under our very noses all this time," Mulrooney called from behind Morgan and the women as he pushed his way forward with other men from his outfit at his side. "Tell us what ya found, darlin'," he instructed the weeping widow.

"Gold and silver," Widow Patton hissed. "She's got gold and silver coins hid out in her cask of salt. Hundreds of dollars in gold and silver by my reckoning, and the greedy little bitch was loathe to share a bit of it with us that was in need when she's got enough to fund all of us and then some on our way to Oregon."

Zack heard murmuring in the crowd and suddenly feared for Charlie's safety. He met Morgan's eyes and knew he was having the same thoughts. "Mr. Stone is correct," Morgan called out. "What Mrs. Byrde carries in her wagon to Oregon is her business. I'm sure you all have a little stashed away somewhere in your wagons for your stake in the new territory, and it's nobody's business but your own."

"Believe you me," Widow Patton called out to those listening, "she's got more than just a little hidden away in her salt keg."

Morgan scowled at the Widow Patton. "You, madam, have violated your agreement with this train and are no longer welcome as part of it."

He turned to Zack. "Deliver her to the sheriff and give him your statement. I don't care what he does with her, but she's not to come back."

"But what about my wagon and team?" the widow whined. "What will become of them and my things?"

"We'll leave them at the livery in town," Morgan replied gruffly, "and when the sheriff is done with you, you can settle with the man there as best you can."

"We're headin' back to the camp to check on our wagons," Mulrooney said as he and his men tried to pass.

"How did you leave things in the camp, Mr. Drake?" Morgan asked in a voice loud enough to stop Mulrooney before he'd gone far.

"Mr. Stone's men are armed and patrolling," Zack announced in a loud, firm voice. "I had your wagon and team moved to sit beside Mrs. Byrde's and Mr. Willard's for safety's sake."

Ellen grabbed Charlie's hand. "Let's go make certain that thieving old bitch didn't make off with anything else."

She began to pull Charlie down the trail toward the

wagons, her arm hugging a white box to her breast. Mary, Emma, and Jimmy followed close behind.

"That woman of yours," Morgan said to Zack as he watched his wife march down the trail with Charlie's hand in hers, "has certainly made this trip memorable." He took off his hat and scratched his graying head. "Just wait 'til I tell ya what she's put into Ellen's head about when we all get to Oregon."

"I can only imagine," Zack said as he began to move forward with the sobbing widow in tow. "And why does everyone think she's *my* woman? Charlotte Byrde has made it very clear that she's nobody's woman but her own."

Morgan and Stone burst out laughing. "If I had the money that bitch has in her salt barrel," the widow sniffed, "I wouldn't want no man around to take it from me neither."

Zack yanked on the rope and said chidingly, "You're one to talk when you were the one tryin' to steal it from her last night."

"Don't they hang thieves out here in Wyoming?" Stone asked, breaking into a grin when the widow's eyes went wide.

"So I hear tell," Zack replied. "They believe in swift justice out here."

Zack and Stone delivered the Widow Patton to the sheriff and then made the walk back to the camp, where they found the Mulrooney outfit crowded into their camp and a huff.

"What's going on?" Zack asked Morgan, who sat in his chair beside the fire with papers in his hand and Jim Willard at his side.

"We ain't gonna stay with no outfit that puts dirty niggers above good whites," Mulrooney yelled, "and we want our fees back."

"The contract you signed," Jim said sharply, "clearly states that should you decide to take your leave from the train at any time before arriving in Oregon, your fees are forfeit and will not be returned to you."

Mulrooney glared at Jimmy. "Damned lawyers ain't good for nothin' but talkin' outta both sides of your mouths." He turned his attention back to Morgan. "So, you ain't gonna return our fees, even in part?"

"You're leaving of your own accords with no good reason I can see," Morgan replied, "so, no, I'm not returning anything to you."

"We've found land here in Laramie," one of the women from Mulrooney's camp said, hugging her crying baby to her breast to quiet it, "and we need that money to put down on it."

"The Mulrooneys ain't beggars, Siobhan," Mulrooney hissed at the young woman. "We only want what's rightfully ours. We've only traveled half the way to Oregon with this bunch of nigger lovers, so we should get half of what we paid back to us."

Mulrooney was quiet for a minute. "As I see it, you owe us a hundred and forty dollars, Mr. Morgan."

Zack saw his face color at the Irishman's remark, and he bent his head to whisper into Charlie's ear. She nodded and disappeared into her wagon.

When she returned, she had seven gold eagles in her hand. "Here, Mrs. Mulrooney." She handed the young mother the coins. "And good luck to you and your family here in Laramie."

Siobhan Mulrooney's mouth fell open in surprise. "Thank you, Mrs. Byrde. This is very gracious of you."

Mr. Mulrooney stormed over to take the gleaming coins from his wife. "I'll be takin' that from ya, Siobhan."

"I think not, Matthew," she said sternly and clutched the gold to her chest, along with her fretting child. "I'll go back into town and make the payment on behalf of the clan for the land we looked at today with Mrs. Sutton's representative. I got the feelin' that woman preferred dealin' with a woman over a man."

Charlie grinned. "You've got the right of that," she said. "Mrs. Sutton will be much more forthcoming with another woman."

Mulrooney spat into the fire. "Women have no place in business or meddling in the affairs of men."

"But this is Wyoming," Charlie said with a smile, "and things are very different out here."

"Will you escort Mrs. Mulrooney into town, Zack?" Morgan asked with a warning glance at her scowling husband. "Perhaps you should get your outfit ready to depart for Laramie, Mr. Mulrooney."

Mulrooney glared at his departing wife and then Charlie and Morgan. "With pleasure," he huffed before turning on his heel and stomping toward his camp.

"That was completely unnecessary, Mrs. Byrde," Morgan said, "but thank you. I'll endeavor to pay you back as soon as I can." The wagon master took a deep breath. "The cash from their payments was deposited into the bank in Independence before we left. I try not to carry too much cash with me on these trips because of the sort of thing that happened last night."

Charlie raised a hand to silence him. "It's perfectly all right, Morgan. We'll work it out in the future. I'm just happy to have that man and his outfit off the train and out of our hair, she said, glancing at Nathan Stone, "without any violence."

"I need to get back to camp," Nathan informed them.

"I'll go along with you," Charlie said. "I have something for Millie." She motioned for Mary to join them with the white boxes from Loretta's.

"You about spoilin' my woman, Miss Charlie?" Nathan asked when he saw the boxes.

"Every gal deserves a treat now and again," Mary said with a wink at Charlie.

"Why don't you let Mr. Stone carry those, Mary? I'm

225

certain Millie would appreciate them much more coming from him than us."

Mary grinned as she handed him the boxes tied with satin ribbons. "She's gonna be very appreciative." Mary giggled. "I'm quite certain."

Millie came running when she saw them approaching. "What you got there, Nathan Stone?"

"Presents for you," he said and handed her the boxes.

Other women from the camp began to gather. Presents in bright white boxes tied with pink satin ribbons were an uncommon sight. Millie took the boxes and dropped them onto a bench. She untied the ribbons and opened the first box.

"Oh, my Lord," she gasped when she saw the pretty pink frock folded inside. "Is this for *me*?"

"I'll take it if you ain't wantin' it," one of the other women said.

Millie took the dress from the box and then set the other box aside on the bench, so she could stand and put the dress up to her body to take measure of the size.

"It's gonna look right pretty on ya, Millie," Nathan said with an uneasy glance at Charlie and Mary.

"What's in the other box?" another anxious woman asked.

"Just wait and give me a minute to take this in," Millie scolded the woman. "It ain't every day my man brings me a new dress from town."

"Mine ain't never brought me even one," the other woman said.

"Open that other box, Miss Millie," another woman pled. "We're all dyin' to see what else he brung ya."

"Oh, all right." Millie folded the dress back into the box and took the other one onto her lap.

There were sighs of delight as Millie took out the bright-white camisole with its lacey collar and pearl buttons and petticoat with its flounced layers.

"It's all so pretty," Millie said with tears brimming in her eyes.

"What else is in that box?" someone asked.

"Well, let me see." Millie lifted out a soft pink flannel nightdress. "Now, ain't this somethin'?"

"Looks as your man has a fondness for pink, Miss Millie," one of the women said, and the others laughed, and Nathan Stone blushed.

Millie folded the new underpinnings back into the box, jumped to her feet, and wrapped her arms around Nathan's neck. "Thank you, Nate," she said happily before kissing his cheek. "I ain't never had nothin' so pretty in my entire life."

"I'm glad you like them," he said with another glance at Charlie.

"He'll be wantin' somethin' special for his supper now," a woman called out.

"Or somethin' special *after* his supper," another chimed in, followed by laughter from the assembled women.

Charlie walked up and handed Millie a small jar. "The man at the Apothecary said this cream would save our faces from lookin' like shriveled apples when we get old."

Millie wrapped her arms around Charlie's neck and whispered, "Thank you for the dress and things, Charlie. I know it was you, and it was sweet of you to let Nate get the credit for it with the other women in the camp."

Charlie stepped away with a smile on her face. "You're a lucky woman to have such a thoughtful man, Millie."

Millie looked up at Nathan, batting her eyes. "Ain't I, though?"

❧ 26 ❧

The train wound its way over the mountain ridges of western Wyoming on the silvery gray trail that had been cut into the earth by the wheels of countless wagons and the hooves of countless draft beasts over the past three decades. The travelers could see it in either direction when they camped on a high plateau.

"Ain't that somethin'?" Zack had said of the trail as he pointed it out to Charlie one evening. "I'd reckon folks will be able to follow it forever."

"Let's not make that public knowledge," Charlie had said with a smile and touched his arm, "or Ellen and Morgan will never get another paying train together."

Zack stared down at her with his face twisted in confusion. "How do you figure?"

"If folks know there is a clear trail cut to Oregon already," she sighed, "they won't think they need to pay a wagon master to lead the way."

Understanding finally dawned on Zack's face as he stared at the trail laid out ahead of them. "Yeah, I can see your point there." He rested a forefinger on his lips. "I'll keep that bit of news to my lonesome."

He built a fire after tending to the animals, and the women put together a supper of stew made from smoked deer and root vegetables, served with biscuits that were beginning to dry with age. It was time to bake again.

"It's a good thing we'll be stopped near Boise for a few days," Mary said as she sliced a biscuit that crumbled into her hand, "we're in need of fresh baked goods."

"I've heard," Emma uttered, "these mountain men build a huge community oven at these gatherings, so they can bake bread and such while they are there."

"That would indeed be a boon if it's the case," Mary said with a curt nod. "I can't fathom a gathering of just men. It'll be a wonder to behold, I reckon."

"I wouldn't go wanderin' out amongst 'em if I were you, Miss Mary," Zack warned. "These are solitary men who live to trap their furs. They don't see much of women, other than Indian squaws they consort with." He took a long swallow of coffee. "You'd best keep your distance or end up being taken off to one of their mountain hideaways," Zack said jokingly.

He'd become easy in his speech with Mary, as well as Charlie and Emma, but she thought he meant it as a warning as well. A pretty young woman might not be safe amongst seasoned men who hadn't been in the company of a white woman in some time.

Mary waved a small pistol in the firelight; it was one Charlie had purchased for her in one of the settlements through which they'd they'd passed. "I've been practicing, Zack," she said with a wide grin on her pretty face. "No man is going to take liberties with me I don't want him to take."

"I reckon Mark Conrad had best watch his wandering hands then," Zack stated, and the others around the fire laughed.

Mark Conrad had taken it into his head that Mary Perry was going to be his girl, and he'd told a number of people he intended to make her his in no uncertain terms.

On more than one occasion, the young man had penned Mary against a wagon or tree in a dark corner and attempted to take her in the manner a man takes a wife in order to claim her as his own. Mary had fought him and told him that in no way would she ever consent to be his wife. He'd even offered Morgan an absurdly low bride price for her hand, and the wagon master had laughed the young man out of his camp.

After one groping, Mary had come to Charlie and begged her to borrow the pistols. They were large and cumbersome in Mary's hands, and Charlie had found her a set of much smaller pistols to carry. Mary, whose late father had taught her to use guns, could shoot a rabbit moving at a respectable speed from a reasonable distance. She wore the guns in holsters on her hips, and Mark Conrad now kept his distance from Mary Perry to everyone's amusement.

"Do you think you'll be able to find your father and brother here?" Mary asked Charlie as she stirred a slurry of flour and water into the pot of boiling stew to thicken it.

Charlie shrugged. "I've been told this rendezvous is the largest in the area and the last of the season. If they were going to attend anything in order to sell their end-of-season pelts, it would be this one."

"Do you think you'd even recognize them after all this time?" Mary asked with tears brimming in her eyes. "It's only been two months, and I'm having a hard time picturing Mama, Daddy, and my sister in my head."

Charlie put an arm around her friend. "I don't know." Her forehead rested on Mary's. "Thomas was just a boy when they left, and he'd be a man of near thirty now, so I probably wouldn't recognize anything, except the scar on his chin where I hit him with a stick when we were children."

Zack snorted, then chuckled. "Those mountain men wear their chin whiskers thick, so I wouldn't count on recognizing him that way."

Charlie put a hand to her hair, which had grown a few

inches since she'd returned to being Charlotte Byrde. "His hair, as I recall, was the same bright yellow as mine and Mama's, but with a bit of Daddy's red," she said, "and curlier than mine."

"Is he short or tall?" Mary continued to stir the stew and poke the potatoes to check for doneness.

"Daddy is a very tall man with bright red hair," Charlie responded with a quick smile, "and Thomas had the look of him, so I assume he is tall as well. They both have striking blue-green eyes, and Daddy spoke with a Scottish accent."

"How many tall, redheaded trappers with blue-green eyes can there be out there?" Zack asked with a chuckle as Mary handed him a steaming plate of stew.

Morgan joined the group at the fire. "You've never been to one of these trappers' rendezvous, Zackary," the wagon master said with a chuckle. "Most all of them come from Scotch-Irish or French families, and most all of them have red hair and beards. Finding Charles and Thomas McCleod at a rendezvous populated with hundreds of redheads may not be as easy as you think."

Mary passed full plates to everyone but Morgan, who had waved her off and offered a broad smile. "I'm eager to see this camp populated with nothing but men."

"I'm certain you'll leave with a pocket full of marriage proposals, Miss Perry," Morgan said with a deep chuckle, but he tempered it with much the same warning Zack had given her. "Keep in mind these men haven't had the company of young white women, other than of those in the traveling brothel wagons, so always mind your surroundings and try to stay in groups of other women for safety's sake."

He narrowed his eyes. "I don't want to have to go runnin' off into the mountains to track down one of you taken as a prospective bride against your will by one of these wild men."

"*Wild* men, huh?" Mary said with a smile and a wink at Emma and Charlie, who giggled at her jest.

Morgan rolled his eyes and groaned before standing. "And my wife is proposing I turn my train into a traveling wedding party for young single women like you. It'll be the damned death of me."

"The concept has merit, Mr. Morgan," Jimmy said between chewing stew.

The big wagon master stopped and turned to face Jimmy Willard, his brow arched. "Yes, counselor? Go on."

"I've been working out the contracts with your wife," Jimmy continued. "I must admit I was skeptical when Emma first presented me with the idea, but after hearing the talk of all these single men at this rendezvous thing, I fear it could work in all our favors. Mrs. Morgan and I intend to set up a table tomorrow to see what interest we can draw from it."

"Mama painted a pretty sign," Grinning, Jenny piped up in her high-pitched voice. "It says: *Sign up to get your Bride from the East here.* And Mary is going to dress up in something pretty to be a model."

"Oh, my Lord," Morgan groaned with his shoulders slumping in defeat. "I'm doomed."

He walked into the darkness, back toward his wagon, with everyone at the fire laughing.

The morning of their trip to the rendezvous dawned cold with a dusting of snow. Zack, bundled in his bulky jacket, added wood to the fire while Charlie filled the coffee pot. She wore mittens made of wool stockings and had a quilt wrapped around her body for warmth.

"I never reckoned on this cold," Charlie said with a shiver.

Jenny leaped from the Willards' wagon dressed in the clothes Charlie had made for her, along with a wool coat and gloves. "Are we ready to go?" the little girl asked, jumping with excitement. "*I'm* ready."

"Have you eaten your breakfast?" Zack asked, "because I haven't, and none of us are going anywhere until I have."

The little girl's face fell at his stern tone, and her lower lip began to quiver.

"You look really pretty, Jenny," Mary said soothingly as she straightened a wrinkle in the bright yellow skirt Charlie had found for her to wear in one of her trunks. "Are you going to be a model with me today too?"

Jenny's face brightened at the prospect. "I wanna be a model, but Daddy says I'm too young for a husband just yet."

"And you will be soon enough, pumpkin," Jimmy told his daughter as he kissed her head from behind, "but not quite yet. Your Daddy wants to have you home for a bit longer, and your Mama is gonna need your help when the new baby gets here in a few months."

Jenny glanced at their wagon, where her mama was still dressing and putting up her hair, and then to Charlie, who wore the dress she'd made from the matching plaid fabric to Jenny's. "I'm gonna have to help Miss Charlie with her baby too," the little girl said with a wide smile on her freckled face. "I'm gonna be very busy."

Jimmy smiled and kissed his daughter's head again. "Yes, you are, pumpkin."

After a hot breakfast of ham, eggs, dry biscuits, and hot coffee, the group made their way to the rendezvous site, where the sight of so many pretty white women drew many men's eyes.

Charlie saw a tent with a hand-painted sign that read "Registration." She went to the empty table and rang the bell set out upon it. A gloved hand pushed aside the canvas flap of the tent.

"What you want so early in the mornin'? A gruff voice asked without looking up to see the person at the table.

"I'm looking for my father and brother," Charlie said in her sweetest voice, and the man's head jerked up.

Bright blue eyes stared at her from beneath the white fur of a fox cap.

"Beg pardon, ma'am," the man said, stumbling out and righting himself on the boards set across two barrels used as a table. "Tweren't expecting no women here." He swiped at his eyes. "Leastwise, not this early in the day. You pleasure women don't usually peek your heads out 'til well after the noon hour."

Charlie gave the man an annoyed smile and snapped, "I'm not a pleasure woman, sir. I'm Mrs. Charlotte McCleod Byrde, and I'm here in search of my father, Charles McCleod, and my brother Thomas McCleod. They are fur trappers, and I've been told they might be in attendance at this festival to sell their goods."

"Charles and Thomas McCleod?" the man said thoughtfully as he studied the woman in front of him. "I might know 'em." When Charlie's face brightened, he smiled added, "What's it worth to ya?"

He stared at Charlie's bosoms. "You could come into me tent here and show your appreciation for what I could tell ya about ol' Charlie and his boy."

Charlie turned so the man could see her swollen belly. "I fear my man might not like that." She reached into her pouch and drew out a small quarter gold coin she held between her thumb and forefinger. "I might be willing to part with this, however, *if* your information is worthwhile."

The man licked his lips at the sight of the gold coin. "Charlie and Tom ain't made their way in from the country around Bend yet," he said, "but I expect 'em any day. Last I saw of 'em, Ol' Charlie said he'd be down to Boise for the rendezvous to collect his take for his summer trappin'." He grinned and held out a grimy hand. "That worth the five-dollar gold to ya?"

Charlie pointed to the spot where Emma, Jenny, and Jimmy were setting up their table in the shade of a large cedar. "My friends and I will be conducting some business at that table over there. I'll give you this five dollars if you promise to direct my father and brother to me when they arrive." Charlie put the coin on the man's dirty palm. "And there might be another if you actually bring them to me *in person*." She patted the pouch that hung heavy from her belt and clinked with the coins inside.

The man stared at the pouch and smiled. "I can do that. I recall Charlie goin' on about a daughter back in Tennessee once, but I never heard him say how pretty she was."

"I was just a little girl when he and Thomas came north." Charlie turned and walked to the table to help Emma hang her sign from the bushy cedar branches behind them.

"Do you even think these men will be able to read this?" Charlie asked in a doubtful tone.

"It's why I added lots of artwork," she said with a grin as she pointed to the sign, "like the two hands on the Bible, a set of gold bands, and a woman in a wedding gown."

"Mama's a real good artist," Jenny said enthusiastically.

"Yes, she is," Jimmy added. "I'm certain this sign will attract the men you're interested in."

"When is Ellen supposed to be here?" Charlie glanced back toward where the train was camped. "I'd have thought she'd want to be here to ramrod the whole operation."

"She'll be along," Zack said with a wink at Charlie. "My sister wants to primp herself all up."

Ellen arrived an hour later, dressed in the clothes she'd purchased from Loretta's window in Laramie. She wore the fancy cameo the Widow Patton had in her pocket and a straw bonnet decorated with silk flowers and satin ribbons to match the dress.

"You look lovely, Ellen," Charlie declared. "The shades of pink and beige complement your skin tone and hair beautifully, just like Loretta said they would."

Ellen blushed at the compliment and touched her cheek. "I've been using that cream you brought me, and I think it's done wonders to reverse the damage done by the sun and dust on this journey."

Mary smiled and held out one of her soft, pink hands. "We've been using it too, and I couldn't agree more."

Jimmy, annoyed by the talk of fashions and skincare, jumped back into business. "Have you decided on a price, Mrs. Morgan, and who should bear the brunt of the expense?"

"I discussed it with Morgan," she replied, "and I think each man should pay a hundred dollars for the transport of his prospective bride across the country."

"I know we'd discussed seventy-five earlier," Jimmy said and frowned. "Don't you fear a hundred dollars will sound excessive to the average man?"

"We'll be supplying the wagons, teams, and foodstuffs for the journey, Mr. Willard," Ellen explained. "The initial investment is going to be astronomical, and I fear we won't be able to bear it." She poured water from a canteen into a cup and sipped. "At a hundred dollars, our initial cash outlay will be eased."

"But you'll be using the same wagons and teams for future trips," he pointed out. "Does that seem fair to the men who are booking these initial trips when the men in the future will be getting the use of second-hand goods?"

Ellen smiled. "Equipment must be maintained, Mr. Willard, and animals get old, wear out, and must be replaced. A certain percentage of the funds collected will go into an operating expense account and used only for those expenses." She took another sip of water. "Profits will only be paid once those expenses have been set aside."

Charlie had to applaud Ellen's business sense. "I've been collecting periodicals, from every town we've stopped in and have a collection of the advertisements for mail-order brides. We can pick through them and chose the ones we feel are the most appealing to copy or adjust for our use."

Emma winked at Charlie. "Putting Mrs. Byrde in charge of advertising was a wise choice. She's familiar with all the popular periodicals and will know where to place advertisements to find the most wholesome candidates for our brides."

"What cities do you suggest, Mrs. Byrde?" Ellen asked in a smug tone.

"New York, Boston, Chicago, Richmond, and Atlanta to begin with," Charlie replied.

"Richmond and Atlanta?" Ellen asked with disgust. "I don't think we want to deal with *those* rebel tarts."

Charlie bristled at her tone. "Thousands of men lost their lives in the war, madam, meaning thousands of women lost their husbands, fathers, and brothers who would have supported them. Southern cities are a rich source of refined and well-bred women who would leap at the chance to escape their current circumstances."

Ellen cocked one of her perfectly plucked eyebrows. "While you may be an example of a well-bred young woman from the South, Mrs. Byrde—and I say that with your present condition aside," she coughed to clear her throat, "we don't want to end up with a wagon full of Miss Jolenes."

❦ 27 ❦

As the day drew on, Ellen and Jimmy signed up a dozen men and collected a hundred dollars from each of them. At next year's rendezvous in Boise, the men would be presented with an assortment of women to choose from to become their brides.

"I can't believe this is going so well," Jimmy gasped as he hefted the wooden cash box again to feel the weight of the coins inside. "We need to search out more of these events to travel to."

"I'm hungry," Jenny whined from her chair at the table.

"I'm hungry too," Charlie said and stood. "I've been smelling the food from that Chinaman's tent up the way all day."

She held a hand out to Jenny. "Let's go have a look and see if it's as good as all these fellas have been saying it is."

"Chinaman Wong makes the best eats at the rendezvous," a man who'd spent the day at their table gawking at Mary said. "And he don't try to gouge a man with his prices like some of the white fellas do for nothin' more than burned bacon and watery beans." He grinned at Mary. "That bein' said, I think you should sell me this here

pretty woman to be my wife at half price 'cause she's
already here and don't need no wagon, team, nor
foodstuffs."

It had been his argument all afternoon, and everyone was
tired of hearing it.

"I'm here as an example only, sir," Mary explained again
in her sweetest voice. "I'm on my way to my aunt's in Oregon
and am not up for auction like one of Mrs. Morgan's brides."

"I trap in Oregon," the man protested, "but along the
rivers in the south, not up there in minin' country."

Charlie rolled her eyes, tired of hearing the same argument again. "Let's go find some food, Jenny." She held out her
hand, and the little girl took it.

"Don't forget what I told you about what Jenny can and
cannot eat," Emma warned.

"We know, Mama," the little girl growled at her mother.
"Charlie knows I can't eat peanut brittle or peanut butter
cookies, or my throat will swell, and my eyes will itch."

They made their way through the crowds of men pulling
sleds loaded with bales of pelts on their way to the buyers'
tents and lined up at tables offering games of faro, whiskey,
and beer. Charlie saw other tents offering coats and mittens
sewn from wool blankets, and she stopped at one to make a
purchase for herself. She slipped into the off-white wool
garment and savored the warmth of it.

"That coat will keep you and your little bundle nice and
warm in the mornin's while you're makin' your man his breakfast," the shop's proprietor said with a toothy smile. "Might I
also suggest a pair of these fur-lined moccasins and mitts
made from the finest beaver pelts to keep your feet and hands
warm in the winter months to come?"

Charlie didn't buy the mittens, but she left the shop with a
pair of the beaded moccasins. "These will save my feet some,"
Charlie told Jenny.

"When you're up making breakfast for your man?" the

little girl parroted the salesman with a girlish giggle. "Mama needs a pair."

They continued on to the canvas tent, with its sides rolled up to expose a fully functioning kitchen with a fire pit. On the fire were unusually shaped iron pans filled with a variety of sliced vegetables, skewers with beef and chicken marinated in a brown sauce, and then grilled, white rice, and a pan of hot oil with small cylinders of dough sizzling in them. A Chinese man called them eggrolls and pulled one open for them to see they were filled with minced chicken, sliced cabbage, and carrot.

Charlie ordered plates for both of them, and they took them to tables and benches set up in the shade to eat. The morning's snow had melted, and the pathways through the camp were muddy. They saw men in all manner of dress but very few women, and of those they did see, none were white. Native women accompanied the trappers in beaded doeskin gowns or bright calico blouses and skirts, their black hair in long braids at the sides of their heads. Some of the women carried babies on their backs in wicker harnesses.

"I can see why the men want to buy women from Daddy and Mrs. Morgan," Jenny observed. "There aren't many here."

"No, there aren't," Charlie agreed.

"Well," Jenny said and pointed, "except for them."

Charlie glanced up to see several white women walking toward them from a group of tents. They were dressed in nothing more than their pantaloons, camisoles, corsets, and dressing gowns, which hung open to expose mounded bosoms above the corsets. Charlie suspected these would be the pleasure women the registrar had mistaken her for.

Men began to flock toward them, making lewd comments and offers. Charlie was glad to see Jenny enjoying her food and ignoring the words of the men and replies of the women, which were equally lewd.

Jenny began to cough and rub at her eyes; they seemed unusually swollen and red. "Are you all right, Jenny?" Charlie was concerned for the child in her care.

Jenny began to gasp for air and claw at her throat. She threw herself from the bench, and Charlie screamed her name as she rushed to kneel at Jenny's side.

People began to mill about as Charlie shouted frantically down the aisle, "Emma, Emma, there's something wrong with Jenny!"

The little girl's face had turned red and was horribly swollen as she lie on her back in the dirt, gasping for air. The heels of her boots beat upon the ground the as she tried to draw air into her windpipe, which had swollen shut.

"Jenny," Charlie screamed as she held the thrashing little girl in her arms.

Emma and Jimmy arrived at a run to throw themselves to the ground at their daughter's side.

"Did you buy her peanut candy, Charlie?" Emma demanded through her tears as she held her daughter, whose struggling had begun to subside. "I told you she couldn't have peanut candy."

"I only bought her a plate of vegetables and rice," Charlie said. "I'd never do anything to hurt Jenny.

The thumping of the little girl's heels stopped, and her body slumped silently in her mother's arms. Emma screamed and pulled the child to her chest.

"You killed my baby," she yelled at Charlie. "I don't know what you did, but you killed her all the same!"

Tears ran down Charlie's face as she watched her friend sob and hold her child in her arms, rocking her back and forth. "I don't know what happened, Emma. We were eating, and she just—"

"Come on, Charlie," Zack said quietly, taking her into his strong arms.

"Zack?" Charlie recognized the man at her side for the

first time. "I don't know what happened, Zack. We were eating, and she just fell off the bench."

"The Chinaman and his damned food probably poisoned her," someone in the crowd called.

"No poison in my food," the man from the tent called back in protest. "Wong, make good food for you. Make good food for years," he said in broken, accented English as the crowd pressed closer, and Charlie could see the fear in his brown almond-shaped eyes as he stared down at Emma sobbing with Jenny's lifeless body in her arms." No poison in Wong's food to hurt little girls."

Something in the kitchen caught Charlie's attention, and she pulled herself to her feet with Zack's help. She pushed past the Chinaman and into the hot kitchen where the man's wife stirred a pan of noodles. She strangled a gasp when she got a better look at the wooden cask above the pan of oil.

In black stencil were the words *Peanut Oil*. "Oh, my Lord," Charlie sobbed. "It's all my fault."

The world went black as she fell into Zack's arms, who had followed her into the tent.

Charlie lost track of time and places. She heard voices around her but couldn't place them.

"Is she going to be all right?" a male voice asked.

"The stresses of her condition upon her body. That combined with the fact that she blames herself for the loss of that little girl have put her and her babe in great peril, sir."

Charlie heard an unfamiliar woman's voice say.

"But is she going to *live*?" the man asked in an angry tone.

Charlie tried to force her eyes open, but they wouldn't budge. Who was this man, and why was he so angry? She heard the sound of little Jenny's heels beating upon the ground again, and tears stung her eyes. Jenny. Her carelessness had killed poor, sweet little Jenny.

"Are you awake, Charlie?" a male voice she recognized as Zack's asked as he squeezed her hand. "You need to wake up,

Charlie. There are some folks here eager to talk with you."
She felt his breath on her cheek as he bent close. "I love you,
Charlotte, Byrde, and I can't lose you now."

"Don't want to talk," she mumbled. "Jenny is dead
because of me."

*He loves me? How can anyone love the likes of me when I cost poor
little Jenny her life?*

"Nobody blames you, Charlie," Zack whispered urgently.
"It wasn't your fault."

Tears streamed down her face. "Emma blames me," she
managed to mumble.

"No, she doesn't," Mary's voice said. "The Chinaman told
her and Jimmy how you made him tear open that eggroll
looking for peanuts inside before you'd let Jenny eat it. He
took all the blame for not tellin' ya he used that oil to cook his
food in, and it was made from peanuts."

"Still my fault," Charlie mumbled before drifting back into
the peaceful darkness where she didn't have to hear the voices
around her or the thumping of Jenny's feet.

The next thing Charlie knew was being jostled in her bed.
Were they moving? Who was driving her team? She opened
her eyes to see the back of a man's head as he sat in the
driver's seat of her wagon with Mary beside him, laughing
and talking. Who was she with? Charlie didn't recall any men
associated with the train who wore buckskins and had long
blonde hair.

"Mary?" Charlie called in a harsh, cracked voice. "Who's
that up there with you?"

Mary turned at the sound of Charlie's voice. "You're
awake," she called with glee and scrambled down from her
place on the bench beside the stranger. "Zack is gonna be so
relieved. You've had us all worried sick, Charlie McCleod."

"We're moving?" Charlie struggled up on her pillow. "And
who's that driving my team?"

The wagon pulled to a stop, and the driver turned.

"You're still as demanding as you ever were, sis," the man said with a broad grin as he climbed into the wagon as well.

Something about the color of the man's eyes touched a chord with Charlie. "Thomas?" she gasped as she recognized her brother.

"Yep," he said as he bent to kiss her forehead. "Papa and that man of yours are gonna be happy to see you've finally woke your lazy ass up."

Charlie noted her stiff muscles when she tried to move her legs. "How long have I been asleep?"

"Too long for my likin'," Mary replied, "but the midwife from Boise and Mrs. Bradshaw as well," she added with a frown, "said to let you rest as long as you and the babe needed."

"What's goin' on?" Zack asked when he stuck his head through the tarped opening at the back of the wagon. "You're awake?" he asked with a grin on his unshaven face. "Well, it's about damned time."

"Why'd they stop?" another male voice asked as a red head poked its way into the opening.

"Hi, Charlie." The man sported a large grin on his bearded face. "It's your papa."

Her papa? Charlie stared at the strange man whose hair and beard were shot through with gray. Well, if Thomas was driving her team, it stood to reason her daddy would be some-where about as well. "All y'all are gonna have to vacate my wagon," Charlie said as she scooted to the edge of the bed to dangle her stiff legs over the edge. "I have a violent urge to use the chamber pot, and I'm not gonna do it with a bunch of men lookin' on."

As Mary helped her to squat over the pot and voices jabbered outside, Millie climbed into the wagon and rushed to wrap Charlie in her arms.

"Damnit, woman," Millie hissed into her ear, "you had all

of us scared to death. You all right now, you awake and pissin'?"

Charlie smiled at the girl's concern. "I'm feeling much relieved now," she said as her stream ended. "I musta been holdin' that for some days now." A cool breeze blew into the wagon and brought on a shiver. "Where are we?"

"We should make Baker City in a few days," Mary stated as she helped Charlie to her feet and slid the chamber pot back beneath the bed.

"Baker City?" Charlie gasped. "We're in Oregon already?"

Millie snorted. "Already?" She giggled. "Woman, you been asleep for nigh on two weeks now."

Charlie heard Morgan's voice outside. "Has our patient regained herself?"

"It would seem so," Charlie said when she stuck her head out the opening to see people gathered around. Her heart fell when she didn't see Emma or Jimmy amongst them.

Charles McCleod stood beside his son and Mary beside him. She couldn't help but notice that her brother held Mary's hand. What had been going on in her absence? Nathan Stone stood beside Luther.

"If you're done with my wife, Miss Charlie," Stone said with a grin, "I'd like to get back to her fixin' my lunch."

"You can fix your own damned lunch, Nathan," Millie yelled from the wagon. "I'm stayin' right here to make certain Charlie is comfortable and catch her up on the gossip."

"His wife?" Charlie gasped when she turned back to stare at Millie, who wore a broad grin on her face. "What in the name of heaven has been going on around here?"

Millie shrugged. "Nathan fancied what's between my legs, but he's a man of honor and wouldn't take it without goin' before a preacher first. We married in Boise before settin' off again after they buried poor Miss Jenny."

Charlie batted back tears as she hugged her friend. "I'm so happy for you, Millie. Nathan Stone is a good man."

Millie smiled. "And the lead security man on Mr. and Mrs. Morgan's Bride Train," she said proudly.

Charlie smiled. "It sounds like I have a lot of catching up to do."

They camped for the night where they'd stopped, and Mary made them a supper of elk roast and fresh bread. The hunting had been good in the mountains, and the train was flush with fresh meat. The sadness of losing a child in the camp had brought more people together than Millie and Nathan. Mary and Thomas had grown close in the weeks they'd been thrown together in the wagon and announced they would marry once they reached her aunt's home in Baker City.

"It appears I gained two daughters at that rendezvous," Charles Mc Cleod said as they finished their meal.

Charlie put a hand on her belly as the baby kicked. "And a grandchild too."

Charles frowned as he exchanged a glance with his son. "Zackary explained to us what happened in Tennessee." He took a deep breath. "When a Sioux woman is defiled and finds herself with child from it, it's not looked down upon by her people for her to take the child out into the woods and leave it to the elements after it's birthed." He stared up at the star-filled night sky. "Your brother and I would be willing to take the child and leave it in a high spot away from the critters, but where the cold would take it all painless."

Charlie wrapped her arms around her belly. "How could you suggest I murder my child—your grandchild?" She gasped with shock. "The babe holds no blame in the way it got here, and if it shames you in some way, you and Thomas can return to your trap lines and forget we exist the way you forgot Mama and me for all those years."

Charles McCleod's eyes went wide and his mouth fell open

at Charlie's harsh words. "We never forgot you and your Mama, Charlie. I promised to come for the two of you when I'd established myself, but I never did, and I couldn't slink back to Fern Hollow, a failure with my tail between my legs."

"Just a letter to let us know you were still alive would have been nice," Charlie hissed. "Mama hoped, but I know she feared you and Thomas were dead after all that time without a word." She shook her head. "We deserved a damned letter, at least, Papa."

"You did," Charles said regretfully as he stood, "and I'm sorry for that failure on my part, daughter."

He and Thomas walked into the dark, leaving Charlie and Zack alone by the fire.

"Don't you think that was a little harsh?" Zack finally asked as he added wood to the fire.

"The man just offered to kill my baby," Charlie spat. "His own grandchild."

Zack squeezed the hand he'd been holding all evening. "I think he meant it as a kindness, Charlie. He and Thomas have been living amongst the savages for some time now and have taken up some of their ways."

Charlie smiled at Zack and remembered the words he'd whispered to her. Had she really heard him say he loved her, or had that been a dream? "They do look a bit savage, don't they?" she finally said with her head slumped against Zack's shoulder.

"Mary seems to like it," he commented with a soft chuckle. "They haven't left one another's side since he and your father came into camp, and that registrar fella brought them to the wagon."

Charlie groaned and sat up. "I suppose he wanted another quarter gold for his delivery."

Zack smiled, then chuckled. "He did make mention of that. Your daddy gave him a good swat on the back of his skull, and he left in a hurry."

"How is Emma?" Charlie asked in a trembling voice.

"Heavy with child," Zack replied without taking his eyes off the fire. "She asks after ya from time to time, when I've seen her."

"They moved their wagon away from ours."

Zack squeezed her hand again. "They're traveling along with Ellen and Morgan now. She's grievin', Charlie," he said and kissed the top of her head. "I'm certain she'll come 'round in her own good time."

"Yeah, Charlie responded with a doubtful sigh, "I'm certain she will."

Zack took a deep breath of his own. "I think we should talk on somethin', Charlie." He took hold of both her shoulders to stare her in the eyes. "I think you should marry me when we get to Baker City and give that child a name."

Charlie put a hand on her belly. "This child will have a name," she said a bit more forcefully than intended. "*Byrde.*"

"And wha-what if I want it . . . and you . . . to have the n-name Drake?" he stammered.

The child kicked and twisted in her belly, and Charlie gasped. "I think it likes that idea," she said with a grin and a hand on her abdomen.

Zack wrapped her in his arms. "I'm so happy, Charlotte." He bent his head and covered her lips with his. The kiss lingered, and soon, his hands were caressing her swollen bosom. "I want you so bad," he whispered as his lips and tongue moved to her throat.

Charlie shivered with the delight of the feeling. Her nipples throbbed, and she pulled away when she realized her camisole was wet with milk.

"What's wrong?" Zack asked, his brow furrowed in confusion. "Did I do somethin' to offend again?"

"No," Charlie replied, her cheeks flushed and her hands over her wet breasts. "You didn't do anything I didn't want you to do. I fear I don't have much control over my pregnant body, or understand how it works just now."

She stood and turned back to the wagon. "I'd be proud to be your wife, Zack, and take the name Drake for myself and this child."

❧ 28 ❧

Word of their engagement spread through the train like fire in dry brush, and folks came by with their best wishes.

"Well, it's about damned time," Millie said when she heard the news.

They were on a steep slope and the train moved slowly, with most folks walking behind their wagons to ease the burden on the draft animals and lend a hand to push the wagons from time to time.

"You sure you shouldn't be in that bed yet?" Millie asked in a scolding tone. "I'd best not see you pushin' on that damned wagon neither, or we'll be scoopin' up that child from this mud."

Charlie laughed at her friend. "By my reckoning," she said and stepped over a runnel of brown water, "I've still got two or three months to go before I have to worry about that."

"You figure a Christmas baby, then?" Millie asked as she pushed on the wagon that spun its wheels in the mud on the slippery trail.

Charlie could hear her brother cursing at the team of

mules as they struggled to pull the wagon. She knew they dared not stop or they'd be mired here for hours if not days to come, and they were only a few miles from Baker City, where they planned to camp for a few days and resupply before moving on toward Portland, and where Ellen planned to set her base of operation.

"You and Zack movin' up to Portland with your new sister and her husband?" Millie asked as the wagons came to the summit and began to move in a downward direction.

Charlie looked out over the grasslands in the valley below and smiled. "No, I want to farm, and this is farmland. I don't want to live in a city crowded up against a neighbor."

The day was cloudy to the east, behind the hills they were skirting, but the sun glistened on the green fields in the valley below.

"You and Zack are gonna homestead then?"

"The two of us together can claim a whole section," Charlie said. "We could do a lot with six hundred and forty acres."

Millie smiled as she plodded through the mud with her skirts hiked up. "Sounds like you have it all planned out already."

"My late husband went to the Agricultural University in Nashville." Charlie gazed out over the green fields with the creeks running through them. "I've been studying some of his books about farming, and I have a few ideas."

She put her hand to her belly when the baby kicked. "I need to talk to some of the local farmers first to learn what grows the best, but this land looks fertile, with good water. I think we can make a good go with a farm here."

Millie nodded as lightning flashed behind the hills, and thunder rolled in the distance. "Miss Ellen's been talking to Nathan about hauling a wagon back, filled with root crops like potatoes, turnips, and onions, and canned-up things like peaches and apples to have for sale to the folks travelin' on the train—sorta her own travelin' mercantile." Millie grinned and rolled her big brown eyes. "She even wants Miss Mary to supply her with men's shirts and trousers, women's dresses and aprons, and children's clothes."

"It sounds like Ellen has big plans for this business." Charlie stepped off the trail so the wagon behind them could pass and then stopped to catch her breath.

"You all right, Charlie?" Millie asked with concern.

"I'm fine," she said and straightened up to stretch a kink from her back. "I should probably catch up with Thomas and Mary in the wagon, though, and ride for a while. It looks like we're going to be on a downhill run for a while."

Millie glanced to the east, where the sky had darkened. "I hope we don't get none of that storm they're gettin' over yonder. Looks to be a bad one."

"What are you doing on your feet, Mrs. Byrde?" Mrs. Bradshaw called down from her wagon in a scolding tone when she came upon them. "You're supposed to be on bedrest for another few weeks. Get yourself back to your wagon before that rain gets here."

Charlie waved at the woman who was acting as the train's official midwife. "I'm headed back to the wagon now, ma'am." To Millie, she mumbled, "I was stuck in that damned bed for two weeks. Every muscle in my body is stiff as a bone. I need to get out and get some fresh air."

Millie giggled. "She just likes lordin' it over them if she thinks she can."

The wagons had slowed to cross a creek, and they got to Charlie's before it went into the water.

"You get some rest now, Mrs. Byrde," Millie said with a giggle as she watched Charlie climb up into the back.

"Oh, I will," she called back and waved.

Charlie left the tarp open to get some air in the stuffy wagon. The tarp behind Thomas and Mary on the driver's bench was closed to keep out the dust, and Charlie tied back the rear flap before unlacing her muddy boots and kicking them off. She crawled up into her bed and grabbed the book she'd been reading on farming when she heard an ungodly roar and then a scream from Mary.

The next minute the wagon began to tumble and items inside were thrown around as the wagon went over on its side. Charlie screamed as she was thrown up against the wooden side of the wagon, and darkness briefly engulfed her.

Her vanity went over, and the old cracked mirror shattered into a hundred pieces. Water rushed in through the open rear tarp, and Charlie rolled off the bed to stumble through the icy gushing water to secure the flap over the opening in a futile attempt to stem the flow.

Her fingers and feet grew numb battling the icy water and slippery ties, but she managed to affix them and slow the water flowing into the wagon. She could feel it floating on its side and wondered what had happened. The creek hadn't been that wide or deep. How could her wagon be floating on its side?

Where were Mary and Thomas? She slogged in her wet skirts toward the front of the wagon and climbed over dislodged crates and barrels of ruined supplies. Charlie yelled for Mary and her brother but got no answer. When she finally got the flap open and gazed outside, she was shocked to see not a narrow creek but what looked to be a vast river of muddy, brown water.

Her team of mules was still hitched to the wagon, but some of them weren't moving in the water while others thrashed in the harnesses and tried to right themselves in the frothing water. Mary and Thomas were nowhere to be seen. She heard someone yell her name, and she called back. A few minutes later, Zack was with her in the wagon.

"What the hell happened?" she asked anxiously when her arms were around him.

"A flash flood from the rain up in those hills," he said.

"Where are Thomas and Mary?" she demanded, shifting her gaze to the empty seat where the two had been sitting only minutes before.

"Gone," was all he could say as he helped her out through the front and onto his horse. "Nathan and his men are mounting a search. Yours wasn't the only wagon caught when the water came through. It grabbed up several on the banks too."

Charlie suddenly remembered waving to Millie before she closed up the rear flap. "Millie?" she breathed, tears stinging her eyes. "Millie was with me before I climbed back in the wagon."

"Nathan and his men are searchin' for all of them washed away," he explained as they made their way back to those waiting on the edge of the water. "And your father is out lookin' for Thomas and Mary in particular."

The banks were gone and the people waiting stood on what had been flat grassland some hundred yards from the banks of the creek, the tops of trees the only things to give any indication of where the edges of the creek had been.

Charlie saw familiar fabric fluttering in the branches of one of the trees and pointed. "There's Millie," she shouted. "That's her dress!"

"Nathan," Zack yelled and pointed. "Charlie says that's Millie down there in that tree."

"I see her," Nathan yelled back. "I got her."

He took off on his horse toward his wife, who was waving her arms and screaming for help.

When Nathan returned, he had both Millie and Mary on his horse. Millie had climbed up the tree to call for help while Mary was in the water, her skirts tangled in branches she couldn't dislodge.

"Where is Thomas?" Charlie wanted to know.

Mary began to sob uncontrollably as she stared down the

fast-moving creek littered with debris from wagons. "I couldn't hold onto him," she wept and held up her pale, trembling hands. "He just slipped away."

Charlie wrapped the sobbing young woman in her arms. "They'll find him, sweetie; they *have* to."

"We're supposed to be married in a few days," Mary sobbed as she held onto Charlie's arm. "I never thought I could love a man the way my mama loved my daddy, but I do. I love Thomas like that, and I don't think I can go on without him."

"I didn't think I'd be able to go on without my Davis when I lost him either," Charlie told her, "but I have."

She took Mary's face in her hands and stared into her weeping eyes. "You're a strong woman, Mary. You've already gone through so much." Charlie brushed aside wet hair and kissed Mary's cold forehead. "You'll get through this too."

Mary fell into her arms, sobbing more intensely. "I don't think I can handle losing someone else."

They found Thomas's body the next day, tangled in debris a mile down the creek bed from where the wagon had been struck. Two of Charlie's mules had drowned, and the wagon severely damaged. They lost three other wagons, including the Bradshaws, who were swept away behind Charlie. Five human souls were lost that day, and Charlie counted Mary amongst them.

Before they reached Baker City and her aunt's, Mary threw herself off a cliff into the river below, leaving a note for Charlie saying she was going to join her lost love and the rest of her family.

Charles McCleod took the body of his son into the hills and gave him a private burial in the mountain man tradition. Charlie suspected it was comprised of Indian ceremonial traditions as well and that he didn't want the whites in the group, including his daughter, to take part. She said good-bye to her brother in private.

Zack joined her beside the body her father had wrapped in a blanket and tied with leather thong. "I'm so sorry, Charlotte," he said, using her full name rather than the boyish moniker she'd recently set aside. He'd told her she was a woman again, and from now on, he'd only address her as a woman with the name Charlotte.

"I understand if you want to put off the wedding," he whispered as he took her hand. "I know it's going to be hard for you after Mary and all."

He grew quiet and let Charlie weep in his arms for her lost brother and friend.

"No." She wiped the tears from her cheeks. "I want us to marry you as soon as we get to Baker City." The baby kicked, and she put a hand to her belly. "The babe and I are ready to start a new life here with you, Zack."

He smiled, bent, and kissed her lips. "I'm ready, too, Charlotte."

The wedding was a private affair in the chambers of the magistrate in Baker City two days after their arrival. The bride wore her plaid polonaise and white flounced underskirt with the hat she'd made topping her blonde head. The groom wore a suit borrowed from his friend Morgan and people from the train filled the small chamber in the courthouse to overflowing.

That night music filled the camp, and they danced merrily around the fire. Women filled the tables with food, and men passed around bottles of whiskey and beer purchased in town for the occasion. Mr. and Mrs. Drake were toasted aplenty that night. They were cheered as they retired to Charlotte's wagon that had been righted, pulled from the creek, and dried as best it could be while the broken wheel and axle were repaired.

The music and laughter continued while the couple consummated their vows in the bed Charlie had shared with both Mary and Millie. She thought sharing it with Zack was going to be much more enjoyable.

They were still living in the wagon on their newly purchased property when Thomas Edwin Drake came into the world at a quarter to midnight on Christmas Eve.

EPILOGUE

The Drakes stood on the porch of their newly constructed farmhouse as the sun set with two-year-old Tommy playing with his set of wagons at their feet.

"It looks like we're going to have a good crop of potatoes this year," Zack said with his arm around Charlotte's waist.

"Sugar beets and onions too," Charlotte nodded. "How is work coming along on the cannery?"

Zack smiled and pulled her closer. "Good enough that Morgan will be adding boxes of tin-tops to his rolling mercantile next year."

"How many trips do they have scheduled now?"

"Ellen said they're adding a southern run out of Fort Smith with three dozen gals headed to California and the two regular runs out of St. Louis to Oregon and Washington, with another three dozen each as well as some families and such as usual."

Charlotte shook her head of long blonde curls and grinned. "It seems the mail-order bride business was a good idea after all." She kissed her husband's cheek.

"Thanks to the management of you and Ellen, it's putting money into all our pockets."

"Millie wishes Nathan was at home more, though. She wants to add another wing on the house to accommodate more sewing machines, so she can hire more gals to sew."

Zack chuckled. "Every time he is home, she ends up with child again. He's gonna need to add another wing just for all the damned young'uns."

Charlotte took his hand and placed it on her abdomen. "Speaking of that," she said with a grin tugging at the corners of her mouth, "it might be time to think on finishing that room upstairs after all."

"You're with child?" He gasped and grabbed her around the waist to twirl her around as Tommy stared up at them wide-eyed. "You're certain?"

"I haven't needed my clouts in three months now, so, yes, I'm pretty certain."

Zack pulled her close and kissed her mouth. "You've just made me the happiest man on Earth, Charlotte Drake."

"You've been making me happy since that first night we met back there in Illinois, Mr. Drake." She kissed him again. "If this one is a girl, I want to name her Mary Rebecca."

"Not Jenny?" he asked with an arched brow.

Charlotte shook her head. "Jenny will always belong to Emma," she replied, a tear stinging her eye.

"Mary Rebecca it is then," Zack said, "but what if it's another boy?"

"We have a few more months to think on it." Charlotte said with a wink and a smile.

Dear reader,

We hope you enjoyed reading *Forty Weeks*. Please take a moment to leave a review, even if it's a short one. Your opinion is important to us.

Discover more books by Lori Beasley Bradley at https://www.nextchapter.pub/authors/lori-beasley-bradley

Want to know when one of our books is free or discounted? Join the newsletter at http://eepurl.com/bqqB3H

Best regards,

Lori Beasley Bradley and the Next Chapter Team

You might also like:
Dolly by Lori Beasley Bradley

To read the first chapter for free, please head to:
https://www.nextchapter.pub/books/dolly

Forty Weeks
ISBN: 978-4-86750-045-3

Published by
Next Chapter
1-60-20 Minami-Otsuka
170-0005 Toshima-Ku, Tokyo
+818035793528

3rd June 2021

Ingram Content Group UK Ltd.
Milton Keynes UK
UKHW010611020523
421079UK00004B/125

9 784867 500453